Augustino and the
Choir of Destruction

MARIE-CLAIRE BLAIS
Translated by Nigel Spencer

ANANSI

Published in 2007 by
House of Anansi Press Inc.
110 Spadina Avenue, Suite 801
Toronto, ON, M5V 2K4
Tel. 416-363-4343
Fax 416-363-1017
www.anansi.ca

Distributed in Canada by
HarperCollins Canada Ltd.
1995 Markham Road
Scarborough, ON, M1B 5M8
Toll free tel. 1-800-387-0117

First published as *Augustino et le choeur de la destruction*
in 2005 by Les Editions du Boréal

11 10 09 08 07 1 2 3 4 5

Library and Archives Canada Cataloguing in Publication

Blais, Marie-Claire, 1939–
[Augustino et le choeur de la destruction. English]
    Augustino and the choir of destruction / Marie-Claire Blais ;
translated by Nigel Spencer

Translation of: Augustino et le choeur de la destruction.
Final volume in the trilogy: These festive nights, Thunder and light,
Augustino and the choir of destruction.
ISBN 978-0-88784-752-3

I. Spencer, Nigel, 1945–   II. Title.   III. Title: Augustino et le choeur
de la destruction. English.

PS8503.L33A913 2007   C843'.54   C2006-903673-X

Cover design: Bill Douglas at The Bang
Text design and typesetting: Laura Brady

 Canada Council
for the Arts
Conseil des Arts
du Canada

ONTARIO ARTS COUNCIL
CONSEIL DES ARTS DE L'ONTARIO

We acknowledge for their financial support of our publishing program the Canada Council for the Arts, the Ontario Arts Council, and the Government of Canada through the Book Publishing Industry Development Program (BPIDP).

Printed and bound in Canada.

For Christiane Teasdale

The longest voyage needs no trunks,
and what I give is all I have.
Take my gaze, rich in its poverty;
It's made from sky, warm air, cool water,
so ugliness can one day be washed.
Take my hands, so alive with caresses
and the rebellions that they've hatched.
Take my hair,
untameable,
it's always shouted.
Take my silence, my giddiness . . . the rest
is for the last great wave,
the first of the first tide.

— Georgette Gaucher Rosenberg,
from *Ocean, Take Me Back*

*P*etites Cendres smelled with disgust, she said, the drunken man's breath on her lips and neck, as this stranger pinned her to the wall of the bar: stop, will you, you're going to suffocate me, what could she say to be safe, no one had any respect for her, the man who had arranged to meet her in the hotel at eight this evening and his strange accent had a heavy violence, a fleshy weight whose oppressiveness she had glimpsed, bald head she didn't like either, nor the baggy eyes of this stranger under his silver-rimmed glasses, leave me alone, Petites Cendres said again, thinking of how she had to drop by briefly at the Porte du Baiser Saloon where she danced every day for customers as dull as this one squeezing her waist and flattening her against the wall, she could see the pink wooden houses lit by the sun on Esmerelda Street and Bahama Street, a dog sniffing vainly for any trace of the owner who had abandoned it, why didn't he just head for the sea, at least there'd be some coolness, he probably hadn't eaten for days she thought, his colour, his colour was the same as hers too, not brown, not black, but at least if she didn't eat it was simply from lack of appetite, she had all she needed from the shade and the vented air in the Saloon, fed also by what had become her unfilled need, yes, the dog was a dark ochre colour like rust, just like Petites Cendres, nobody was going to feel sorry for him, too old, forty they all said, too late, the man was dragging her out into the street, and she was ashamed that everyone would see her now, hear her whimpering, leave me alone you kids, because that's what they called her, Ashley, hey Little Ashes . . . Petites Cendres . . . forty years old and you're teetering on the brink, laughing as they called out the numbers coming up in the Saloon that night, in their evening clothes and stiletto heels, coarse heavily built men, she thought, but they don't give a damn what happens to me, they'll see, they'll see later on, nobody gets respect at this age, nobody, and one of the boys who didn't have a wig, yawning on the sidewalk, no wig, just earrings and short, slicked-back hair, she noticed, he just thought it was funny, the john's tattooed arm across her throat, then he tapped the drunk on the shoulder, hey, loosen up on her a bit, will you, you don't want her to croak on us, do you, and the man shook himself out of his stupor and flung her onto the sidewalk like a rag, don't forget . . . be at the hotel by eight, girl, he said; that's it, show him you're a man yelled the bare-headed, kid with no wig, so are you a man, I'm the man that I am, the way the Lord made me, said Petites Cendres as he watched the bottom-feeder slouch away from him, yes, that's how he made you all right, said the kid with no wig, bit stuck-up aren't you Ashley, with those jeans so tight on your skanky ass, your black corset, the zits on your face, your plastic tits, aintcha got a little angel-dust for me while you're at it, it's a black silk corset, he said, and I am just the way I am, you get nothing from me, the kid with no wig went on, watch out for your john, he looks like a wrestler in the ring, get a load of that ox-neck of his, he'll beat you to a pulp, afraid are you,

Ashley, come on and prove you're a man, then they all started laughing again, in their evening wear, Petites Cendres did not know if they were just indolent, mean or ferocious, he saw the sea glittering under an incandescent sun at the far end of the long, narrow street, on the shoreline of Atlantic Boulevard, any moment now that sun would burst into a ball of flame, a furnace to stifle the heart of Petites Cendres, his soul felt blood-raw, liquefied deep down inside him, in a pale, cold sea where the need that gnawed at him would break your heart, a fire burnt out, his heart, that dog should not have been there on Esmeralda or Bahama Street, hunger tottering on all fours, night-prowling around the Porte du Baiser Saloon where he just would not stop living despite all odds; in thunder and light, Lazaro launched his boat from the side of the wharf, thinking he would rather work at sea than be a student and live with his mother Caridad and those brothers and sisters of his, all of them born here of a man not his father, not even a Muslim, his mother had betrayed him by pardoning Carlos for his murderous act against her son, none of them, not one, knew who this Lazaro really was, sitting, hatching his revenge against Carlos, ready to kill him when he got out of jail, unless of course Justice did it for him, oh yes, maybe Justice would be fair and kill Carlos, then Lazaro would be recruited for some grander mission, and not only Carlos would disappear but all the others, Caridad the charitable who mangled the faith of their ancestors, her pardon was just a caricature of pity, there should be pity for no one, not Carlos or the others, from a grumpy fisherman resigned to working the sea with his hands, a student with no diploma, Lazaro would become someone, someone . . . who knows what, he needed a pitiless role, one to light a fire under the whole of the earth, he had written to his uncles and cousins, recruit me, I'll volunteer, be a missionary for some dark work, for he had known from childhood, hadn't he, that one day the earth would belong to the militant and soldier tribes alone, no more women, certainly none like his mother, Caridad — changing countries so they could unveil their faces and drive cars — none of these anymore . . . the sullen, strong-willed, dry and thirsty planet would be reserved for the young and angry, those destined to sensitive missions of martyrdom, thousands of them, unnamed and unnameable, candidates for suicide, flourishing in disordered ranks worldwide, staging attacks anywhere and everywhere — supermarkets in Jerusalem, hotels in New York — they would be heard if not believed, because of the panache of their murders, the toll rung by the belt-activated bombs they all would conceal under their clothes and in handbags, girls breaking off engagements and hiding mortar shells beneath folds of scarves, in bags, at store entrances, in stations, holding them so close to their own organs, these innumerable unnamed brigades alone would inherit the earth, bombs would be housed in their young and healthy bodies and holy terror would reign, oh yes, in whole cities, on tiled floors in cafeterias of Hebrew universities, where squads of nurses would lean over pools of blood — here seven people died — quickly wrap them in sheets just as quickly soaked in blood, and still gloved, the nurse would take the wheel and drive home to his family at night, something sticky still on his fingers . . . ah, he would say, may God have pity on this blood; in every town and village, on walls of homes and schools, there would be pictures of suicide-bombers with crowns of flowers, brigades of pious volunteers, nurses constantly on call and on the move to massacre-sites, gloved alike, and surgeon-like, who would say that blood is the seat of the soul, and like the kamikazes these new angels of death would become heroes subjected to a familiar ritual, here, in this cafeteria, where seven people died, and now the pile of bodies must be removed amid shards of glass, broken tables, and tomorrow it would be the same thing somewhere else, in a bar another woman would be sitting with her elbow on the counter, eyes open, glass in hand, a marbled statue in sudden death, tomorrow

more streets and houses, tanks splitting the pavement, footsteps in the smoking dust of exploded houses, such was the
world Lazaro had contemplated since childhood, or it might
have been when his father Mohammed beat his mother before
he was born, blows that came from a long way off, when his
mother said, we must get away from Egypt, this country, this
man . . . might there be still more streets and houses or gassy
smells, smoke billowing from the sky, I'll get him, I'll get that
Carlos one of these days, Lazaro said to himself over and over
as he walked down Atlantic Boulevard, where the sun was red
as it prepared to vanish into the sea, and the air was so sweet
you'd think you were swallowing it and getting drunk; Lazaro
waded barefoot through the sea, his body shaking with rage
as he soaked his face and hair in the salt water, remembered
Carlos, and heard a heavy flapping of wings, the sudden, troubled passing of a wounded pelican, frightened and desper-
ately try to scoop up fish and stay alive, still lumbering
awkwardly over the water, but seeming only to skim the hard
surface of the waves with his beak, the sound of his one good
wing racketing skywards; Lazaro climbed the stairs to a terrace
and tried to get help for the wounded bird, thinking petulantly
that his mother would have done the same, talking on and on
as she did about respecting nature . . . Lazaro spotted the bird
from the terrace, apparently staying close to shore, looking for
shelter beneath a bridge, flying more and more lamely, and
panicked now, the weakened pelican suddenly abandoned
the protection of the shoreline and headed for open water,
and Lazaro could no longer see the yellow-gold plumage of
the bird's head, as though some malevolent fate had snatched
the endangered bird away from him, and he felt a moment's
anguish, this world of small and larger birds that could be
seen in the wakes of boats, sailboats used by fishermen, and
wasn't this after all the last domain which could still win
Lazaro over with its vitality, its diversity and its courage in the
face of an uncertain ocean, a world not yet reflecting a dark,

deathly light like the mission he could not stop thinking about — avenging himself on Carlos or the militant action he wanted to carry out — when these thoughts of his future were frequently fleshed out and freighted with primitive foreshadowings, this majestic world of birds, for instance, he came close to fainting, he thought, and Mère, whose birthday they were celebrating, heard her daughter Mélanie saying to Jermaine's parents, oh, but Jermaine doesn't play with Samuel anymore . . . before yes, but not now, he's a handsome young man whose Asian features resemble his mother more an more, but didn't he just spoil it all, thought Mère, by bleaching his hair blonde like that and making it stick straight up on his head, Mélanie was saying, women must learn to govern, we need a woman president, because when men are in charge they start wars, but Chuan replied that when women governed, they could be just as cruel and ambitious as men, think about those "enlightened despots," said Jermaine's mother, like Catherine the Great they crushed an entire population of serfs and peasants under feudalism, entirely indifferent to the suffering of their people, and it's often been that way — even nowadays — oh, I don't mean you, Mélanie dear, we could never get enough of your sincerity in the Senate, but my husband, one of the first black senators ever elected, won't tolerate any talk of politics in this house, and now he's retired, he channels his protest through writing, often alone in the cottage over by the ocean there . . . just down the path and through the hibiscus from the house . . . he often phones me, and we talk several times a day, when I'm not off designing in Paris or Milan or Hong Kong, his real home is here on this island near his family, Olivier's not a nomad like me; Mère told Chuan how delighted she was by her house and everything she created by way of decoration, Chuan knew how to pare things down to their essential forms, and her houses in the Dominican Republic and here, facing the ocean, were as light as Thai cottages out on the water which reflected onto the white blinds of the living room, air

wafting through the row of palm trees in the garden, luxuri-
ance and weightlessness, Mère said, thinking neither of her
daughter nor of Chuan to whom she addressed these polite
words, but seeming to ask herself vague questions, or rather
afraid to ask them, at almost eighty, she had made a success of
her life, though what that meant for a woman she wasn't sure
. . . on her deathbed with an insidious anaemia, Marie Curie
had told her daughter Eve, "I don't want what you're going to
do to me. I just want to be left alone," and Mère too wondered
what will they do to me when they see my right hand trembling, and some other things are not quite right, Mélanie, who
notices everything, what will she do to me, I want to be left
alone, her last words must be like those of the great apostle of
pure science, "I do not wish it," but it wasn't about to happen
anytime soon, you never change, Esther dear, they always told
her as she sipped her cocktail in the warm breeze, naturally, I
still have plenty of time to think about all that, "Sleep," Marie
Curie had said as she closed her eyes, sleep. Yet Marie Curie
was a woman of renown, the Mozart of science, Mère thought,
but still, born a woman, she might not have thought her life a
success, is it possible she left this world with doubts, saying
over and over to her daughter that she wanted to be left in
peace, not bothered anymore, that this life was just too much,
so many tribulations, so little grandeur, just too much to bear,
she would die with the true scale of her work unknown, just
to be allowed to sleep at last; might an accomplished life go
hand-in-hand with success? Maria Sklodowska's childhood in
Poland had not been especially promising, brothers and sisters
dying around her of tuberculosis or typhus, very early on she
became an agnostic and had to do without whatever support
was not as solid as science, the disappearance of God, the
loss of her parents . . . all this left her mind free and clear,
Maria knew this, the straightforwardness of thought alone
would yield rewards, no wandering across snowy fields, no
sleigh rides for this little girl, perhaps the companionship of

a dog in her study, wars and insurrections had drained the world of its blood, but through the dark emerged the thoughts of one who did not yet know who she was, she could not say with the authority of others before her, I am Darwin, I am Mendeleyev — their theories had penetrated her mind even before she knew who she was, what was success in life, born like Marie Curie, in Poland oppressed by the Russians, and no voting rights for women, in England or anywhere else, to discover as one grew older that academicians and intellectuals were imprisoned in Siberia, then to be swept up in an era of positivity when the emancipation of women would be justified, or to be assassinated for revolutionary politics like her friend Rosa Luxembourg, whose young body would be found floating in a Berlin canal, what was success in life, wondered Mère, knowing how to design, plan and build harmonious coral pathways — as Chuan had done in front of her house — or being Rosa Luxembourg, the falterings, the failings bearing down on Maria's life, whether teacher or housewife, poverty ground people down everywhere, were the grumblings and ingratitude of others all she could ever expect? In this far-away Polish village, so alone in her mansard-roofed cottage that one had to get to it in winter by a stairway, she devoured literature and natural science, read in French and Russian, got up at five in the grey dawn, stuck doggedly to her physics and math books, still not knowing who she was, a failed schoolteacher, a creature petrified by the sheer concentration of all her faculties, waiting under that mansard roof for her father to send her money from home, and when none came, she sent her own salary to help her brother with his studies, in her isolation, Maria wrote to her family that she had no plans for the future, or at least such banal ones they were not worth mentioning, she would get by as best she could, and one day, so she wrote, she would bid farewell to this petty life, and the harm would not be great, neither Darwin nor Freud, just an ordinary being, it was the time of year when everything was frozen, the sky, the earth, there was revulsion against any physical contact, this too she felt, and why mend your clothes when there was no one to dress up for, nerves were the last thing alive under that ice and clothing and body and soul, all lying uncared-for beneath this deathless winter, the spark came from learning chemistry, though she had written her brother that she had given up all hope of ever becoming someone, failure, thought Mère, yes, the unbearable failure of every successful life, the ascetic face of Maria Sklodowska bent over her work and assembling so many pictures and voices that Mère no longer found her way through them, Chuan had taken her by the arm and was inviting her to meet the guests she called her European group, writers and artists newly arrived on our island: Valérie and her husband Bernard, Christiensen and Nora from even farther away — Northern Europe; of course, arriving in Paris was more stimulating for Maria than stagnating in her village, thought Mère, Chuan shouldn't have bothered to introduce her to all these charming people, she mused, she would never have time to get to know them, night began to dim everything, and nothing would remain of these hand-shakings or glances as they said I've heard a lot about you Esther, dear, and your daughter Mélanie with such wonderful children, Mère was thinking they should have left her in peace for the rest of this life journey of hers which seemed so short, or perhaps Paris shocked the austere Maria, so earnest she was for a city that, after so many fires, revelled in lightness of being, or perhaps she was afraid, then there was that annoying click of Augustino's computer, the picture of a hundred dolphins on the screen, carcasses rolled over by the waves and deposited on the white sands of an island in Venezuela, what had happened to provoke this mass suicide in just a few short hours, or what poison at the very depths had cheated them of their lives? Mère said to Augustino, turn that computer off, I can't stand it anymore, Augustino, you don't seem to understand that an old lady just can't look at everything, there are things I do not want to see, and he had looked at his grandmother without understanding, it was the first time they had not got through to one another, she was always saying, please don't bother me, and yet yesterday he had done it constantly without her ever complaining once, I mean, who knows, in a few years you might be an intellectual or a philosopher, and your grandmother will read a book of your thoughts with pride, how many fingers could you count those years on, or how many hands, Augustino asked, his eyes suspicious under long lashes, well, right now you're only sixteen, she said as though she held his youthfulness against him, their social instinct and their psychic skills are more developed than ours, so why couldn't their ultrasound guide them, and why these multiple beachings on the white sands of l'île de la Tortue, can you tell me, Augustino, she once would have said to him, but her clouded blue eye stared at him as if to say, never mind, don't say a thing, what's the point, I don't want to know, they're just poor dolphins, one of many species that will soon cease to exist, and Augustino thought she hasn't answered my question about how many fingers for how many years, it must be because she doesn't believe they exist, she's taken so long to get old, and I may not have very long to become young, bottle-nose dolphins are very smart, Augustino had said, but they aren't suspicious enough of us, and they are often victims of our mistakes, who knows, repeated Mère, perhaps one day I'll read your thoughts in a book, she could not wish anything more distinguished for him, she thought, something Jermaine's parents could never say, because their son never even read a book, let alone wrote, sports cars were all he cared about, his father Olivier regretted that, yes, sports cars and those harmful video games, he had them all, and children developed the same indifference, lack of interest to the handling of massive war machines, engines of destruction that no longer make the slightest impression on them, at least, Mère thought, Augustino has no use for them, more restrained

than Jermaine, he did not burst into his father's study, his inti-
mate writing hideaway, in the morning and teary-eyed say, I
love you, Dad, can you lend me some money or the car or
both; Olivier, holding back a bit, asked his son once more, say
you love me, is it true, you didn't write to me when you were
at university, Chuan retold all these little events to Mère, my
husband's very close to his family, she said, but he shuts himself up with his dogs too much and refuses to come out, he's
the one I worry most about, it's depression that comes out in
this paralyzing thoughtfulness, you know; Chuan suddenly fell
silent, and Mère thought she could hear the world turning in
her silence, it was un-intriguing tumult which took hold, every
pore of the flesh was offered up, listening, lies and noise, and
Mère said to Chuan, I know what your husband is feeling, but
why don't you come and dance for us like last year, this year I
don't dare do what is forbidden, Chuan said, I borrow a little
of that ecstasy I criticize my son for taking, and as she listened,
Mère thought how deprived of rest Marie Curie's life had
been, even when she was only twenty-five, Maria shied away
from amphitheatres and exam halls where she would be first,
what a day it was for Maria, a woman, what a day it was when
she came in first for the Physical Science degree, this reticent
woman with nervous afflictions, and how she showed her joy
despite her persistent fear of succeeding, of easy triumph, yes,
Mère thought she heard the turning of the world with its
bump and jolts within Chuan's silence, they might have
spoken up, with all that's going on nowadays, for the earth
and its inhabitants, she thought, whether it be surrender or
death, perhaps people were aware that a minuscule part of the
planet had been wiped out, still life had to go on, and even
Chuan must have sensed that night it was her duty to dance,
yes, singing and dancing had to go on whatever racket they
made, turning the world on itself, or was it fair and sane to
think this way beneath a deluge of gigantic explosions any
sensate human being had got used to, however bored

Jermaine had become by the on-screen manœuvres of his demonic games, entire territories disappearing, the spectacles of huge structures crumbling, seeing them over and over, we no longer felt disturbed by them, these glimpses orchestrated by an invisible choir no longer troubled us, so now we had, it seems, been won over *en masse* to our own devastation, these dark thoughts were not Mère's but Olivier's, whose articles she had read in the island newspaper, and what exactly was it we wanted for ourselves, surrender or death? Yes, of course I'll dance tonight, Chuan said, her smile a twin to her son's, and it distresses me that my husband shares such sad thoughts with his readers since he has retired here, but there's nothing I can do to change that, so Chuan was going to dance once more and Mère was going to enjoy her solitude with the operas of Puccini, though Mélanie her daughter kept suggesting she get to know the symphonies of César Franck or the operas of Benjamin Britten, and why did Mélanie want every classical rule broken and monumental works filled with metallic sounds and songs of unbearable sorrow in which the human voice was distorted and sometimes silenced, to which absentee gods were these cathedrals, these fortresses of modern sound erected, and these lamentations of the poet Owen contained in Britten's *War Requiem*, to what dove of peace lost forever? The *Requiem*, that Franz (ageing rebel conductor that he was) refused to perform in churches, but only out in the open and under the sun, on terraces and in pavilions by the sea, could be heard in Daniel and Mélanie's house and across the island, the choir's *libera me* wafting to the heavens and toward who-knows-what abysses and resurrections, and Mère thought if only they could just leave me alone, just as Marie Curie said at the end of her life, Puccini would always be a spellbinder to her; Chuan was gone now, running off in her bright red dress and black leather sandals to the vast kitchen she had painted carmine, saying the Cuban architecture of the house demanded these tints of burning sunlight on her walls, and her husband had gone to greet a young man from the caterer's with an immaculate white singlet and pants under a black apron at the entrance to the garden who was telling Olivier that his wife had ordered the tray of fish he held in his hands, but our table's already groaning complained Olivier, look, put that down, it's too heavy for you, what's your name son, it's Lazaro, he often comes here said Chuan sidling up to him as Lazaro gazed impenetrably at Jermaine over Olivier's head and his wife's as he held it, and Jermaine was laughing with his friends, well-off children all of them, drinking and laughing around the pool, the green water iris-like in the daytime, playing wild reflections across their faces, all of them with the same bleach-blonde hair Jermaine had, the same necklaces, in their festive circle they were no more disparate, no less outlandish, thought Lazaro, than Jermaine's parents, the father a moody African-American, a giant in this house next to his delicate oriental wife whose smile might have been rebellious or kind — it wasn't clear — these people were so self-assured living here on life's margins, far from the troublesome struggle for survival Lazaro had to wage, whether it meant taking to the sea with rough men or working for a caterer or as a waiter in a restaurant, nothing hemmed them in or confined them, Lazaro thought with clenched teeth; to Chuan he said, as she looked astonished at him, look at these kids, they have to drink to have fun, when you could do it just drinking tea or fruit juice, alcohol is forbidden in my religion, it's poison; Olivier got annoyed and said we don't talk about religion around here, religion will destroy the world, and who was this sectarian young man that his wife treated like a son, out of kindness of course, Olivier thought, to bridge the class divide, for we are all equal, all equally unhappy, some wearing masks to cover faces streaked with blood from mutilation and slavery, Chuan had been born into it in Japan where for a long time it would have been better not to be born at all and simply wait a long time for the embers to cool just a little, as far as Olivier was concerned, one of the few black senators elected, had he actually put an end to segregation, if only Jermaine loved him genuinely, that would be his true happiness, Jermaine coming into his office in the morning and saying, Dad, you know I love you, I say it often, sidetracked from life, that's what they are, thought Lazaro, all of them, with their alcohol and seafood banquets, so Jermaine and his friends might as well have fun while they can, said Chuan, because university vacation days would soon be over, and then we won't see the kids for months, besides what do they know about the other side of town, Lazaro thought, Lazaro's zone, Carlos, the gang-fights on Bahama and Esmerelda, suddenly Lazaro had a flash of rapists being executed in Tehran, a vision which could only emerge from past shame, perhaps he'd been present at public executions with his mother and she had said, cover your eyes, let's get out of here, don't open them, was he one of the ten thousand people of Tehran one cursed dawn, numbed into compulsive stupefaction and fascination, like all the rest, as they saw five condemned twenty-five-year-olds hanged from a crane for rape and racketeering . . . a long, agonizing time dying at the end of a rope hoisted from the back of a truck, the crowd chanting in unison, good, that's what they deserve, so thought the families of their victims in amongst the crowd, not a voice raised in pity, and the dawn called forth a misty day, a pink dawn already dipped in rain, five black vultures as they called themselves, the black vulture gang, hanged from the backs of truck-mounted cranes, a journalist counting the five to six minutes of their death-throes and jotting it down in his notebook, at Lavizan, Lavizan Square, rapists, of course, but what if they were falsely accused, not really rapists, conning and robbing young women in parks, what if it was a plot by women, for it was they who had called for their public hanging, after all, these women had all been seen later on in Lavizan Square with their children at the dawn executions, men, women and children, everyone a hungry spectator, some perched on fences or electricity poles, a vendor of dry cakes weaving through the crowd, and if this wasn't a conspiracy, thought Lazaro, then these five black vultures had been hanged for no reason, hadn't they? Yet it was a man who carried out the contemptible ritual, slipping the knot over their heads, and two of them had murmured their innocence at the last second, and a third had asked for forgiveness, another who resembled Lazaro had held out, and before the bodies were lifted skyward, held himself upright, hands and neck bound, contemplating the early dawn and reddened mists, defiant, plump lips barely moving in an impassive face, this is how Lazaro would have done it, he thought, thinking they were hanging him by mistake, it was a conspiracy; what's wrong, Olivier asked Lazaro, let us give you a strawberry drink before you go off on that motorcycle again, but Lazaro was suddenly heading off toward Atlantic Boulevard, walking rapidly, his black apron flapping in the wind, that boy gives me a strange feeling, Olivier told Chuan, you're the one who's always too serious, don't blame me tomorrow if that loud music of Jermaine's makes me deaf, said Olivier impatiently, I just love it, said Chuan, loud and screaming, said Olivier, Mélanie says Benjamin Britten's music illustrates the anxiety of our time, thought Mère, that fugue with such stunning energy like the hammering boots of young soldiers marching impetuously, joyfully to battle, that old European youth and its longing for battle . . . isn't it still true, that's what scares me about this music, Mère thought, it would be better if it were just soft and melodious without the sound of cannons to the beat of the young soldiers' march, but rather the early spring-song, the cooing of doves, white pigeons of love's time, letting us feel the joy of their coupling, so hasty to unite these pigeons or doves that they bump into one another's bluish breasts in flight, perhaps Mère might have said, like Mélanie, that Britten's *War Requiem* was really the opposite — a solemn mass for peace — so exclaims the choir, "Lord, grant them eternal rest, and let the perpetual light shine upon them," but alas, what rest can Britten's work bring to those already dead, laid to rest beneath their arms, surrounded by officiants holding candles and praying for them, better the music should be solely melodic and soft, like the protracted song of mourning-doves or the cosmic chant of Olivier Messiaen, composer and ornithologist, in nuanced notes of birdsong, hearing the birds stirring at morning makes one think the world is reborn, it was he who wrote *Réveil des oiseaux* for piano and orchestra, thought Mère, he felt for a moment, didn't he, that he had created a garden of wonders, the original paradise complete with all its beasts and trees, the birthplace of music, the initial song of birds still coming to us in distant crystalline echoes, as though spilling forth from a tunnel and through our assimilated rhythms and sounds as musicians use them, surprizing and multifarious, from brass to Martenot waves in works with bird-whistles and chirps of nestlings, thus for a moment the composer had re-created the world, decomposed it like Britten's requiem, showing us who we really were, incapable of change, the same annoying portrait of ourselves, violent and warring; in his physical adoration of nature, Messiaen was saying, listen to this redemptive song, spilling out so pure from the tunnel of darkness, a pious music of belief, borne away by faith, something Mère could not understand, better if it were not so, just this magnificently gifted composer, lyricism a mere short breath of beauty, but that was not belief nor what he felt of our way through life, the composer dared to weave, insistently sometimes, into this birdsong awakening amid the rustle of leaves, this whistling outburst of joy, the idea that there was a beyond, there were cities, colours, a divine kingdom somewhere, in his harmonic prophecies he went so far as to describe colours, dawns which could only exist in heavenly cities, and where were these cities without crime or meanness, by what marvel could a musician still be able to dream of these mere decades ago in a death-camp at Terezin, where a choir of emaciated men and women sang another requiem by Verdi or Mozart before their executioner music-lovers, a requiem for their own interment, music with which they would be buried alive, the men and women of this choir, voices suddenly suspended, cut out, sliced off, on what bird-like migrations would these requiem voices and notes wend their way back to the city free of peril evoked by the musician? Mère was right to like Puccini best, a musician of feeling who understood women so well, and the Britten requiem conducted by Franz could be heard everywhere on the island, through the rumble of ocean and lower, quite audibly, the muffled, filtered carnage on TV, this was no longer a place of rest for Franz between his European tours with his wife and children, lingering in sleazy bars late into the night, it was now late, he thought, and you would think they had heard the anger spread through Britten's *War Requiem*, yesterday he had taken refuge in a house rented from a mistress, now today he was alone, wandering from one rooming-house to another along the ocean-front, once you could sail off to Cuba and be even more isolated, no one looking for you, no phone, no mail out there, he'd write his sonata for clarinet and piano, just back from a concert-tour of Vienna, London and Mexico City, he'd be straight off again, Franz was unstable, a wild sort, Mère thought, a man with everything who wants still more, he piled up knowledge as well as doubt, love and disappointment, and where was the procession that preceded him in triumph yesterday when he arrived on the island with his wife, children and sister Lilia — herself a musician — with friends, assistants, a maid or two . . . an unending feverish round of solid friendships and chance acquaintances sent him ranging round the beaches meeting fake artists and pushers who robbed him, all in the same day he played tennis with illustrious poet-friends, dined in splendid restaurants opening onto the sea, and what laughs and tipsiness tinged the air on those nights, even though Franz always held onto a side of himself that remained obscure to those who knew him, some irrepressible force whose strength was unknown to him, he would put his wife and children to bed with the vision in his head of the stranger he absolutely had to embrace tonight, the face was Renata's, or perhaps, later on, another woman's, for those who knew him, thought Mère, a whiff of scandal always clung to Franz, how could someone compose a sonata, often even an entire commissioned opera, and still get stiff drunk with whiskey in sailors' bars where he would recite Milton and Blake, poets he knew by heart: *Songs of Experience, Paradise Lost*, his anarchic thoughts overriding memory, as though his long hands (also capable of memory) rested on the piano keys, a man whose spirit and senses certainly bathed in the darkest waters, thought Mère, but now he was bereft and alone, alone to guide himself when not at the helm of his orchestra, dropping anchor alone on his barque, incipient songs lingering always on his lips, the first act of an opera he knew by heart, voices, a song to which, crying, he had rocked his first grandson many years later . . . oh, he'd see them all once more, but now it was time, time for Britten's *War Requiem*, and for dreaming of all, all those women and children, all those songs and fruits of experience, his paradise lost, limitless, his happiness and his sentence, it was time to silence for them the too-intimate music hidden beneath the immense *War Requiem*, just as life ebbed away tomorrow, who knows by what means, a heart attack or something more insidious, he, Franz, born to music, must spread his great arms over those he loved and protect them from that formidable and ineluctable choir, for the warriors had breached the room where Lilia, his musician sister, held his sleeping grandson in her arms, Britten's requiem had to be heard, voices unfurling like waves on the sea, Mère thought she heard the trace of song languishing on Franz's lips, do not come in here, let our children sleep, while Franz glided solo towards port, where his too-active imagination, although untroubled, free of Franz's

dark shadows, was still as aware as he was where he would
be in ten years, perhaps like Mère he would be afflicted with
a disturbing tremor of the right hand, Mélanie had noticed
this anomaly but said nothing, always on the lookout for
her mother, she was suddenly cautious, stepping ahead of her
mother into that night, sensing the same premonitions in the
symptom sketched in air by a trembling right hand, Mélanie
told her mother you must not overdo it and tire yourself out
like that, Augustino can carry packages for you while he's at
home, do the gardening, her gardening, even that they would
take away from her, her roses, banks of acacia, already they
were pressuring her into renunciation and Mère recalled that
dream, more than a sign it was, but still prescient, and in it
Mère held out a glass of wine to Mélanie, which split in two
before Mélanie could ever grasp it, Mère's fingers, her right
hand, bled onto the crystal, and she awoke with a sharp pain
as though in the breakage her daughter Mélanie had been
snatched from her, so it was true that the day would come
when she no longer saw Mélanie, the jewel of her life would
be gone, although they were so different — the maternal
instinct Mère did not have but Mélanie did, Mai was only six
but a difficult child, often worrying her mother by disappearing, would she one day disappear forever like the little girl
whose name she bore, and Mélanie would have a lot to worry
about with this much-desired child, a daughter, Esther, my
mother, I will have a daughter, the glass was beyond repair,
the augury irrevocable in that trembling right hand, the fabric
of life folding into the gap of mourning, one must simply wait
and not flee, hands cut by the glass, and Mère's fingers hurt
only remotely as in a dream, there Mélanie was beside Daniel
in Chuan's flowered courtyard, and Mère dared not look at her
for fear of loving her too much, all they could talk about was
how well Samuel was doing in New York in Arnie Graal, his
teacher's, latest choreography, it was wrong that Mère felt
more love for her daughter than for the others, even Samuel

and Augustino whom she adored, but Mère could not touch
the heart of all these young beings anymore, it was a world
she couldn't reach anymore, thinking of Mai was as dizzying
as any moonscape, who knows what it was filled with, all the
perils life held piling up around that little head which bowed
to no one, while Mélanie would rather have a sweet, cuddly
child, all-seeing Mélanie had noticed the trembling right hand
but said nothing, she had felt the glass slivering away, my fingers gushing blood on the edges, thought Mère the way she
would like to have said to Mélanie, my thoughts pouring out
to you, perhaps also a flood of thankful tears at having borne
you, Mère did not say these words out loud, all they discussed
was Samuel's success in New York, and in still another dream,
perhaps in ancient temples or in a Scottish castle, the dimen-
sions of the place were overwhelming, one could see the rows
of mortuary rooms, dressed all in furs, Mère approached one
of them, removing her furs and jewels as she went, and knowing fearfully all the while that she was never leaving this place,
temples, morbid nests, Mère was walled up, in another dream,
she and Augustino were out looking for Mai and got lost
themselves off the polar shores, what were they doing so far
away calling Mai and getting no answer, Mai where are you
cried Augustino, it was the day Jean-Mathieu's ashes were
scattered off The-Island-Nobody-Owns, when Mai had disappeared just after being photographed by Caroline, they called
out to her all along the oceanfront, and she never answered,
turning up only in the evening under some Australian
pines, and in this dream, she continued to refuse to answer,
Mère and Augustino had swum in freezing waters beneath
packs of ice all the way to an iceberg, and there Augustino
saw a bureau with Mai inside it, but we have no key to open
it, he said, then suddenly they heard a voice begging them,
Grandma, Augustino, I'm here, let me out, and Mère awoke
from the weight of these dreams thinking she would no
longer be there to help Mai grow up when Mélanie was in

Washington, the nanny Marie-Sylvie really only felt over-whelming affection for Vincent, and Daniel had already been forced to forbid her to take him to the seaside, even on wind-less days, she might be responsible for more of his repeated episodes, Samuel's boat *Southern Light* tempted them toward the waves, *Southern Light,* said Vincent, *Southern Light,* and he may have loved Marie-Sylvie more than his own mother, and it may have been to Mai's detriment that they never left each other's side, and Mère again thought, yes, it's true, one day or one night, I'll not open my eyes, not see my daughter Mélanie, so many regrets, especially at being so far from per-fect, I'll miss her, she is so attentive, I'll say to myself I did everything there was to do here, at least all I could, but was it really enough, things will go on without me, manoeuvres, bat-tles, cities decimated under a rain of missiles, generals, minis-ters taking refuge from the sound of these bombings on women, men and children in their country-house for the weekend, life is well-worn habit for the good and the evil, that I will no longer be able to talk about with my daughter, what is a successful life anyway, Marie Curie herself never knew, the upright and misogynist Pasteur grew old, a young woman who might have been resplendent wore herself down acquir-ing knowledge, sharpening her devotion to science all the while, and she would soon have a husband as brilliant and disinterested as herself, like kindred spirits meeting and fusing into one another, did she recall the young man she had met writing one day that there were few women of genius, or at least he had written, said, affirmed somehow, that women of genius were rare, the phrase she heard in the interweaving of marriage, the abandonment of marriage, but the young Marie Curie bowed her head and said nothing, she needed most of all to act, not to interrupt her thoughts, her inner discourse, also to be wary of a long tradition of prejudice when in the company of men, she would be no rival to her husband Pierre nor to anyone else, all feelings of rivalry would be banished, she must be mistress of herself, and how beneficial it would be, this rigour, uninterrupted self-discipline, bringing into the world two daughters, two Mélanies, one consumed by love of the pure sciences like her mother, a blazing and attractive replica, just as independent, straightforward, disinterested, and — like her mother — destroyed, sacrificed too soon to radioactivity, both working hard into the night in uncomfortable sheds, suffering from the dampness in the walls; Marie serious always, drably dressed, absorbed in her thoughts about uranium rays, orderly, minute, here in this shed, radium is treated exclusively, while the first little Mélanie was cutting her teeth, Marie Curie's first daughter, later to be her own mother's colleague, and whose studious shadow would in turn later haunt the laboratories in this shed, but before growing up, as Mère had done with her own daughter, Marie kept a diary recording the fifth, the sixth teeth to come through the baby's gums, her bath in the pond, the cries as the child refused to drink milk, *Irène cried today, I hope she'll stop*, though Mère thought Mélanie cried relatively little, at least wrote nothing to that effect in her own diary, along with the study of new rays, Marie had dated her discomforts shortly after Irène had been born, suddenly this phantom lesion diagnosed in the lung, it was this shed with walls that dripped humidity in autumn and winter, the stubborn adherence to work, still Pierre was by her side with so much to lighten her life, so close as the day wore on, a friend, a companion to go home with at night on foot or by bicycle, that too she had written in her diary at the same time as the baby's teeth and tears, few words in a solid hand, a hundred-and-fifty times more active than uranium, then there was the phantom, the shadow of the lesion, atrophied lung and those fingers, why were they suddenly so chapped and swollen from handling murderous substances, Irène may have been her mother's cherished one, but so was research as well, radioactivity is my life and my child as well, and what is my future life to be if

not devoted to it, usually so discreet, this she confided to a
disciple, a young girl who would study with her, she was
mother to her work, a creation slow in coming to birth, and
who knows if the student remarked on the bloodless face of
her teacher there in that shed, that factory for heating poisons,
that airless shed, heated by an iron stove in winter, and what
was she to think of this diminutive woman, working silently
on chemical operations amid the odours of gas burners, her
creation on the point of consuming her at the very moment
her daughter Irène needed her at home, working on her first
teeth, crying ceaselessly, later her mother was to say I'll tolerate no cries of sadness or of joy, my husband and children
must be silent, no, no noise at all, and Mère thought that if
Mélanie had cried very little, it was because her mother was
always with her, no, Mère was wrong about that, Mélanie had
cried the day her parents divorced, the day her grandmother
was buried, when the distance between her parents suddenly
showed itself in such savage hostility, they no longer saw each
other, spoke together, even on a day like that, her grandmother's funeral, and Mère recalled Mélanie shedding finally
the tears she had held back the day of the communicants in
the Pyrenees, when one little girl had separated herself from
the line of communicants on the edge of a highway and had
in an instant been struck down by a bus, the flash of white
thread from her dress caught between the wheels, Why Mama?
Mélanie had asked her, her long hair masking her crying face,
she was the same age as Mélanie, what was unexplained,
what failed to explain the undefinable, the indefensible, and
above all the word not to be spoken in front of Mélanie, Mère
had managed to extricate herself from all these entanglements
. . . you see, it's like a moth, it comes, it flies away, the com-
municant was that white moth, the shining blood on the snow,
Mama, tell me why? Don't look back my dear, Mère had said,
we must learn that in life, don't look back, I can't explain any
of it, Mélanie, except that when a child is struck down like

that, it is a crime, a crime of God, this was how she tried to distract Mélanie from her sadness, for Mère had never spoken to her of God, and Mélanie fell quiet, never did Mère see her cry again, yes, perhaps on the day Samuel left for New York, but it was her son, her flesh, pulling away from her, she had been expecting that, hadn't she, Einstein said glory had not corrupted Marie Curie, but how could such glory corrupt a woman who deemed herself so ordinary, who had never considered this glory for herself? Notoriety was a man's business, a ridiculous ambition which did not concern her there in her shed, her shadowy laboratory, and with these numb, swollen hands impeding her progress, would she have time to finish, thus was the simple, pain-filled woman Albert Einstein was to meet later on, someone who thought of herself as she had been before, an ordinary being riddled with doubts and privation, then Mère remembered Chuan's question, Why aren't your sons here for your birthday, Esther? Oh, I invited them, but they don't have much time to visit their mother, Mère had replied abruptly, my sons take after their father, cosmetic surgeons, they don't have time for me anymore, Mère slid out from under Chuan's questioning intrusion into her family life, which seemed complex to her, forcing deeper inside the shame her sons had made her feel, lining up as they had with their father at a time when he was unfaithful to her, she saw her sons again on the back seat of the white limousine, they had mortified her, but still why couldn't she forgive them, it was time to erase past wrongs, these boys were young and already successful in life, she ought to have spoken of them with pride to Chuan and Olivier who were covered with pride in their son, well yes, Jermaine was charming, not contemptuous of his mother for being a woman, if you could call life successful when it concerns only material wealth, thought Mère bitterly, neither of her sons was as sensitive as Mélanie, though really she could not complain about them, whether she felt humiliated or not, the boys were her triumph like

Mélanie, they had a considerable place in society, even if they
did have precious little time to visit their mother, and they did
live far away in California but phoned often, more polite than
before, not like a friend of hers who had no news from her
son for years, and then suddenly learned by accident that he
had died of AIDS in a Los Angeles hospital, or had she found
out by messenger or letter, the mother had often said our son
Thomas never told us anything about his life, we know nothing about him, and why had these middle-class parents
entered into a pact of mystery when they suspected how their
son lived his life, the same bourgeoisie as Mère with its way of
plastering over its shameful secrets, rejection, when really
Thomas' parents had known all along where he was and how
he lived, but they did not want to know, rejection, dismissal
suited them better, like a bum living in the street or under
bridges, they covered up for him, he would die alone with his
skin diseases and rapidly deteriorating eyesight, an outcast in
a Los Angeles hospital where he had come for pneumonia,
and then without understanding why, he had died from the
radical rejection that had befallen him, depressed, hopeless of
any cure, might his mother have received a last phone call
from him begging her to take him in, and had she perhaps
refused, saying no, Thomas, you cannot come back to us, thus
the bourgeoisie patched up its shortcomings, one more scandalous than the next, like the wounds on Thomas' face, denying everything, seeing nothing, so Mère could not really
complain about her own sons, she would tell Mélanie how
proud she was to see them so well set in life, and if she didn't
forgive them now for her birthday, when would she, who
knows which will be the last birthday, this right hand trembling more and more, and Mère recalled her dreams once
more, each one perhaps the symbol of life's approaching end
refined to the point of sadism, an indicator of failing health,
wasn't that to be feared more than all the nastiness of dreams,
in one such dream, Mère was asleep in her room, a little after-

noon nap in the languid heat, it would have been so sweet if Mélanie had not suddenly burst into the room and her bed with a suffocating mass of lilies and delicately spread them around Mère's face, I'm just resting, Mère wanted to say, Mélanie can't you see my eyes are open, it's not yet time for flowers, they're choking me, wouldn't they be better opening out by the Mediterranean than here in this room where we'll all suffocate together, they're for you, Mama, said Mélanie, no, no, Mère wanted to cry, but no sound passed her lips, and when she awoke, Mélanie was no longer there, that was the day she took Vincent to the doctor's, so she couldn't have been in the room, could she, still the choking smell of Asian tiger lilies seemed to linger, sometimes in a dream, the putrefaction seemed to be stealing some other body than hers, one of her sons returning disfigured from a war, then leaning over him she realized it was herself, her eye colour, the son's pained mutterings became her own, this too seemed to her too hard to put into words, Mère wanted to tell her sons she had always refused to send them to war, she had not done this, but still she was mute, dimly aware that a disproportionate and sinister misfortune hung around her, and Mère remembered the story of Caroline's little bag, a small, flat, cloth handbag that she had mislaid that day they scattered Jean-Mathieu's ashes near The-Island-Nobody-Owns, the story of the bag was an absurd one, Caroline asking everyone if they had seen it, when, only seconds before, Jean-Mathieu had been scattered on the ocean, but this event still seemed fantastic for Caroline, who could not believe that her friend was really dead, expecting him to come home from Italy that evening, as he had so often done, she said he had given her that bag, almost as though he might scold her that evening for having lost this old gift, just a little bag with a compact, house keys, never mind the car keys, the chauffeur would be waiting for them in the port at sunset, Mère had noticed Caroline's sudden mental dislocation, usually so haughty, and now here she was asking everyone, where's my cloth bag, have you seen it, her face largely hidden by her broad-brimmed hat, but Mère heard increasingly rapid breathing, and Mélanie at the same time worriedly asking everyone if they had seen her daughter Mai, yes, she's run away again, Mélanie fixing her gaze on the empty swing where Mai, yes, we saw her there, swinging, but where is she now, and there was Mélanie, beside herself with worry, who had said to Caroline, here's your bag, you forgot it in the wicker armchair on the patio, and possibly there had been wicked smiles all around when Caroline had confidently mentioned her chauffeur, because they all knew Charly was an addict, all perhaps thinking, like Mère, about how they could get rid of this unsavoury character who might even be drugging her, Caroline hasn't been the same lately, she needs help soon, expressing child-like gratitude, Caroline had taken up the bag, thanking Mélanie, thank-you, thank-you, young lady, lady — a dated, old-fashioned word to address Mélanie, and she, a mother of two big boys, was at a loss to respond, eyes riveted on the swing Mai had abandoned, and where was she anyway, it would soon be time to get back to the boat she murmured, and Caroline went on, my dear young lady, Mélanie, I call you that because I was present at your birth, and yet here you are pursuing that frightful thing called politics, now her handbag was recovered, Caroline's face had composed itself again and become protective of Mélanie, reassuring, don't torment yourself, Mélanie, your little daughter never wanders far, you know, I used to want to slip away from my nanny at her age, and perhaps they had all noticed beneath the broad-brimmed hat the child Caroline who was every bit as unreasonable, an ageing adult now, still mixing with bad company like Charly because she fancied herself still young and had a fondness for youth, and although Caroline's friends showed her respect, knowing that with the loss of Jean-Mathieu today she was the most desolate of creatures, the thought that someone pitied her was repugnant, and Mère

thought I am Caroline, this sudden dislocation is me, and perhaps today, five years later at Mère's birthday celebration in
Chuan's garden, Mère would have loved to know where
Caroline was, why did she go out so rarely, was she still in
town, well, of course, it was gossip, vicious talk when people
said they saw her silhouette sliding around at night, walking
around the block with her dog in front of her unable to recognize her own house, none of it was true, Mère thought,
rumours and nasty tongue-wagging, but still why had Caroline
missed the party, she never would have skipped one before,
of course she would have been with Jean-Mathieu, what a
touching couple, travelling together, learned about painting
and opera, unparalleled friends, an accomplished life she had,
her photographs known round the world after those last exhi-
bitions in Paris and London, and his life too was a success as a
renowned poet Adrien said he envied, how had a poor boy, a
sailor from the port of Halifax, so mastered his art, the love of
Caroline had won him over, would he have travelled and written so much without her, she had never known he was born
poor, she had learned not to speak of her modest fortune in
front of him, he not realizing she was sharing it with him, and
where were they now Jean-Mathieu and Caroline, and what
was an accomplished life, the life of doubt led by Marie Curie
there in the greyish photograph talking to Einstein, they were
in Geneva by a lake, a prematurely aged woman draped in a
shawl, shivering with cold, a life without triumph it would
seem, a life triumphed over by the word solitude, solitude by
Lake Leman, talking to Einstein — was he even listening,
heavy in his coat and smoking his pipe, the immovable
empire of knowledge and absent-mindedness, not listening,
actually, and she knew it, just an enfeebled woman with
numbed hands and wrapped in a shawl, more isolated next to
this man than in her laboratory at the Institute, alone she was
able to make advances on all fronts, visiting a radium plant or
on the arm of an American president in the White House,

always the lone woman at international commissions, alone
next to Einstein, or to the right of Bergson and male colleagues, the only one at conventions, an elevating personality
notable by her austere face, from its white hair among all
those men, never smiling, and that ultimate triumph, thought
Mère, that word solitude on the verge of death, when Marie
Curie contemplated through eyes gas-burned and uranium-
seared in her lab, that which approached her and which she
awaited uncompromisingly, death, the end of a life she still
thought of as too banal in her abhorrence of vanity, she
demanded only one thing, to be left in peace, and Mère
strolled among Chuan and Olivier's guests wondering why
Caroline, who professed to love her, had not shown up, if she
had, Mère would have embraced her joyously, she might have
told her what was really on her mind, my dear Caroline, here
we are, you and I, about to make the same journey across,
whatever lies in the past for either of us, we could say we
weren't meant to be the motherly sort, I had several children,
and you a fruitful career instead and so many lovers and
adventures, and finally Jean-Mathieu who gave you the gift of
charming companionship, and the art with which you froze
time through the play of light on so many faces of writers and
poets, and in each photograph recreated a place, a time or an
elite spirit fixed, immortal it would seem, like the English poet
resembling a crucified Christ emerging from a trellis, how did
you capture that tortured pose, and the artist's studio, the office,
were not for you, better to go off and travel, intrigued always
by the complexity of your subjects, adventurer and portrait-
painter, with only the arm of Jean-Mathieu to lean on, around
the world you went, while I, often with children to look after,
would remain in one place, then suddenly you turn humbly to
us and ask where is it, my little cloth bag, how time has
passed, and if you were with us tonight, Caroline, I would
hold you with joy, for who knows what is going to become of
you or me, who can really tell, Mère thought, pretence and

lies are the thorny gifts that parents leave to their children, Daniel thought, Vincent would be spending the summer at camp, he'd have everything he could need up there in the mountains, riding, biking, footpaths through the woods, but why so far away from you Papa and Mama and Marie-Sylvie and the beaches and Samuel's boat *Southern Light*, why Papa, they have rooms and dormitories there, and in winter you can travel by dog-sled, catch whitefish, you'll have tasty meals, you'll see, and you'll be back here before the fall, you need to learn to breathe better, Vincent, and there's only the mountain, why not tell the truth, Papa, your inn or your castle is for sick kids, but Vincent, ever docile, said nothing and let his father take him there to woods in Vermont, Daniel thought with shame he had not been truthful, sure they would camp out in tents, in cottages and pavilions and dormitories, they would ride and fish and bike, naturally, two lakes, the view of the turrets and the river, but what wasn't said was that not one of these young campers could exhale properly, at night one could hear the whistling noises from their narrow chests raised up under the sheets by convulsions, the spasms, the contractions, pneumonia or bronchial asthma would go from one child to another, without ever alleviating the nightime breathing difficulties, come, it's time to sleep, they would say at the window as they watched the mist rise over the fir-trees, goodness how could their blood not manage to regenerate itself in such pure air, and through the rooms and dormitories the whistling noises Daniel could not bear to hear, but put his son in the care of specialists in hope of a cure, never would Vincent dare to complain, his father felt the tensing, the spasms, the father who forced these distant visits on him, for all at once, Vincent was the bird flying around, trapped in a prison of cables in Madrid, a pair of bees, flies or horse-flies, Daniel had seen them so often, their eggs frozen in their first winter, Daniel had lied to Vincent once again, he thought, never telling him what had to be said, and what Chuan and

Mère were saying about Caroline, that, yes, if she's not here
with us tonight, it's because someone won't let her out,
because she must be kept inside that residence, what residence Mère called out to Chuan as she disappeared, there was
so much for her to do with the friends and husband and son
who were looking for her, and Mère stubbornly went on, what
sort of residence, a residence for women artists of her ability
and social class, idle chatter and slander, Mère thought, none
of it could be true, nasty gossip, leave me alone, that was
what Marie Curie insisted on, a bit of peace, and said Caroline,
I've got my hat and gloves, I want to go out, they've invited
me to dinner, but a voice came back, no Ma'am, you're not
going out tonight, it's her, I know it, my black governess,
Caroline thought, she's got back into this house I used to live
in with my mother when I was small, though that was in
Louisiana, not here in New England, Charly my chauffeur is
waiting for me in the car, or rather the car I gave her, and all
the gifts I have given people, all those presents are lost to me
now, Caroline thought, for she felt she could no longer run
her own life as she used to, what was she doing in a house
she was told she could not leave, but a voice — she recognized it from the warm, melodious timbre as Harriet the black
governess' — kept saying to her, Ma'am, if we pull up your armchair, you can see the bay and hear chickadees singing in the
pine trees, but what's the point if I can't go out and play with
my cousin or take my pony out past the dunes, said Caroline,
Beauty he was called, do you remember, Harriet, my father
and grandfather were wonderful sailors, and we always lived
near the sea, I'm sure that's why I'm here by the ocean now,
dear, exactly where are we, can you tell me, the walls weren't
this high before, and I could play with my cousin, although
my upbringing was always too rigorous, in the morning when
my mother welcomed her lovers, everything was forbidden
me, that's when my cousin and I used to wander off with the
pony among the dunes, Beauty, that's what our pony was

called, Caroline knew she was repeating the same long sentence whose words eventually faded towards the end, a vague, nebulous sentence, occasionally lit by memories and vivid, elusive images, but it had to be enunciated right to the end, this sentence hammering the brain and the heart, Charly, where is Charly, I really don't like those young people she hangs around with, Madam, please do not use that name, the voice said, my name is not Harriet, I am Miss Désirée, I do remember you, why are you always contradicting me, Caroline said, irritated all of a sudden, I knew you long ago, remember Mississippi, my photographs of the South are famous, remember that mother with two children, that was you, Harriet, erect and so proud with your children, almost a haughty expression, and that's how I photographed you, a poor but majestic woman standing on that veranda with rotted boards, and that other photograph, who could forget that, our shame it was, a restaurant façade with words written in wood and stone: whites only here, reserved for whites, a black passer-by wearing a cap is reading this, remember Harriet, I took that photo myself, how strangely numb I felt, as though I were making a film, photographing without feeling anything, sometimes these poor people, with broken bottles placed in the spindly branches of trees to ward off evil spirits, spelled out on the roofs of their huts, where will you spend eternity, I didn't know we were those evil spirits, it was a way of calling up the dead to help them, strange isn't it, where will you spend eternity like a preacher's threatening finger, the sky seemed close, the plaintive wind whipping into the glass bottles like gunshots, it seemed, how sharp it sounded, I remember, far better to feel nothing, believe me, Harriet, especially when I took pictures of the gazelle-hunt in the desert from my first husband's convertible, that was certainly sobering, killing them while the car tore through whirlwinds of sand, it's always been wiser to numb oneself, we weren't alone in this grotesque appetite for hunting, I remember the cruel falconers

in the desert with their trained birds, eagles tracking the buz-
zards or perhaps some sand-coloured bird behind the odd
bush, unless the eagles and falcons cut its throat first, the falconers killed it amid strident cries, and I still hear their shrillness
like the sound of bullets, go falcons, kill, kill, and we ate the
bird, which tasted like pheasant, wild turkey, falconers who
could not eat the meat themselves because it was on offering
to Allah the merciful, the compassionate, I heard them praying
and offering the slit throat of their prey to the falcons and
eagles they prized so highly and raised on the taste of blood,
possibly they would one day cut our throats as well, and we
expecting none of this, once more by Mère's side in her red
dress with ruffles, Chuan was not reassuring, if Caroline has to
be confined to the house, she said, you can well imagine, my
dear, that it for her own good, so she can detox, what are you
talking about, Mère replied, well, you have guessed that our
dear friend has been addicted to morphine more and more
each day, the stillest waters run deepest, you know, the more
quiet and respectable one seems outwardly . . . Chuan's attention swiftly turned to her husband who was speaking very
loudly, and she reddened with distress, oh my poor husband
is making his speech, I warned him to steer away from certain
topics, to lighten up, still Olivier's voice seem to redouble in
volume, we are toys in the hands of religious hypocrites who
want to tell us what to do, he was saying, beware of those
who cling to a land of redemption and oppress us with their
prophecies and biblical presages, they build in the desert
where a bloodbath is sure to follow, beware these messianic
madmen, we are no longer ruled by reason, God, why doesn't
he shut up, Chuan said, wait, this arrow will come back at us,
Olivier continued to those who were still listening scattered
around the pool, only Mélanie seemed to be listening with an
air of utter gravity, she knew the retired senator's oratory fire
when addressing a crowd, and wasn't there some truth to it
when he said we are no longer guided by reason, and what

might that mean for the future of her children, she wondered, beside herself at the thought it might be true, were we nothing more than playthings in the hands of madmen, was this our ludicrous fate, was that it for us, to be falcons so falconers could revel in our decay, Caroline thought, imperiously she had demanded that her armchair be moved near the window with the angora cat she never let go of in her lap, the cat Charly had given her, my Charly, one day at a bullfight I filmed in detail at Lima the delirious, enthusiastic shouts of the bloodthirsty spectators burned on my temples, women, men, the killing of the bulls, and this is us . . . as corruptible as the animal hanging on to life amid their cries and their joy, and that image, fixed forever, of three horses in harness and ten men, workers recruited at the last minute, dragging the defeated bull from his dusty arena with ropes, as they will remove me one day, head dragging on the ground, last-minute hires with their lifting gear, and I won't want to go, the laughter and shouting were contagious, the dance of the bull during the rites, always the same ending, I lingered over that image of the bull being led to burial, lying on his side in the dust, feet still raised, their sharp cries, oh I remember, where are my hat and gloves, Harriet, I want to go out and not hear those shouts anymore, and that summer trip to Italy in 1946, I think, who was it who went with me, was it Jean, what was his name . . . what did he look like, a short while ago, when I wanted to see him, they told me Italy was the last place he went, he was so close to me, wasn't he, so why has he broken things off, why is he withdrawing, no letter, no nothing, that interference when I phoned him, no connection, no voice, the cries of Charly who really didn't like him, who was he, when his body had been reduced to ashes, I wanted to keep them near me, but they made me give them up, it was at the Palazzo Vecchio, and I had bought a new camera, you should have seen the flash set-up, the pictures, my fevered longing to capture the energy of those shadows, statues, sculptures, bronze horses

and eroded clock-towers, Palazzio Vecchio, just him and me
alone, the last place he travelled to, they said, I don't remember much of him, but they tell me I was there on no one's
Island, The-Island-Nobody-Owns, that's not true though, my
hat and gloves, they say they saw me, and dragged him away
from me, but that's not true, that word *him* weighed on
Caroline's spirit and was just a pronoun referring to a blank
face or a sudden absence of any face, but still I knew him
well, she repeated to herself, the lightweight scarves he wore,
his citronella colognes, *him*, what wavering, what dismay at
not knowing who *he* was, didn't we argue in the Paris
museum about the pre-Raphaelites, that assertive male tone of
voice when *he* insisted there were no precursors to Raphael,
and my cheeks were purple with anger, I had indeed
succeeded in capturing the energy, the firm shadow of
Michaelangelo's sculpture, and there *he* was next to me, saying, put down that camera dear friend, and let's talk a bit, look
how full the shadow in that statue is, he was fidgeting impatiently next to me, the walk has put me out of shape, he said,
no memory-lapse there, *he,* a hole, an air-pocket, a perforation
in the heart, I was holding the little casket, they snatched it
away from me, a perforation, open the box where the ashes
lie, never mind, I'll forget him, something Adrien whispered in
my ear, Caroline, the boat's waiting, Caroline, we'll all slide
into that perilous sea, a word, a remark about *him*, I know
how much you've loved him, they forcibly took the box from
my hands, *he* was the one who would slip into the ocean
waters, unfeeling *he,* slipping from my hands by accident, and
there was nothing I could do, in the summer of 1946, I had left
a tiresome husband for *him*, eyes scarcely find a place in a
forehead too vast, how wearisome when everything was so
standard and precise, the proportions of shadow in the sculpture, the stimulation of my eye behind the lens, then suddenly
this void surrounding a head, was it a beautiful one, off-
centre, and here it was bursting out of its frame, fruitless,

uprooted, the body and head of *him*, even his name no longer within my grasp, am I to blame, *he* had not been accessible for quite some time, perforated brain cells and heart, better to picture Italian Renaissance architecture instead and forget *him*, think about him no more, for there is no horizon in the gap of a viewfinder, schools and colleagues will study my photographs, I had no assistant to help me to the Tower of Giotto, they had been thinking of all those Renaissance engineers, then once up there, it was as though the light obscured my vision, veiled it, just as now I am losing the ability to register the light from *his* face and head, what I do know is that *he* was right to see that shadow, that veil over the face of the young London painter, whereas my unaware eyes hung greedily on the shadow, the veil over the face and head in their migration toward death, *he* said, it alarms me, don't photograph that young man, what you're photographing is not the life he transmits, it's the hand that holds the pencil, chalk on the open notebook, of a young man about to kill himself, tomorrow, in a few hours, it will be motionless, motionless perspiration on my brow and under the dark hair over my left ear, and I saw neither the shadow nor the veil that kept me from seeing, for the light from that dark sun stuck to my eyes, concentrating especially on the painter's right hand as it held the pencil to the book, and you could see the knot of veins and the squareness of nails, who could have detected the death sentence already on this body while it still breathed and perspired, it was like that when they asked me to photograph a group of soldiers just after a mission that had nearly proved fatal to them, I felt like suppressing what I say beneath those laden, hallucinating brows on a respite in some rest-house, it was as though the Grand Inquisitor had laid hands on them and caged them in their tormented postures, like the Allegories in the paintings by Max Beckmann, heads and bodies sadistically vice-gripped, or was I able to read in their hollow eyes what they were able to rescue of themselves from the trenches, cut off, decapitated, but still imprinted there on the painter's canvas, still breathing and alive, like marching ghosts, Max Beckmann, labelled a degenerate and forced to flee Germany, banished, had carved out the future of all monsters, the demons of a darker Europe, and there they were before me, sprung from the triptych panels by a painter who himself was demolished, painter or poet of the trench-mud, I said to myself, and is this how we face tomorrow, and our destiny still further on, and I wanted to suppress all I saw, for I was young then, barely out of my university internships, then the very same day, in that dark, ruined Europe, I heard a choir of voices so intensely jubilant that I just froze there in that dark, cold street, through the hearth of a destroyed building, I saw a stairway leading to a music academy, the teacher was a woman smiling at her students and letting herself be carried away irresistibly, guiding them with the baton and a wilful hand, it was a dress rehearsal of *Così Fan Tutte* by some very young people with voices that seemed already round and per-fect with notes of joy spilling forth on this glacial night under the rhythm of the hand that led them, the banality of the libretto was forgotten — the drama of a few infidelities — all gave way to the songs of love and desire, almost the whistling of a bird or a mocking child warning you of the perils of love, and those who had burned the earth in hatred and vengeance were no more, each and every one joyfully buoyant on stage, a delicate tumult giving voice to the sensuality of living, Mozart, acute psychologist that he was, knew in the end that loving was needed and nothing more, of course it seemed that every struggle was pointless combat, senseless stubbornness, voices, notes of a purity we somehow could no longer hear in our bellicose moods, notes of joy in this glacial night, pitiless, and listening, I said to myself, yes, I will face my fate, but how, if only the ecstasy had endured, if only I were still preceded everywhere by these voices, their enchantment, and tomorrow that young man I photographed, his artist's pencil between his fingers, sad-eyed and melancholy, would have had enough time to end it all, to leave his studio and his house empty, and I would have been helpless to stop his over-thought act, helpless to say to him, come hear this music with me, *Così Fan Tutte*, a flight of birds or laughing angels brushing against your deep shadows, cold halo around your body, come, follow me, and why was I not able to communicate this knowledge of joy, because it was not just for me, do you hear Harriet, Désirée, Miss Désirée, in complete dismay, one must still sing, Désirée says, when you're shining white folks' shoes, or washing floors in airports and public places, you've got to sing, my mother said, for God is there to listen, and I don't know if my mother was right to say this: you must sing through gritted teeth or right out loud, but do not be silent, pray, she said, spare me the prayers, Caroline said grumpily, how can a black servant, a simple girl, call her back to God's existence or resign herself to it, you're getting on my nerves, I told you to move my armchair over by the window, how can one love a God of cold, Frédéric said, just as I thought, oh, I hope, Mélanie said to Olivier as she breathed the perfumed night air drunk on music filtering into the gardens and up to the open doors of Chuan's house, she was saying, I hope that this doesn't come back to haunt us, she had the impression Olivier had forgotten his pride in oratory, so as to listen to her with full attention and anticipation he had placed his hand on her shoulder and said, I think of you often, you're a very active woman, full of fight, and you look out for the general good; your children will inherit those values too, but be careful who you rub the wrong way, their exasperation will quickly turn to intolerance and irresponsible fury, every day in the papers I read the sad story of anonymous madmen killing activists, one had founded two hospitals in Somalia and taken care of tuberculosis patients for thirty years, be careful my dear Mélanie, how serious you are, Chuan said, come dance with me, or shall I just dance by myself, Olivier, stop weighing Mélanie down with your advice, Chuan's red dress rippled by them like a wave, and suddenly the lightness of her spirit settled on Mélanie and Olivier, welded to one another by the weight of their thoughts: could it be that Samuel has really found the path of commitment in dance, Mélanie said, our children will go farther than us, accomplish more, and Mélanie replayed in her head the new choreography by Arnie Graal, it seemed that the work in which Samuel represented his dance school was defiance in the teeth of cruelty, or might she be thinking oner-ously of the over-wrought cruelty in the pillaging of scenes, tableaux, even dance steps which appeared fragmented and deformed? All at once, musical norms were fractured, and the show — one they had watched all night without sitting, no passivity, no seats, the inflexible choreographer said — could be compared to electronic music which was abstract in colour, was no more, and how was it that a show demonstrat-ing such discomfort elicited so much popularity, Mélanie won-dered, for the textures and sounds of synthesizers and sequencers, entangled with noise of a funereal fanfare, fires, the exceeding slowness of the dancers emerging like ghosts from walls of concrete and burnt asphalt, some on skate-boards, toy vehicles, attacked in their positions by fire, could only increase in us this sense of uneasiness, indeed, the insis-tence and unbearable slowness of these bodies tumbling into the void became oppressive, one saw in it what one did not wish to, the huge collapse of a city, multitudes of inhabitants fleeing into one another, like bees smoked out of their hive, was Arnie Graal's choreography too suggestive or was the spectator too suggestible, moulded in the clay of dance-steps and images he saw, there was no mistaking the terror still inspired by the event from which Arnie and his dancers had created an almost too-vivid creation, you have to think, Arnie said, of the collapse of a cathedral in ancient times, when artisans and sculptors hung onto tower stones, tools in hand, constantly working, tied to the translucent wall stones, stained-glass, huge windows, luminescent at this hour, and from where all these bodies, stooped or spread-eagled under the violent shock, will plunge into the void with a slowness accentuated by stupefaction at the very moment the glass cathedral moves in seismic oscillations to its foundations, Mélanie thought she disliked Samuel's being one of these dancers, like a dominant, isolated figure falling headlong past a wall, his left leg advanced in a lamentable gesture of revolt against heaven, all of it was only too true, she thought in horror, it seemed to her that her son, in that fall to rocky ground, forgetting the stage onto which he would re-emerge . . . Arnie had so masked the sight-lines . . . would have his spine, kidneys, and neck broken, when for too long his head, brain, and all his faculties would be intact, and his memory-centre would have too much time, if only two seconds, to think, suffer the ultimate, in a reflection too agile, many a mother had lost sons thus, Arnie would have told them, she ought to have added that in the inconsolable part of herself, she was close to those mothers and sons, but Arnie also distracted the audience, those bodies falling with a slowness exacerbated by the artifice of choreography, he said, are bodies that have been thrown from helicopters into the sea in their hundreds by dictator-generals, a lone man capable of carrying out all these villainies with his military apparatus, prisoners and political detainees were tossed, still breathing, above the Pacific waters, and these operations are still going on, what do you feel when you are the pilot or mechanic of these helicopters after dropping their human bundles from Santiago or wherever it is into the sea, those who disappeared into the waters will say nothing, of course, but what do you feel when one by one the bodies fall with measured, concentrated slowness, Chuan said to Mélanie, remember, tomorrow at dawn will be the flotilla of sailboats for the summer festival, and at night the quays will shimmer with swaths of light, we'll see an exquisite chain of white boats beneath banners and decorations, I'll be up at

dawn to see who wins the race, *Walzer* or *Compass Rose*, we
won't sleep all night, of course, my wife's active and indefati-
gable, while my strength wanes, thought Olivier, admiring
Chuan's intense appetite for life, the night is just beginning
and she's already talking about tomorrow, did he need to
approve of her agreeing with Jermaine on this hard-driving
music that filled the house, and those boat-races on the ocean
were so boring and especially loud, it's so hard to write my
articles at this time of year, Olivier told Mélanie, but at least I
see more of my son, he's like his mother, he also loves partying too much, Samuel's teacher in New York, Mélanie
resumed, is our black Balanchine, that's what my son says, it's
too bad everything he creates is so close to real life, you do
have to respect tradition a bit after all, Olivier said absently,
while admitting he understood nothing about the choreographer's controversial ballets when Mélanie referred to him, perhaps he's too innovative, don't people criticize him for
pushing the limits of the human body too far? Is it necessary to
break these young dancers at the beginning of their repertory,
Mélanie wondered, then she remembered seeing her mother
in a dream the night before, another of those same dreams,
obsessing, rampant, perhaps indicative of Esther's difficulties
and shoals; Mère invited Mélanie to dinner in her gazebo, but
instead of the place settings, there were two black leather
gloves on the tablecloth, difficulties and shoals, Mélanie
thought when she saw her mother's serene and smiling face
among the evening's guests, Esther always sprang to life when
the conversation touched on something she knew about, no,
Mélanie's mother was not showing any sign of weakness,
except perhaps a trembling in the right hand, scarcely notice-
able, a dream to be forgotten, except that the scene of the two
gloves seemed bothersome, and Mélanie couldn't manage to
rid herself of it, why not wait for dawn and the arrival of the
boats on calm waters with Chuan and her impetuous feelings
of joy and astonishment, all these forebodings would vanish

out there on the beach, face and hair wet with the salt and the air, how could Augustino be left out, transparent water at dawn, salt air, and Caroline said, thank you Désirée, I am finally comfortable here by the window with Charly's cat on my knee, I don't want him taken away, he's fine here, affectionate creature, all that remains of Charly, I loved Charles too, when the man with thinning hair, whose name escapes me, still came to visit, till everyone began withdrawing from me, Charles who once confided in me, only you, dear Caroline, can understand me, he said, because you are a woman and a great spirit, shouldn't I admit that this wonderful essence of a spirit, so great that nothing can quench it, was really more Charles' than mine, noble ascetic of poetry that he was, perhaps he shared with me only that affinity, out of love, and he agreed to lose his soul, if soul is the flesh that submits to the tortures of love, if soul is also the body that marches on blindly, what do we really know, Charles had a loyal companion in Frédéric, with whom he shared a life in Greece whose splendours he praised in his books, already a distant happiness, so many books read and written, then suddenly those wrinkles at the corners of Frédéric's mouth, his first dizzy-spells, his fall when he was smoking by the pool, Charles thought the grey curtain of mortality was descending on them without warning, he thought he could heal his reluctance to write in his room with the blinds drawn and through which the emanations of jasmine and acacia drifted when opened, but denser than these perfumes was the melancholy that gripped his chest, he thought he was doing the right thing by withdrawing, this time so inaccessible, the misanthropy of the unapproachable poet was well known, every year he left like this, all alone and no one knew where, Eduardo stood his green Sunday-outing bicycle against the fence, where it rusted while he did the gardening, Charles preferred to spend Sundays in the deserted town, going by in my car, I pretended not to recognize him by the water-line, though that neck and delicate man's head were familiar to me,

so often I had photographed them throughout Charles' literary
life, from its precocious beginnings, I knew him as well as if
he had been my own child, a dreamed-of adolescent that time
altered so very little, now so impenetrable that no one could
find him out, he would go to India, an ashram in Delhi, and
that would be his fortress where he could meditate and write.
He didn't know who was expecting him there, or under what
sun he would melt, cook and be struck down, was he forgetting, in these spiritual shadows he looked for, the meditation,
the going-beyond individual consciousness, a denatured mental concentration, how could Charles forget that, beyond this
iron thought supported by pride, there was another Charles,
still a man of the flesh, subject to temptation as others were.
We never know when a star will detach itself from the vault of
heaven and make us stumble. I can say that I knew nothing of
it, yet love came easy to me, before I met the man whose
ashes now sleep at the bottom of the sea, at that island no one
owns, and as for Charly, you forbid me to speak her name, as
if you had any right, Harriett, she phoned yesterday and asked
to speak to me, didn't she? Now why can't I see her, you're all
plotting against me here, my hat and gloves, I want to go out,
you say I might fall down in those rainy avenues with my dog,
and I assure you it was the dog that got me lost that time,
don't give me any of that medication, tell Charly to come and
see me, I can show you the club she goes to in the evenings,
it's just a matter of cheques and stolen goods, I can forgive for
all of it, you, Harriett, and Miss Désirée, you misjudge her, you're
a zealous woman, always off to church to pray when you're not
here with me, and if I decided to stop eating, what would you
do, let me die in peace, just one star detached from the heavens
and we see nothing anymore. I don't think it's good for you to
pray so much, good thing you sing as well when you're in
church, and sometimes I go to sleep to the sound of your
voice, but I sense too much begging and prayer in it, as
though you were reciting psalms to get on my nerves, yes, like

you were doing it on purpose, Désirée, remember how I used to love hearing the guitar-players in the streets of New Orleans, the rhythm of those blues, and the Mardi Gras celebrations, remember, Harriett, my mother used to say those rhythms set me loose, even then I felt myself possessed and ready to break all the rules, though they left everything up to you, Harriett, because my family didn't have much time to bring me up, so you had to decide everything for me, like Mai, that girl of Mélanie's, you couldn't do anything with me, and if that one is already a runaway, just wait and see how much trouble Mélanie's going to have with her, and in Delhi Charles meet his devastating angel without knowing it, theatre was Cyril's stock-in-trade, true or false, was Cyril a comedian, lazy and unemployed? The young man certainly had the key to reciting poetry with a deep voice, you like the contemplative poets, like me, Charles said, Milton, Blake, how could one be still in the company of a thirty-year-old, whether it was all lies or truth, and Cyril said to Charles, wasn't it like a fiancé's promise, and Cyril lacked Charles' modesty, Charles who was truly great, I will read your poems all over the world, here in Delhi, later in Holland where they've invited you, not without vanity, Charles basked in this new discovery, Cyril was excessively lanky, more than Charles liked, without being wiry, his back and shoulders being muscular, it would be very pleasant to travel, continue those professional travels that Charles had told everyone he was giving up, but meeting Cyril changed everything, he would go off tomorrow to those conference halls he so hated with this alter-ego whose clear and azure eyes — so clear one saw nothing in them — one got lost in, this double lyrically reciting Charles' poetry, contemplative, reflective, like the work of Milton to whom the critics compared him, Charles, who was reserved, relating to his admirers only through letters, forgot his reserve, welcomed Cyril's spontaneity, he who dressed Charles up in his cajolery, and how can those accustomed to discreet, almost cold, personal relations with others, not be suspicious of the comfortable bodies of such liars? Perhaps at this moment Charles missed the peace and safety of his correspondence over many years with Vladislav, the young Russian poet, one of Charles' passionate admirers, whose face, praise heaven, he had never seen nor whose tempestuous heat he had never felt close to him. Cyril, though, was simply there, never asking Charles if he was wanted or not, but just there waiting to be taken in his arms, at once abandoned and compromising. Heavier still, and bulkier than Charles had ever imagined, when he constantly felt the attraction of eyes so very clear, yes, perhaps at those moments he missed the unpremeditated quality of Frédéric, the subtle words of Vladislav, the Russian that Charles knew how to translate, disconcerted, Charles wondered what was happening in his life, he felt spoiled and put upon, like his friend Caroline, where had he stumbled and into what trap? He recalled Jacques, so loved by Tanjou, and who knows, these things are as unavoidable as they are brief . . . he would write to Frédéric, he would phone him tonight from Delhi to say he would soon be back, as a prisoner of his senses, he did feel so unworthy of the Hindu tradition he'd wanted to take up, didn't he? Frédéric understood him, didn't he? He had just written to him, warning him to be financially prudent and not to let into their house everyone who came to the door begging for help, Frédéric's weak point was never being able to say no to the most off-the-wall and marginal of people. Whenever Charles was not keeping an eye on him, wasn't he always giving his money to whoever needed it without discriminating, it seemed an incorrigible fault in him, Charles thought, exhorting his friend to exercise caution and not go out to jazz sessions alone at night, but in his declining health to make sure Edouardo was always nearby. In his letters to Frédéric, Charles omitted Cyril's name, surely it was better that way, and he repeated to himself that the burn he got in India would certainly heal soon. My dear Caroline, he wrote me, I can tell you everything, including what to do, but I no longer know what to think. The problems I have with Charly, her disobedience, her nastiness, keep me from replying to Charles. I think it all began with Jacques, who left us before he was fifty, the just man, the Kafka specialist, impartial, exuberant, how is it he was struck down like the patriarch Job on his bed of manure, with wounds, low blows, and so on — for that is how he is seen in paintings — Jacques the first of wave in an infinite ocean? The first breaker before so many others? He left us so suddenly, we all felt ourselves going with him. We were dismayed, not even able to shed a tear, unlike Tanjou, to whom Jacques had promised to return every evening as the sun set on the sea, his faithful visits would be heralded in pink to recall his exuberance in life, Tanjou waited, but Jacques never came, perhaps only in a slight breeze, a summer's breath on Tanjou's mouth. We need to be concerned when we completely change our habits or build up fantasies, Charles, however, wasn't, he walked down Delhi's lush green streets, hand-in-hand with Cyril, seeming to put on his partner's daring, his limitless temerity, and his former virtue of temperance was gone, now his life was stormy and exalting, and he wrote these new verses as soon as he was alone in his room by the river, no dryness, no dessicated regimentation for him, there were no rules for poets, all at once his lines took on a volcanic quality, ardent and sensual as his writing had rarely been, that he had always avoided these excesses and was now metamorphosed did not bother him. I wrote to tell Charles that his friend, the poet Jean, had let me down badly, never answering the letter I sent via Charly. Never. I was certainly not expecting that moment of ashes on the ocean near The-Island-Nobody-Owns. I thought we all had so much time ahead of us, Charles did too. Jacques was the one who caused all this upset, Harriett, Miss Désirée, he shook us all up, the last time I took his picture, it was summer, but he was cold, and I could sense him shivering under his corduroy pants and turquoise sweater—almost the colour of his eyes—do you know what Tanjou says to me, Caroline, that I don't love him enough, is it true, Caroline, I'm not detached nor impassive, or that's just the way I am, this feigned frigidity, and then he wept, poor child, and went on repeating, you don't love me enough, God what can you do, tomorrow, later on, tell him Jacques loved him well enough, very much, don't forget, and through my lens I captured Jacques like a painter, his ironic expression, his pale cheeks, saying good-bye to him all the while. Was it the loss of the little cloth handbag or the loss of her memory that affected Caroline more on The-Island-Nobody-Owns, it seemed catastrophic to Mère that she had dreamed about two opaque travel bags someone had put on that rough, back lawn in autumn and winter that had gone unmown for a long time, what was the figure two that ran through some of her presentiments, or that confrontation between Mélanie and her mother, two women telescoped into one when death made its entry, the faded condition of the garden had moved Mère to call Julio, Jenny and Marie-Sylvie to help her with the clearing of it, and where were they all, why weren't they answering, an icy wind whipped at the windows, they've all run off and left me alone, even my daughter, she'd thought, when just at that moment, Augustino appeared with one of his birds sitting on his shoulder, not Samuel's parrot, but an odd sort of parakeet that moved bizarrely on his shoulder, you called me, Grandmother, he asked, look at our garden, where did all this rain come from, the frost on the palm-leaves, and why are the trees so bent over, as soon as Mère and Augustino were outside, the parakeet flew off its familiar perch but seemed to have forgotten how to fly, don't let it get away, Grandma, Augustino yelled, where's it going anyway, it might break a bone, whose travel-bags are those, Mère asked him, two, always the figure two, and as she awoke from her nap, she saw Augustino next to her with the parakeet sitting meekly on his shoulder, could you keep an eye on her

Grandma, I'm going for a swim, isn't too cold, said Mère still in her dream environment, then she felt the bird's plumage on her cheek, saved again, she thought, she had been saved, and those bags were there ready for her visit to her sons in California, it reassured her that Augustino had woken her up before dinnertime, she'd have time to get dressed before the evening meal, it seemed that whenever his grandmother insisted they all get dressed for dinner, Augustino went out, she'd put the parakeet back in its cage, it bit everyone with its pointed beak, except Augustino, whom it loved, yes, those travel-bags would come in handy, she thought, if ever she decided to visit her sons; what a magnificent night it was in Chuan's gardens for Mère's birthday, now just bury the thought of those bad dreams, nightmares actually, she smiled and spoke to everyone but was concerned that Caroline was not among them, there were very few friends of her own venerable age, some did not seem to change over time, like Suzanne or Adrien in his black jacket and white pants, listening to Daniel with polite coolness, what was it they were talking about, the lengthy follow-up to his novel *Les Etranges annees*, ah yes, said Adrien in his professorial tone, I'll be most curious to read you soon, a lie Daniel paid no attention to, thinking he would retreat to his monastery in Spain, worn out by this boring socializing, he'd only gone along with this party to please Mélanie, his book was his whole life, so why did he let himself get torn away from it so easily? Yes, he thought, if he had let off Hitler's dog, why not also exculpate the children of treacherous, reprobate officials, what would he, Daniel, have done if he had been the son not of one of history's victims, but of one of its executioners like Himmler or Göring, if his birth had been in that apocalyptic shipwreck? If his parents, his father, had held macabre sway over the execution of so many innocents, they would have revolted him, but he and his offspring, what would they have done? He'd have been the son of a man hanged at Nuremberg whose vicious ghost would have tormented him everywhere, destitute, he would not have hesitated to sell his father's story for food, even if he knew nothing of it except what they told him — though would he believe it, missing his guilty suicide-father, hanged in some murky past, he'd have been like all children, reliving family scenes in which he sat by his mother's and sister's sides and felt a kind father stroke his hair, no denying that hand, a kind, always affable father, blameless except for an affair with his secretary, something the son only learned about much later, and with chagrin, the sons and daughters of cursed, reprobate men would always have to hide, flee the partisans of hate, and why were they hated, they wondered, fleeing from interrogation, little children locked in with these men's wives in hotel rooms with no way out, internment camps, the pretty estates given to their father by the good Führer in times past, where were their dolls, their croquet set, they no longer knew where they could live or hide, these little ones and their mothers suddenly stripped of everything, taken in by nuns in homes for the sick, these little ones and their mothers, bereft, had not understood that, if these hotel rooms were empty and the beds deserted, it was because the whole place had been purged of its infirm, all injected or gassed, and the stoic nuns welcomed the offspring and wives of those who had committed these crimes, saying God will not forgive them, God will not forgive them, and they, so little, had understood nothing the nuns said to them, because they were the sons and daughters of those who would never be pardoned by Man or by God, and they gave the sons and daughters of these officials chocolate and sweets out of pity, knowing well that these small ones must be rendered blameless, if they had known, if they had seen their fathers enter here to get rid of all the defenceless infirm and sick, the ones their fathers called rubbish, garbage, if the sons and daughters of these fathers had seen what they had, the injections and the excruciating agony, they would not have wanted to live a second longer, no, faced with all those cries, these sons and daughters would not have wanted to live and carry the seed of evil, these sons and daughters of the same age as those who were gassed, four or five years old some of them, understood nothing of what the nuns were saying to them, where were the dolls, the croquet set and the pretty German estate given to their father by the good Führer, you must never say your name, your father's name, because you too will never be pardoned for anything, innocent as Hitler's dog and with that same animal candour, betrayed, they listened wide-eyed in fright, still you will grow up like all the others and be courageous, the nuns said as they washed them and cared for them, just like the infirm and feeble in spirit, tomorrow, bringers of justice await you in their hundreds, and what will you say to them, we will pray for you, little angels, and already judged by the justice-bringers in their hundreds, they listened in tears, where was Daddy, would their kind daddy come, these sons and daughters had no idea that at the same time, their fathers, conceivers of carnage and irredeemable, definitive solutions, would be signing agreements this January on the shores of Lake Wannsee, it was too bad that this time, indeed, the problem could not be solved, the conceivers said as they signed, ordinary bureaucrats following protocol, they had no choice but to eliminate human beings, signed it was now in the building on the edge of Lake Wannsee, one of the bureaucrats had picked a few scavengers to pick up belongings after it was all over, death was a factory, an industry from which fabulous gifts flowed: hair and jewels, an operation their fathers were be proud of, the kind fathers of little ones called Gudrun, Sylke, and Lina, safe in their infirmaries, would these nice daddies be home for the holidays, their mothers barely survived out wandering the streets disguised as peasants, and destitute, paperless, in an exodus like a soldier's flight, pushing carts filled with vegetables and rabbits, in this month of January, in this locale near Lake Wannsee, the fathers of Klaus, Sylke, and Gudrun had opened their secret files and smoked cigars as they put the finishing touches on their strategy, oh yes, this time there would be an unredeemable, final solution, the decision had been made, Sylke and Klaus wondered why their fathers had forgotten them here with these nuns, would they ever be a family again, or would they just visit their fathers' graves once a year, and tomorrow each one would have their father's ghost sticking to their skin, each would have a hanged man or suicide, why would no one have pity on these innocents? You're wandering into forbidden territory, Adrien said with that professorial voice of his . . . which interests nobody, he might have added, it might be different if Joseph, your father, were the writer in the family, but you weren't a prisoner in Buchenwald like him, he seized control of himself under Daniel's smouldering gaze, is he fishing for compliments the way all these young authors do, Adrien wondered, well, bravo, my friend, I'm glad to see that you've been doing such good work, say, is your father still going to play the violin tonight the way he did for the millennium festivities, it was very moving to hear, Daniel knew only too well these gambits of Adrien's when he refused to talk about Daniel's books, this attitude was one more reason to retreat to the monastery in Spain, he thought as he explained that his father had little time for the violin now that he was Chairman of the Institute of Marine Biology, and so his technique had suffered, talking to Adrien, Daniel had the feeling that he was just chatting, going on, when he would rather be talking literature with the nationally renowned poet who was snubbing him and whose wife then came over and hugged Daniel as if to intercede for him, Suzanne's sudden kiss, full of spontaneity, and Daniel blushed with pleasure, when you're in Spain, I'm going to miss our Friday breakfasts on the terrace when I can read you my poems, she said, you're not hard on me the way my husband is, too bad so few writers of your generation like being around us, Daniel, sometimes I say to myself, you are my only friend, at least I know you won't make fun of me if I laugh and push away that word, old-age, which is the enemy of joyfulness. Children inherit their father's past, even if it's only partially revealed to them, Daniel thought, and Ari walked farther out onto the jetty with his daughter Lou in his arms, look at all the stars in the sky and the boats lit up like cakes with candles on them, tomorrow's the race all those sailboats are waiting for, too bad one of them way over there is the eerie recreation of a torpedo-boat, your real name is Marie-Louise, no, Lou, stammered the child, then she let out screams that pained her father's ears, Lou, Lou, Lou, father and daughter, wrapped up in the same night-shadow, high on the stone road, so small-seeming, so far, at the far end of the wharf, Lou's face showing the grimace of pain that comes so quickly to small children, resolute, she did not cry, but her father saw that the large movements of the waves under the planks of the jetty did not scare her, though she didn't much like it, all that blackness around them, the stars that barely lit the rippling waves, why did her father make her do this walk every evening, water and waves didn't reassure her much, except when they were warm, calm, and contained in the pool at home, where she could wade after she had painted her body with her father's pencils and brushes, that liner over there, that's *Le Commodore*, Ari said, that's a pretty big vessel that's going to pollute our beaches, and the boat watching us is *L'Ange de la paix, The Angel of Peace* is watching all of us, hear that, Lou, that's nothing but the wind and the waves, the ocean breeze forever in you hair and mine, as everlasting as the sky and the sea, as you and me, and these thirty-kilometre winds are common at sea, later I'll teach you to navigate, then Ari buttoned Lou's sweater, the one with kittens on it, she'd never be cold in her chequered overalls, though her feet were bare, how good the wind is, how much good it does us, he felt as infuriated as this sea and wind, not wanting his daughter to be baptized, but no one had paid attention to him, and he hated the idea that a priest, a complete stranger and signed by the message of a religion, put ablutions on the forehead of Marie-Louise, a child born free, listen Lou, what your mother did in that church that day made me mad, it's a fraud that I, your father, would never have allowed, a mistake, a misunderstanding, you're as free as the wind and the air, and always will be, that religion always takes advantage of newborns, and what could you do about it, loud cries, I don't believe a thing they say, your mother wanted you in that ridiculous white dress and bonnet, and me there in church too, a day of futility and humiliation for you and me both, non, she and I will never understand one another, it's low tide, you'd like to back to the car, sweetheart, you're already instinctively good in the water, and soon you'll be able to swim, OK, let's go home if you're going to sulk, if that's what you want, you have to want to, that's fine, why didn't I just grab you out of that priest's hands before all those ridiculous immersions and ablutions, but no, your mother, Ingrid, forced me to be reasonable, standing there in that church, not angry, remember, you are free, and the monk Asoka had written to him, oh dear Ari, be as patient as those oriental flowers, so persistent they flourish and bloom in the mud, be respectful of your child's mother, unfortunately, you are not separated or divorced, sad really, Ingrid is entitled to the Christian sacrament of baptism for her daughter, isn't she, just as you are a convert to Buddhism late in life, cultivate the flowers of patience and acceptance in yourself, my dear Ari, be persistent as the tea bush, the camellia flower, for we are different, all of us, I am in England after a trip to the south-central United States, I was meditating with some students in Dallas when a large man came up to me with hostility and said, aren't you ridiculous in your orange robe from shaved head to toe, I am an itinerant monk, and in my country this is how monks dress, it is the habit of poverty, well, if that's the god-awful way you dress where you live, why don't you just go back there, the big man tried to insult me, but I just threw

him off balance by being gentle, which, as you know, my dear
Ari, is also a form of patience, then suddenly I started questioning this man, a man piqued to hostility by my appearance
— what is appearance anyway — and little by little he started
to tell me about his family, his house in the country, and forgot all about my orange pilgrim's robe, when you get bitter
with your wife Ingrid, you are certainly not free from desire or
hurtful thoughts, Buddhism is based on responsibility for oneself and the fulfilment that emanates from it in adulthood, Ari
thought, they baptized my daughter when she was barely
born, and without her willing consent, Ingrid, her mother,
even had her own doubts about some of the mysteries of faith,
Christianity defined hell as the place where souls were tormented perpetually, but if those souls were damned, hadn't
they already had enough in this world, Ingrid could not understand how a subterranean place discharging rivers of fire onto
spirits could exist, Lou, her daughter, her lamb, would not
have her mind tarnished by the sadism of such a mystery, after
all, they both told her, each one separately every day, that she
lived in a paradise, they knew how cruel the world could be,
this reality of a true hell, and Lou would realize it quickly
enough, Ingrid and Ari had been ideal couple so recently, and
already that was no more, Ari thought as he held his daughter
close against the wind, the perfection of it had been poisoned
by so many disputes and quarrels, and who bore the brunt of
them, thought Ari, Lou, Marie-Louise who got bundled from
her father's big house to her mother's cramped apartment,
where she shared an apartment with Jules, Ingrid's first child,
Lou, an unhoped-for child in parents over forty, their gift, a
couple once perfect and now in dissension, gradually dissi-
pated, scattered after the birth of their daughter, Ari had
painted and drawn the couple, and on this solid foundation,
this beauty and love, had sketched out several plans for sculptures, sketches he felt were so irresistibly sexual, but which he
did not dare destroy, and which he looked at with regret in his

studio, could it be the influence of these religious notions that
had split them apart as it split and annihilated nations; having
scattered and reduced one another to nothing, Ingrid and Ari
still had Lou, and who knew where she was going to sleep
tonight, at Daddy's till Sunday maybe, then on Monday her
mother would take her back, still Ari would so have loved
them all to be inseparable, be patient my dear Ari, Asoka
wrote his friend, I'll be in Mali in a few days, where so many
children carry their mothers' viruses, already I am wondering if
it isn't too late, if the situation isn't desperate, what will I say
to those mothers who ask me for help, when I know how
badly the whole of West Africa is ravaged, meditate and pray
for us all, my dear Ari, kiss Lou for me, this will be my third
trip to Mali, and Petites Cendres waded through the sauna at
the Porte du Baiser Saloon, it was not him, Ashley, looking
mismatched and ugly, that men came looking for here, he
thought, there was a fresh crop of New York models hanging
out in the bar, too young perhaps, but tantalizing to the old
guys . . . sweet, nice, white boys with milky skin, Ashley
thought, must have just let go of their mothers' apron-strings,
all very with it in their tight-fitting tops, strutting like models
in a magazine, and one, slender as a girl with straight blond
hair, insolent, but sweet as candy, didn't laugh like the others
when he saw me come in, just smiled, hey Ashley, there you
are, where've you been, someone was looking for you, guy
with a thick neck you should stay away from, if you want to
know, we're clean, all three of us, going to a show tonight,
and the cocktails are cheap here, I bet they don't pay you
much either, though you're a good guy, Ashley, there were the
milky-skinned boys and the blonde with straight hair who'd
smiled at me, and near him, noses in their martinis, a couple
more teenagers, one was a model too, I bet, a graceful, Asian
kid that the straight-haired blonde was hugging, his brother he
said, and the third with a dark fringe over his forehead, a
Mexican, Ashley thought, the trio formed a circle, then these

kids waltzed, hands on shoulders and laughing, their teasing relaxed Petites Cendres, and after the show, they were going to surprise the Queen of the Desert with splashes of champagne in her dressing room all over her expensive feathered coat, but she wouldn't mind, she'd say, come on you jokers, let's do some dancing and singing in the streets, but watch out for the cop and his checkpoint, and these rowdy kids would say, oh how beautiful you are, Queen of the Desert, pearls wet with bubbly and all, you're why we came to this island, to whistle and stomp at your shows when you can't get mad at us, how could anyone get mad, she said, you're way too cute, where've you been anyway, come on into the dressing-room and let's talk awhile, and Ashley would be alone in the sauna, did you know the instructor wouldn't let me into the gym today, she said in a plaintive voice to the three boys who weren't listening anyway, yeah, he had the nerve to say that to me, he didn't mind my darkish skin, he said, he lives with a black boxer, it was the marks, these swellings on my skin that might infect the other athletes, one of the boys raised his head and said, we'll beat him up for you, though he hadn't listened to Petites Cendres' complaints, they were playing, having fun, see those swellings and marks, it wasn't true, he just said that so he could throw me out, how can I infect the others just working out on the mat or the parallel bars, then the instructor said, what about hugs in the shower, sweat, sperm, this is a classy gym here Ashley, not a bordello like those hook-up joints, is that any way to talk to me, I feel humiliated, I'm a real person, yes me, said Petites Cendres, but an offended person, said the joking boy, God bless you, Petites Cendres said to the straight-haired blond, you smiled at me when you came into the saloon, it makes me feel better after what the gym instructor did, if my ancestors hadn't prayed to God, they'd still have chains on their wrists and ankles, but God was there to beg to and sing for in their misery, though he watched helpless as they were lynched and their blood dried in the sun, with God they had everything, no matter if they were humiliated with dirty work day after day, may God always smile on you and protect you from people's meanness, boys, Petites Cendres said with his hand over his heart, for he felt the God he praised was inside him, others may have empires, but Petites Cendres had God within the temple of his withered flesh, although the rejection by the gym instructor who had shut the door on him that morning had left an impression like spittle on his face . . . was this the Manhattan street where Samuel had seen Our Lady of the Bags, a thirteen-year-old itinerant with a delicate face haloed in golden curls, an unlettered child in a pleated skirt, sitting on the sidewalk with an open Bible in her lap, the same one Samuel had shouted jeers at from his car, you and your predictions, lies, that's all they are, lies, when are you going to shut up, you liar, and what are you going to do when heaven unmasks every one of you, children of the shadows, Our Lady of the Bags had recited in a monotone, when the heavens open and engulf your houses and buildings in flames, then what will you say? Yes, this was the spot where Samuel had seen and mocked the destitute prophetess, more in high spirits than in hardened ill-will, what had become of her, where was she, if among the disappeared, under what pile of rubble would she be, and if alive, maybe she would come back to this street and Samuel could apologize to her, for however ignorant and desolate she was, Our Lady of the Bags seemed to be right, Samuel would have told her he danced every night in that unwieldy choreography of Arnie Graal's from which he barely seemed to emerge in pieces each dawn, so crushing and rigid was the discipline that, if he danced these steps with a fire that the art of dance could reproduce in its physical depth and density — at least with the images of bodies broken in pieces, taken apart — it was so no one could forget what he had seen and lived through that day when the predictions of the unlearned Lady of the Bags came true, and so no one

could forget that, no sooner did one recover from these pun-
ishments than others went on elsewhere or had been continuing for such a long time, and Samuel wanted to say to Our
Lady of the Bags how perplexed and torn he was, unable to
confide in any one, except perhaps to her whom he had
derided, the unlettered, uneducated little girl with her diaboli-
cal reflections on that sunny day in New York, but where was
she, under what mountain of granite was she lying, her halo
of hair beneath the muck and stones, he would like to tell her,
I dance too, as others have done around me, in fact that very
day with their tributes, saying, come, let me give you a bit of
joy, a caress, a moment of happiness in the roar and the
calamity, so that hope for the young like us revives and does-
n't die, and she would have said, the unlearned Lady of the
Bags, I can't read, I don't know what I'm saying either, it's
delirium of revelation from heaven, for Our Lady of the Bags
did not know that both latent and overt terrorism had threat-
ened her country for a long time, and she had no country but
the street and the greyness of the psychiatric clinic she had
escaped from, now sitting out on the city sidewalks, with an
open Bible on her lap and surrounded by bags, he thought he
sensed a turbulence surrounding her, whirlwinds raised as a
closing to her hymn of imprecations, she had asked Samuel
where she would sleep tonight, whether it would be in the
park where she listened to the preaching of the Apostle in the
morning dew who had said to her, go to your parents, you
cannot follow me, for my mission is to live alone and preach
hope everywhere, whether it be in a station where hoodlums
and skinheads persecuted her, Samuel had a home and parents, but Our Lady of the Bags had nothing, like so many others of her wandering tribe, she knew nothing of a country that
would defend her or protected her rights, and Samuel, who
had it all, had mocked her, saying, what are you talking about,
you little idiot, shut up, will you, and she had said, at last you
understand, son of darkness, and it will be too late, Samuel's

inheritance was the earth, he thought, handed down from his parents and grandparents, and they had read and heard everything about goodness over decades and centuries, they knew what belonged to them, and they had their saints: Gandhi, Martin Luther King, philosophers and poets to awaken the conscience of nations, pell-mell in the same pack as leaders, presidents, thieving out-of-favour ministers, passing nobility and others, how was Samuel supposed to guess what had been plotted against those near to him, before he had even come into this world, in 1924 by an insignificant political agitator writing a book in his comfortable Munich prison and free from any sanction, dictating his memoirs to advisers every bit as poisonous as he was — Rudolph Hess, his chauffeur and associates, dictating a book that would soon sell in the thousands, a subversive anthem to racial hatred followed by millions of deaths, including distant cousins in the village of Lukow, Poland, and the great-uncle whose name Samuel bore and who was shot in the winter of 1942, Daniel his father had told him that he, Samuel, would be the rebirth, the continuity of all that had been irretrievably lost in the village of Lukow, the rebirth and the life he would be, and now it seems, thought Samuel, that nothing can erase those words from the Book of Hate, the inheritance from Samuel's grandfather Joseph and his great-uncle shot there in the snow, it had so distraught Daniel in his youth that his sole refuge from the memory had been in drugs, and now it was Samuel who was torn apart by the revealed violence of the world, history's spectator assimilated all he saw of the unfolding documentary, the filmed events were confusing, here one recalled Lenin's death mask held up to the crowd, why, though, had an unidentified young anarchist woman shot but not killed him, for a long time the bullet from the revolver had stayed in the revolutionary's neck, and it troubled Samuel that this young anarchist had carried out this irrational act of courage, but why, there would be no answer because the anarchist was killed, what was it that made her throw away her life and youth for some never-to-be-understood higher purpose, our lives are just such ephemeral gestures as hers, ending in the death she intended to deliver to someone else, she had learned her radical lessons from master theoreticians she had read or contacted, and become the enemy of all hierarchies and states, but in taking aim at Lenin, she had acted alone, a sterile act of suicide in which perhaps she had seen a liberating, evangelical dimension, who would know since she had been killed on the spot, something comparable would have happened to her today, piloting a plane with which she would go down in flames on embassies in Africa, the army of terror to which she would belong would send her to destroy herself along with the consuls and consulates, and no one would ever know her name any more than they would have in Lenin's time, because these volunteers were punished with silenced names, even though every day they were there ready to die, everywhere the anarchist would be the archangel of death with her wings striking Kenya yesterday, Tanzania tomorrow, or maybe even Samuel's dance school, or again the theatre that performed Arnie Graal's choreography each night, perhaps he lived, Samuel thought, lived and breathed inside the unstable framework over which the deity of anarchy reigned from on high, like the painting by Hiraki Sawa, which was both animated film and a changing black-and-white picture, the artist who paints or dances in his studio while airplanes take off from his kitchen table and land on his bed, the sky of studio and bedroom intermingling with the sky outside where impersonal planes do criss-cross, and this now is how we live, watching the stormy trajectories in the sky from over a cupboard, as in the Japanese painting or from his unmade bed, the planes streaking at high speed across the plasma screens that broadcast their jagged and wavering journey, the life and art of Samuel, his predilection for music and dance were, after all, transposed onto a living drama, the immense tension of an immediate present not yet ready to be archived like his parents' and grandparents' past, while the planes seemed to take off from the kitchen table in Samuel's little studio and land on his bed — like in Hiraki Sawa's filmed self-portrait — a voice said beware, we are here at your door, whether you want us or not, you are part of our design, on the grid, woven into us, the design of your future life, whatever happens, you must bend to our service, and Samuel walked along the street where he had seen Our Lady of the Bags, wondering where she was now, under what pile of rocks or toxic stones, he longed to say to her, as the morning sun dawned on the city, maybe you were right, Lady of the Bags, won't we both be, as you said, you and me tomorrow or whenever, witness to all killings, where are you living, I can't find you, and Caroline said, I don't want this breakfast, Harriett, I don't want anything, oh I know they're all just waiting around to get the inheritance, cousins and all, but they won't get a thing, I'm giving it all to Charly, it isn't much of a fortune now, Ma'am, said Miss Désirée, that girl Charly that you let in here, why what a shame, be quiet Harriett, said Caroline, she waited on me, so don't speak ill of her, but I will have a bit of tea before I go out, where are my hat and gloves and cloth handbag, the one with the compact and keys, Miss Désirée, and why am I shut up here like this? Will Adrien and Suzanne be coming to dinner tonight, and Charly, where is she? I must go out, I just have to see her, I understand everything, her meanness, her thieving, her swindles, when I pretended not to notice, she told me all about it, even where all the injustice began: no one wants to remember, but the memory punctuated her life, her delinquency and her mistakes, the *Henrietta Marie* left all those African and Jamaican slaves to drown, that's memorable enough, so why would Charly, as a Jamaican, not remember? I couldn't bear it, I was as guilty as the others of the *Henrietta Marie*, and what if the servants in my parents' home were well treated, I was the one who said to Charly, take everything I have, send this money to your family in Jamaica, no, she said, now wasn't that honest and upright, because of the white man, my father and his pirate ancestors, slave-merchants, alone carried the blame, or maybe when I could no longer stand seeing that boat at night with the pitiful shadows swimming around its machinery, I said, Charly, what's mine is yours, you sign these cheques for me, it's OK, I'll let you, why would I want to live now that Jean-Mathieu is gone, there now, his name isn't slipping away from me, Jean-Mathieu, that was his name, without him, why was I living anyway, and the vessel *Henrietta Marie* massaged the waters, that was the nightmare that haunted my nights, obliterating all, chewing up one-by-one all those who were lost, including Charly's mother and sisters whom I photographed on the beach, and I said take it all, Charly, then she kissed me and said, aren't we great together, just the two of us, Caroline, please get rid of that cook and that secretary and that maid, and let's just be alone together, and I told her they've been with me for many years, from my parents' house to here, I can't live without them, nor could I offend them, like Charles with Cyril, how did it come about that I obeyed and submitted to all her whims, when more than ever the *Henrietta Marie* went down in my dreams leaving behind her a wake of slaves, in the pool naked, Charly snorted out water, so perhaps I liberated her by giving her what she wanted, didn't I? Charles wrote me that Cyril was under contract and often had to leave for England or the US, was that really true or not, he was hailed in plays by Tennessee Williams, Charles wrote, he and the heroes of the plays shared the same sensibility and aversions, I don't know if Charles was exaggerating, but he was often alone in the Indian springtime, writing solitary in his ashram, springtime and his flowers, the greed of Cyril's young and tempestuous body along with the ecstasy of Indian spring, perhaps it was a bit evanescent, where Charles saw in Cyril a vigorous animal of youth, and I wonder if Cyril was as acclaimed as all that, perhaps he was more like an illusory peacock spreading his magnificent plumage around Charles, bewitching him with the metallic glint of eyes so very clear that Charles did not properly realize their numbing effect, was this what it meant to love, he wrote, these departures and absences, I'm still waiting for the reviews that will prove all this really necessary, but so far, nothing, doubtless, Cyril's being so non-conformist and visited with a natural disobedience, he must have shared the nervous sensibility of the great Southern author's main characters, just one thing missing, though, no matter what he did, Cyril was never at fault like those heroes he played; he was never culpable or unpardonable, though Charles often had proof to the contrary, he was a being devoid of any sense of culpability, no matter what he did, and yet didn't an actor have to experience every state of being? It was something missing in Cyril, wrote Charles, and where was he, why hadn't he written yet, and I thought, here we are, Charles and I, under the spells of our respective witches, waiting for a word on the cell phone, a letter, the parsimonious charity of a friendly word, when Jean-Mathieu hadn't written or phoned, I used to ask Charly, what's that liquid you pour into my glass, and she said, it's to help you sleep tonight. The *Henrietta Marie* dissolved into the night waters, I did sleep better and stopped waiting up for Charly when she came in at dawn and the noise of her shoes thrown against the wall. The sad part is that Cyril glories in seducing women as much as men, Charles wrote, imagine all the hearts he breaks, but he never gives them a thought, it's like the way he crushes beer cans one after another between those long fingers of his, I can't stand the noise or the damage he does to himself with too much alcohol, women and boys, of course he did not actually write any of this, but I could read it in what his solitude left out, his disappointed tenderness, or maybe it was my own, I asked Charly, what is that you're pouring into my glass and why? She would say, well, it's to stop your migraines, you'll see, you won't feel a thing, and she was right, I gave in to the mysterious numbing of pain and slept better for it, all at once, I got a letter from Charles, Cyril was back from Delhi, and they were happy together, really, no lie, oh Charles, how could you have been touched by doubt, he reproached himself, Cyril had been hailed in London and Boston, what a gifted actor and friend, whether it was true or not, I believed it too, after all, Cyril could probably play any role, including the gigolo with a loving and unfathomable heart, or a character with more sophisticated inner disapproval, he was as stimulating on the stage as in life, awoke the sleeping flesh, and people threw themselves at his feet with gratitude, I dreamed around that time that a letter arrived from Charles in India, no words, just staples, needles and pins glittering like delicate silver signs on matte paper, my eyes burned to read these symbols, each one finely chiselled, was it my concession to Charly, or did I simply hear about it from Charles, like each one of his concessions to Cyril, an increasing number of them by both Charles and me, I don't know how I ended up arguing with Charly, I think she had her eye on a piece of jewelry I could not give her, a family gift I held very dear, it was crazy, but all of sudden I dug my heels in and said to myself, no, not that, my fierce child, I'm not giving in to you, must you strip me of everything, well, what had I done for her to become violent like that, her hand on my face, I could have fired her on the spot, but I didn't, I just locked myself in my room for days, although she begged forgiveness, seeing the mark on my face, I decided to stay there and not come out, after all, what would my friends say, Adrien, Suzanne, Chuan, Olivier and all the others, Charles hit his head accidentally against a tree during a race with Cyril, and both of us were degraded and humiliated, we were shot through with pins and needles as Charly had done many times to her voodoo dolls, so why didn't I fire her then, and Charles wrote that what happened with Cyril was a little accident, you know, dear, how hopeless I am at sports racing, I should simply not have been so hardy, that's all, young people are always right to be intrepid and daring, but us never, we're going to Holland for a few days, Cyril and I, was it a mere accident or not, still I mustn't see my friends like that, no matter how slight the mark, in fact under a wide straw hat it didn't show at all, just vanity of course, but I got in the habit of not going out, not that Charly had to force me to it, that was what I wanted, or at least my will was like a flickering lamp, and thought about the time when my villa, with its gazebos and cottages, my house had welcomed all of glittering society, oh, it wasn't like Mélanie and Daniel's, which became a home for refugees like Julio, Jenny, Marie-Sylvie de la Toussaint, but I did host an intelligent elite with Charles, and Frédéric in my garden and around my pool, if I was a woman of the world, it was with artistic passion and the intention of photographing all those faces around me, I had the impression of being the architect of all this . . . I had retained something of my unused training in architecture, studies interrupted by the war, plunging into a first marriage, so many mistakes, I still had the feel and manual bent for plans, constructions, faces, and images of friends and people I knew less well, I felt like an architect when I collected and consolidated them with my camera eye, put them into a structure and aesthetic ordering, that was before Charly, when I was with Jean-Mathieu and dignified, I used to say, welcome to my house and my table everybody, it wasn't Charly adding something to my drink back then, it was the euphoria from an intoxication I really benefited from, drops of a deadlier poison; ah yes, a feeling of guilt I had never had before, what wasn't yet in my nature became so, actions, even those I hadn't performed, were prejudicial, the boat *Henrietta Marie* with all those drowned aboard began appearing in my dreams, why had the worthy, light-hearted, complacent woman in me never before had this impression of letting others down, this poison was the shadow of all my thoughts, I could have told Charly, enough, I won't hear any more, but I didn't, perhaps my whole started to go tip with the *Henrietta Marie* as it went down amid the waves, the memory of the falconer's return and of the child, the little girl that we dropped from the boat at sea, my first husband and I, there you go, we don't want you, you have to be gone from your mother's womb before you are viable, this was neither the time nor the epoch to be born, quick, let's throw her overboard, for many women abortion was butchery in those days, I was hatefully indifferent, I felt mutilated but indifferent, true or false, we went out so much it was dizzying, shallow, cruel amusements, hunting gazelle from an open convertible, deer captured dying on the railway tracks, either this is how we thought of it or this is what he said, this is not the time nor the epoch, dark days, a fascist era in Europe, darkness over the earth, the disillusioned unemployed, the hungry everywhere waiting for bread, lines of men and women in the streets hopeful for what never comes, desperate farmers, women sitting on barrels in front of tents, young immigrants already so tired in their cotton dresses, worn down by poverty, cold and hungry November days, the brutal forces advancing everywhere on women and children, we had no choice, that's just the way it was, everything went too fast, perhaps we simply had no time, and in the darkness there was nothing else to be done, the child was not to be born, come to grips with it, yes, those drops Charly put in my glass every evening weren't good for me, the child, one of the wrecks, the *Henrietta Marie* in the sea, said to me at night, Mummy, I can't get back up to the surface, help me, and I answered, it isn't me, it's this darkness all around, there's nothing I can do, I never wanted a child to hear the explosions in Pearl Harbor while eating his pancakes in the morning, nor to run in fear through the rice paddies, no, no, I did not want that, the Pacific waters may be far away, but we cannot cut ourselves off from others in a few instants of fear, the sand of the bay, the banks, the keys extending all the way to the ocean, and the entire town of Aiea were covered with corpses, was this a time to be born, when life itself was scarcely viable, I could not think about it nor about all those other embryos that mothers were getting rid of, so many wrecks to surround the *Henrietta Marie*, small hands and feet malformed, not yet perfected, undulating on the waves, true or false, I could not think about them but saw them in my dreams, when a voice fraught with indecision said, regretfulness is not for you, you may have given up on architecture, but you can still defend your country, where now women can learn jobs usually meant only for men, airplane pilot, marine lieutenant, and who knows what else, but I was forgetting the little one, her life hardly viable, I didn't have the nobility of Justin, whose book I'd later discuss with him, a book that came out amid controversy and which I judged harshly, I envied these scientists with the secrets that went into building their bombs, holding the future of humanity in their hands, I envied and admired the physicists, gods of learning, without understanding the idea of superiority's universal triumph, this is the thinking of those who feel inferior, women and children admiring what they think of as being on high, beyond their station, in a burst of sincerity, no doubt, but where would this pride and superiority of those I admired lead us? Justin could never get me to admit I was wrong, I just couldn't side with him, the so-doubtful life of my child forbade it, have you never thought, he said, two young boys playing in the yard under a cool August sun, who then fall down in the grass unconscious, both of them, and their sisters barely turn to look at them as reddish bits of flesh are torn from their bodies, those who recall it saw that August sun consume itself in seconds and drop black rain on them, they call it the black rain of ruins, the instant ruins of liquefied glass, everywhere a dusty fluidity smelling of death, have you never thought, Caroline, for several days in a row, as though it was never enough, never ever enough, that black rain, a rain of oil on the bodies and faces, was just an idea thought up in some scientist's office and written out on a blackboard in a classroom, a superiority that would taste victory though not vengeance, in this time of such scarcely viable life, and he won me around, thinking of these great men in their conference rooms, I said to myself, who are they protecting with so many secrets, it was the explosion of the sun with all its black rain, aren't these men defending and protecting me, without them, wouldn't I be more vulnerable, haven't you ever thought, Justin would say in his soft voice and wanted to repress any desire for victory I had, no victory is good, you see, we have proof of it, he was moral, I was not, but above all I was alone with my first husband, I had committed my act of expelling this barely viable life out of me when the oily rains devoured a population, and this is the poison of blame that Charly insinuated into my veins every night that she worked for me. Immobile on the glittering waters of dawn, Julio waited in his motorboat, what peacefulness when the waves were calm, Julio thought, only the rocking of the boat could be heard, the cries of the seagulls as they streaked in to make off with the pelicans' prey, landing as though squatting, so as to snatch in an agile twist the whitefish hanging from their beaks, the grey herons and egrets unfolded their feet on the water, perhaps this was the hour when all was mirrors and mirage like the first day of flowering on the planet, thought Julio, he would see the ghosts of Oreste, Ramon and Edna at the oars, shaking the air, in their inflatable boat, voiceless rowers, lying down or upright on their floating platforms, no, they weren't what Julio was watching for like José Garcia's mother, they would never be coming back to shore, it was for him, José Garcia, the Cubans and Haitians that Julio was looking out, though he did not hold out much hope, still it is true, or was it an illusion, it was here, among the marble-necked doves and lilies, that fishermen had spotted and picked up José Garcia one Thanksgiving, a miracle of fate, he said, crying, where's my mother, where's the boat that brought them from

Cuba into deep water, where had it sunk, dehydrated and lips chapped with fever, José Garcia asked, where is my mother — who thought of everything — who had wrapped her son in her own clothes, taking them off now one by one, she knew which ones she would not be needing anymore, and she touched her son's forehead, saying, go there for me, be free and happy, don't forget, he saw her plunge beneath the waves under a fiery sun, was it an illusion, a mirage, he asked the fishermen, where is my mother, but they said nothing so as to spare him further pain and to let him recover from the strange sort of coma he was in after being carried by the Atlantic waters for several days and nights, why did my mother and all the others with us suddenly stop rowing or did they just wait till nightfall to slip one by one alone into the ocean, so that he, José Garcia, could remain unaware, you know his mother was only twenty-five, yes, better that he continue to know nothing, illusion, mirage, they had thought he would not know what was happening at night, wrapped up in his warm nest under the stars, José Garcia had fallen asleep on his raft, dreaming of his kites back there at home, would his brothers and cousins bring them for him, and what was it that weighed so heavily on the back of the beat-up little boat, what, maybe the weight of one or two of the drowned, lying among the knotted ropes as though they'd been strangled, an illusion, a mirage, when José Garcia slept under the stars, and when they had all fled, his mother had said to him, good-bye and sleep well, my angel, may your kites fly to you on your makeshift raft, my son, farewell, life is made of courage and innumerable fears such as this, I have dressed you, fear nothing, sleep, and you will have other toys where you are going, I want you to get an education, like your brothers at the Little Havana school, goodbye José, José Garcia heard these words as his mother watched over him while he slept, the sea voyage would be long, his raft constantly surrounded by sharks, a single drop of blood at the temples of one drowned man would have been enough to draw them, my mother, where is my mother, he asked those who had picked him up, my mother, breeze, sweet breath of wind, breeze, breeze of his mother's fingers in his hair, warm breeze of the fishing village where he had grown up, he drifted along the channels of seas and oceans suddenly grown cold, where was that breeze, under what clouds swollen with rains and storms, where had they all gone, his mothers, their companions, balseros, balseros, was it an illusion, a mirage, suddenly they were invisible on the water, but they saw a thin bundle drifting toward them on the waves, what was it, a child, and, so small, the body of a man who had clung to the knotted ropes drifting behind the boat, the fishermen took pity and called the Coast Guard, a bundle so small, was it an optical illusion, we almost didn't see him, he recalled, José Garcia, delirious from thirst, his mother and the balseros, too poor to pay thousands of dollars, a boat with a faulty motor, did he remember the price of this journey, depopulating their forests of the most beautiful birds, no longer hesitating to sell them for a more-than-ten-hour night on the water, and the crown of these captive birds sold on the black market, might it be drifting somewhere in the wake of José Garcia's raft, resplendent birds with nothing left of their song, torn away from their trees and forests, José Garcia thought he heard them, and wouldn't he too be bought and sold once the Coast Guard handed him over to the all-mighty of all countries, the rapacious interests already divided among themselves, in cities everywhere, José Garcia's face on plac-ards, posters, and highways, some saying you belong to us, other saying we're sending you back home, they split him among them in their greed and ambition, José Garcia, sold, a media phenomenon, scarcely saved from the waters and already the owner of a bicycle, phosphorescent green phones, so many toys he did not know what to do with them, birds silent with fear, birds sold by the balseros on the black market, where were they, José wondered, and my mother, who has seen my mother, on one of phones hanging from the belt of his new jeans he heard his father's voice saying, come home to me, son, you know I was against leaving, and now, look, you have no mother, I am all you have now, don't listen to your uncles, come back, my hair has grown long, and I'm waiting for you to come home before we go cut it at the village barber's, only when you come home will it be cut, not before, I love you son, come home, I don't want you studying in that school in Little Havana, you're going to be a communist like me, that's what we've chosen, I'll explain it to you later, come back to your village, your friends wait for you every day, I had to sell everything to phone you, I know our choice is the right one, you have to be the pride of the country and do as I say, I let my hair grow thinking of you, José Garcia, come home my exiled son or it is something you will regret, there are penalties for those who break the law as your mother did, I'm your father, I am all you have, I've had to sell everything I own to phone you, you are mine, do you hear, José Garcia didn't know how to get away from all this shouting and gossip, my mother, where is my mother, he seemed to be saying to all those who assailed him, from the colossal poster on the highway, or in his striped shirt, he seemed to be asking the crowd this question, do you know what will happen to me tomorrow, Julio watched and waited, what was that black dot on the horizon, an illusion or a mirage, could it be a wreck filled with men and children, many without mothers, and if they were Cuban, a ridiculous minimum of legal protection would be given them, but if they were Haitian, they would be sent right back out to sea on their rafts, and Julio thought they would be shut out of this country, not what you could call a promised land, more likely conquered by owners wherever they were, from one coast to another, they expelled these pitiful cargoes of Chinese, Haitians, deaf to their laments and cries, but Julio would continue to watch and wait, he wrote to Samuel in New York that he and Daniel, with the help of a Cuban association in town, had founded a House of Refuge for the survivors, and that he, Julio, waited and watched from dawn to dusk in his boat, Samuel, whom Julio had loved so much as a child and who had replaced Ramon and Oreste, lost at sea, he had changed, a little more distant now, more remote, Mélanie said he didn't show the same attachment to her either, though he didn't hold out much hope, Julio continued to watch and wait for the dark dot on the horizon, illusion or mirage, it seemed amid shouts of joy that the silhouettes of Ramon, Oreste, and Edna were outlined against the sky, Augustino got up early like his father, often before dawn, and wrote, reading the words he had written from a screen placed up high where he could see the ocean, an invisible choir of destruction, I'm convinced that there are strategic missiles hidden on this island, but no one really knows, how was Augustino to face his father, Daniel, who adamantly resisted his son's desire to become a writer, what was this craziness about writing alone in his room for hours when Augustino had received a sports education, you can't see these missiles, Augustino had written, but they're here everywhere in the light of dawn and on the water, in the luke-warm colours of the sky, though he felt too inexperienced to describe the hold of outside forces on his life, inexorable as they appeared to him, living sheltered from all outer conflict in his family's home, and this further jumbled his thoughts, it was this dream, so real and palpable for him, this story of missiles he was writing, the weight of this dream that he could feel beneath his sleeping eyelids, he was certain he had seen his grandmother holding her arms out to him in another life, and moving toward her — though she no longer existed, yet still seemed the same — very small now that he had grown so big, seemed to be crying on her shoulder, please don't leave, sweet Grandma, for she had always been so tender and refined, and remembering this dream in a diaphanous mist, Augustino felt tears run down his cheeks, it was true, one day his grandmother would no longer be there with him, as adoring of her grandson as constraining, imperious as this insistence that he dress for dinner in the evening, Augustino thought, how could one give in to all these rules, children sitting in morose silence in their stiff suits at dinner time, and that other tyranny of hers, insisting on exaggerated politeness toward the ill-tempered nanny, Marie-Sylvie, who camouflaged her cuddlesome moods, keeping them only for Vincent, and annoying Augustino with sly smiles, a little off-kilter like her brother's, He-who-never-sleeps, whom she had coddled too much in his madness, sure the problem had been eating away at her brother for a long time, she said, since they'd left the Cité du Soleil by boat, look at that country burning up, bursting into flame, savannahs and bare-boned plains, how could you cultivate bananas, cotton, or cocoa now, and look at Augustino outrageously taking three meals a day, it was from listening to the imprecations of Marie-Sylvie de la Toussaint that he thought, I'll be a writer, this nanny's not fair to me, she may have her reasons, but I'll write her story and Julio's, however repressive his grandmother might be, she had always accepted that Augustino would be a writer or philosopher, Samuel's dyslexia would prevent him form lengthy schooling, and you had to admit he had unusual gifts for theatre and dance, and that's all there was to it, it was in him, and Augustino, well, his grandmother said, it's true he was born to write, first he must study and learn, now to what prestigious college or university would he be sent this fall, to the math and science college where two thousand students of the twenty-first century would have the benefits of the latest technology, then later Yale or Harvard, the list of well-known universities drawn up for him by his father and grandmother would be a long one, Mélanie preferred to steer clear of the scheming, and she was still tormented by Samuel's absence, is this how our children are torn away from us one by one, frowning, Augustino imagined groups of students on the campuses, in the labs and libraries, destined to graduate studies,

the crowning glory of knowledge, victory at university, each
with a late-model car of his own, insolently parked in the campus lot, Saab, PT Cruiser Turbo, performance car and performance student alike, how do you place a value on a life like
that, when Augustino thought about the miserable existence
Marie-Sylvie de la Toussaint had led before, like her convict
brother, He-who-never-sleeps, would he, Augustino with his
intelligence, be the one at the head of this elite class of two
thousand students of the twenty-first century, would it make
any sense that the century was meant to be cut short and
determined by the launching of missiles that all refused to see?
If Daniel, his father, had really determined that he was going
to a doctor of neurology, not a poet or a writer, well, then
Augustino would study the afflictions of the nervous system,
his father would effectively have assigned him that role, not
writing, which would unbalance his health, all he had to do
was think of Kafka's tuberculosis, if that's how it was for
Augustino's future, whom the missiles pierced like spears,
then he would be the doctor to trace a neurological cause for
his brother Vincent's shortness of breath, his spasms and his
convulsions, whether he became researcher, a doctor, or a
poet, Augustino could not conceive of a future without his
grandmother, without her it would be like walking through
the storm-tossed thickness of an unknown jungle, and this
night perfumed with jasmine in Chuan's garden, Daniel
thought about Augustino writing next to the lamp near the
covered perch where his parakeets slept, what a pity if the
boy got it into his head to write, Daniel thought, he felt pres-
sured by his own book, thinking that if Hitler's dog could be
declared innocent, like the children of out-of-favour officials,
where would the fertile infamy of these fathers lead, for it
could not be expunged, but would influence several generations, suddenly sheltered like atomic dust in the wind, just as
deadly, in the hearts of two young boys: Alex, age twelve;
Derek, thirteen; pious altar boys, hair nicely combed, with

barely a hint of pink ear showing, tight collars, white shirts and grey ties, church angels, how had they come to condemn their father, by what mysterious tribunal, brutalizing him under a rain of blows from a baseball bat till he died, surely they knew that the aluminium covering of the bat would cause pain, but the ineffaceable infamy had lighted on them, how many times did you hit him, asked the judge, ten times, maybe eleven, then we set fire to the house, our parents' room first, then we took off, it was at home in Pensacola, and Dad was sitting on the sofa drinking his coffee and relaxing after work. What time was it, Derek, just after midnight, Your Honour, Dad called us his little masterminds, and he was right, we'd been planning to get someone else caught instead of us, Rick the child molester who'd already been in prison, our dad was one too, so we punished him, Alex and Derek's biological mother had denied all the accusations, the father of my kids was a good, protective man, she said, so were Alex and Derek just piling one trick on top of another, or were they telling the truth, the choirboys in this criminal ritual would be tried separately, sent to juvenile detention separately, but what did they feel together as they delivered blows to their father's head, Daniel wondered, one of them told a detective, boy, was it ugly, that hole in his head, his face all swollen like a really bad cold, nose blocked up, really gross, but things just couldn't go on the way they were, we'll wait till we're twenty-three, then we'll be free, what were Derek and Alex really, if not a fetid swamp, their two souls mere receptacles for the unspeakable things of the past, those of nazi fathers and torturers whose work was still being carried out, Derek and Alex in white shirts and grey ties, angelic, lying faces, a cesspool, two spirits numbed by cruelty, shouldn't they too be declared innocent, wondered Daniel, and looking around to make eye-contact with Mélanie, who was talking with Olivier, late as it was, but what sweetness this night under the stars, the ringing of his phone sounded like a crystalline harness-bell, and holding the thin object to his temple, in an effervescent glow he heard the breathless voice of Vincent, Dad, it's me, I can't get to sleep, Dad, and Daniel replied that it was time to sleep, and hadn't he already phoned twice today, so tell me Vincent, did you like that outing in the kayak, tell me all about it, hectares and hectares of mountains and lakes, you know, many years ago the entire northern part of the continent was covered in ice, you do go for a walk in those leafy forests every day, don't you, and before you were born, Vincent, your mother and I climbed Mt. Mansfield — don't forget your raincoat when you go out on the trails with your instructor — your mother got the tent ready, and I prepared the stove for the meal, what we liked the most was going to sleep that way, it was like being at the top of the world among the deer that would come to drink at the ponds and rivers, are you listening Vincent, never go out without your raincoat, you're still coughing a bit, do you feel any better, Vincent, but was Daniel really hearing his son's voice this late in the night, Dad, said the breathless voice cut short, I want to see Marie-Sylvie again, even though you say I shouldn't, the sea air, Dad, *Southern Light,* oh *Southern Light,* our boat anchored in the marina, and Mélanie your mother, don't you want to see her, Daniel asked, she's here with me at Chuan and Olivier's, did you remember it was your grandmother's birthday, all Daniel could hear was a murmur in the fog, Marie-Sylvie, the sea, Samuel's boat *Lumière, Southern Light,* yes, it really would be better, thought Daniel, that his son Augustino never become a writer, and Olivier was saying to Mélanie, you'd never think so, but there's been progress since that August 28th, 1963, when we marched on Washington, president of the black students in our student committee for non-violence, I felt very alone despite the huge audience, white cops eyeing us and our speakers with hostility, maybe I was very much afraid, even in that crowd of 300,000, I said to myself, pray Olivier, concentrate and pray that you behave like a leader and a man, then all of a sudden, it was as though I'd been lifted up by the waves on the sea, and what I saw calmed me again, to my left, groups of young people on their feet and sitting in trees, listening to me, I was floating with those close to me on this sea of humanity, and all around me, every single person seemed to be saying, shouting out the words with me so all could hear, they call us niggers in this rich country, Mr. President, and regardless of what you want, we're not moving from here till something changes . . . here we are, marching through the streets of Washington towards you, Mr. President, these streets belong to us now . . . we've been patient, too patient, but we aren't anymore, doubting that their society had really evolved after all, Mélanie was listening to Olivier, and these women who not so long ago were still gagged, censored, and imprisoned like Margaret Sanger the obstetrics nurse, simply because her ideas were my ideas and those of so many women today, that every woman had a right to contraception and safe birth-control, did Olivier shrug knowingly, seem less attentive to Mélanie's words, though it was a splendid evening, and the arbour Mélanie and Olivier were in, a little way from the noise of the celebration, was embalmed with the insidious intoxication of an assortment of bougainvilleas and African lilies, Mélanie was distraught at not being properly understood by the man she so admired, but perhaps it was not so, Olivier seemed carefree and amused as his dogs bounded toward him, my friends, my fine friends, he said, I just can't get away from you, and Mélanie saw his strong hand seize an orange from a vase Chuan had filled with them and with lemons, what delicious fruit, he said as he peeled it with his teeth, it quenches one's thirst on a hot night, if Olivier could be so easily distracted from what he was saying, well, of course on a party night, Mélanie thought, a heady, sensuous evening to which even Olivier had to give in, tasting an orange, scenting the corollas of African lilies that seemed to spill from the arcade of the bower right down to their faces, while Mélanie could not help being preoccupied by her own struggle, they would see tomorrow, not thousands, but millions of them, she mused, women marching through the streets of Washington, emerging from every epoch of their history, daughter of an Irish Catholic mother of eleven who died so young, Margaret Sanger would no longer be alone, in the rush, eager to judge their obscene censors, we will be seeing those who had kept them so long in ignorance, the perpetrators of epidemic deaths of newborns and mothers, perpetrators of secret shames, syphilis and gonorrhoea, yes, we'd meet them all again, Mélanie thought, a living mural by young artists from New Mexico like Erin Currier who painted political demands with collages, like that grandiose mural of women cut off from the world, veiled and showing their hands tied, widowed of their lives, eyes submerged in fatalistic pain, hundreds, thousands of them, when Mélanie thought this tableau of widows, grieving women beneath the veil, would be broken and fragmented, baited by a new ethic, that by painting slavery, the artist proclaimed liberty, now, now, you'll make me all dirty with your paws, Olivier was saying to his dogs, it was true, wasn't it, what Mère was saying about the African lilies, you could get drunk on their perfume, dizzy in fact, like an intoxication of the senses, and Petites Cendres left the Saloon and went out into the street, lower back soaked in sweat after the dry vapour of the sauna, there were all kinds of people, cop cars screaming through the night, what's going on, Ashley asked the Queen of the Desert, who showed up wig in hand, a cloud of red streaks she held onto carefully, it's one of the New York models, my favourite, Blondie, she said, he's stolen a motorbike, and he doesn't even have a license, practically still at his mother's teat, Petites Cendres said, they won't arrest him, will they, he's the boy who smiled at me so nicely, button up your front and zip your pants, said the Queen of the Desert, what do you want to go out in the street like that for, I heard the siren, and God, I just knew, said Petites Cendres, they're putting cuffs on him and

humiliating him the way they did me so many times with
those chained bracelets, oh those stinking rats, they've
arrested my boy, we've· got to call his mother in New York,
she lamented, wait, let's be reasonable, said the Queen of the
Desert pointing to two of the blond kid's friends, the charming
Asian and the Mexican with the dark fringe, look at how those
three kids carry themselves, each one has a lover who's a fashion designer and maybe a constellation of handsome gentle-
men, so don't you worry, Petites Cendres, he won't be behind
bars for long, stinking rats, Petites Cendres repeated, snatching
up a child like that, the other two boys bent their heads in
astonishment in the direction of their friend who'd been
admonished by the police, like some bundle on the back seat
of their car, he's innocent, they were saying, it was just a
game, we all bet he'd drive the motorcycle without a license,
we're tolerant of minors in this town, said one of the cops, but
theft is theft, Petites Cendres saw the hubbub was subsiding
beyond the barricade of police cars, when suddenly she saw
the blond boy, barely visible on the other side of the car window, smiling under his curtain of hair and making a sign with
his cuffed hands, as if to tell her, I'll be OK, you'll see, God
bless you, sweet ruffian, yelled Petites Cendres, Christ be with
you, after all, he was the one that said, suffer all the children
to come unto me, yeah, well, it's nearly time for my second
show, said the Queen of the Desert, don't worry too much
about them, they've got good uncles, godfathers (though
maybe not real fathers) and mothers, it's not the same as those
boys who sell themselves in the streets of Moscow and sleep
in cardboard boxes, shivering from cold, huddled against their
puppies, Petites Cendres said, I always said, God help this furnace of an earth, God has nothing to do with it, I don't even
know who you're talking about, said the Queen of the Desert,
if this earth is a furnace, it's because cold and indifference
reign supreme, I've got to get going or I'll be late, and you'd
better get dressed, Ashley, what a way to go out in the street,

all undone like that, God help you, said Petites Cendres blown away that the blond kid had smiled at him, you may not know it, but God exists, I get proof of it every day and every night of my miserable existence, you and your chatter, interrupted Timothy appearing on the doorstep of the Vendredi Décadent piano bar, one of the pubs where he hung out, Timo, my Timo, said Petites Cendres, you look like some kind of businessman or banker, well, hey, said Timothy, that's what I am, and no familiarities, don't kiss me in public, I've got a chic clientele, you know, a journalist interviewed me inside the pub, I didn't tell him my name, you're no ordinary pusher, Ashley told him as they went down toward the ocean walking side by side, as Timothy covered Petites Cendres' eyelids and forehead with cigarette smoke, a somewhat saliva-laden smoke, she thought, you've shined that leather jacket up nicely, and brushed your hair so it's glossy, I could help you pluck those eyebrows, though, they often get me to do that at the sauna, nope, you're no ordinary sex-trader, Petites Cendres said, and what did you say to this reporter, that for me it didn't count with men, it was just about the money, but my relationships with women last a long time, maybe a year or two sometimes, they don't know anything about what I do down here, I said one day I'd be an oceanographer and study algae and oceans, that's all we really have, that I'd go back to Savannah, when, asked Petites Cendres, oh in a few years, but first I have to get rich, said Timothy, that idiot asked me about my family, nothing to say, my moral values are my own, since I was ten I've made it alone, and drugs, he wanted to know all about that, whether my clients were old or young, up to seventy-five, I said, and I don't like the cops, in this business they beat you up, not all of them, he was particularly concerned about condoms, I said, once in a while, but I often forget, oceanography, that would be a cool profession, Petites Cendres interrupted, there's no future for you on this island, you need customers who get around less than the ones in the Vendredi

Décadent, then Timothy tapped him on the shoulder and said he had an appointment with someone in the navy, I'm due there now, and off he went, confidence in his stride and a cigarette between his lips, Ashley thought back to the thick-necked man who had ordered him to come up to his hotel, brutish he thought, well, he wouldn't, he just wouldn't . . . unless the envelope of white powder in his front ran out before the night was over, unless his need began to hollow him out like the point of a knife, what a furnace of torture it was to need, he often thought that, the earth was a furnace — cold for some, comfortably tepid for others — so what can you do, that's life, Timo was a lucky one, all nicely slicked up and groomed, no buttons, he wasn't going to get hurt, and they weren't going to call him Black Dog, but God would look out for Petites Cendres, as He had always done, tonight or tomorrow when dawn broke over the ocean, as cigarette smoke rose in the air, and doves cooed, Ashley knew for certain that God would come to the aid of His son Petites Cendres, and His voice would burst forth in the singing of the waves, and He would say, they have offended you to your face, wash it in this water, my son, and be relieved of all your pain, I say unto you verily, it is you I love. Mai could see a ray of light under her brother's bedroom door, she'd have loved to know what time her parents were coming home, Daddy had said it would be very late, and he'd be angry to know Augustino's lamp was still on and he was writing at his desk, and that Mai refused to go to sleep as well, with her cats rolled up in a ball against her knees, sometimes she thought she was asleep in her bed and dreamt of an empty swing, and the day they scattered Jean-Mathieu's ashes near The-Island-Nobody-Owns, she also thought she was awake, stretched out on her bed with the cats, the scenes that tumbled pell-mell into her brain also seemed real, although she was afraid of their being true; when Mélanie had noticed Mai was not on the swing anymore, the seat was empty, she had asked everyone, Mai,

where is Mai, have you seen her, Mummy's voice was overlaid
by the slightly cracked voice of an old lady, Caroline, asking
them each where her little cloth bag was, and that must have
annoyed my mother, thought Mai, suddenly the shouts of
Mummy, Caroline, and Augustino echoed to the sky, Mai
where are you, I could hear them, but there was a little boat
near a rock that I really wanted to get to, my feet and my
sandals were covered in mud, what would my mother and
grandmother say, you were so pretty this morning, that never-
ending funeral service gave me plenty of time, walking along
the low tide to the sky-blue boat that seemed to be tied to a
stake, there was this mist on the sea because it was summer,
the closer I wandered to the boat, the more I could see beach
after beach of white sand, deserted clearings, then all of a sudden I was under an umbrella of Australian pines, Daddy told
me these were the tallest and the strongest, and as I sat under
them, I could see the boat was still there, and I knew there
was a man in it, a fisherman dozing with his hat over his face,
the boat shifting on the waves, Mai, where are you, they were
all yelling, the voices of my parents faded to echoes as I went
over to the boat, in that thin film of water where my feet sank
in among the seashells, the man in the boat woke up with a
start, isn't this a surprise, where are your parents, he asked,
not far, I went off while they were reading Jean-Mathieu's
poems on the podium, they were crying because their friend is
dead, dead how, the fisherman asked, stowing a supply of
shellfish in the bottom of the boat, Daddy says old age, but
my Grandma says you only die from living well, don't you
want to get into my boat, asked the man from beneath his hat,
eyes reddened by the sun, is this how it was supposed to be,
Mai wondered, why should she get into a wet, dirty boat with
her nice dress on, or would you rather go collect some rare
shells on the beach, that would be over by the Australian
pines, Mai thought, she could find her way back more easily,
by now they must have noticed the swing was empty and

maybe begun to worry a lot, she could still hear them calling out, Mai, where is Mai, the man jumped out of his boat, let's get to the wharf before the tide comes in, he said, because I have to make out to that other boat over there, see, imagine all the men fishing for days out in the middle of the ocean, the things they say about women, boy, you wouldn't want to hear that, they're drunk and raunchy when they get into port, women waiting for them everywhere, sometimes very young ones, I only like delicate creatures though, as brittle as shell-fish, you're OK, just a little girl, no need to be afraid, we won't get lost, when Mai asked his name he grumbled back, it's not nice to want to know everything, I don't have a name, the men on my boat call me a lunatic hermit, I don't have a name any more than The-Island-Nobody-Owns, and don't forget, everything between us is a secret, no yammering to your Ma about the man with the bushy beard and hair and no name, here give me your hand so we can walk over to the pine wood, what are you waiting for, I won't hurt you, Mai begged him to let her hand go, it's full of fine bones this hand, l like subtle, delicate things, look at the eagles and hawks up in the sky, I know the Caribbean well, you know, and the Antilles Sea, the Inner and Outer Antilles, I'd love to take you there later on, anyway, how to remember the rest of the story, no telling tales, no gossiping, and Mai wouldn't say a thing, after all, she had promised bushy-beard-and-hair, about how he had sheltered her from the wind with his smelly shirt, now you're under my wing, next to my skin, and what had he done besides defend her from the eagles and the hawks that would rapidly have preyed on her, like mice and ferrets, caressing her legs under the dress with the neck undone, what would Marie-Sylvie have said, dressing her that morning, the fisher-man had stood up in that cave under the pines, thought Mai, he would row to his boat on the incoming tide, with a single expert finger he seemed to trace the perfect line of Mai's legs, he said, and listen, no chattering, don't tell anyone anything, or else the eagles, hawks, and all those vultures will descend on your parents' house, and your little brother's the first one they'll gobble up, there's your mother calling, can you hear her, quick, go find them, you careless kid, 'bye, it was nearly night, and the sun was setting on the water, Daddy was there saying, Sweetie, Sweetie, and sat Mai on his shoulders, and he didn't ask any questions, though her dress was soiled and she was missing a sandal, he said, Mai you had your mother really worried, you must never disappear like that again, besides what could a little girl be playing at alone in the pine woods like that so far from her parents who are looking for her everywhere, no telling tales, no gossiping, I saw some big vultures, Mai said, her legs hanging over his chest on either side, he seemed very hot, and she understood she had upset him, there were tears behind the tremor in his voice, she had upset him, and he was pretending to forget as she returned triumphant on his shoulders, everyone running to make a fuss of her, even Caroline, the elderly lady with a cracking voice, showing veiled sympathy by admitting that she too had tended to run away at that age, but they were all so happy to see her that she felt it was more a holiday than a day for ashes as they were saying, down they went in clusters aboard electric carts to the marina where they would all meet on the *Grand Catamaran*, and the captain had iced drinks ready for them, they had spent a long time at sea, Mai, still perched on her father's shoulders, had managed to fall asleep there amid the staccato sounds of the motor; she no longer remembered the rest once she saw the sliver of light under Augustino's door, what did she have to fear from those vultures in the sky, and when would her parents be coming home, no one had better be able to come in through the half-open window, she'd tell Marie-Sylvie to keep it closed, you could sit on the window-seat with the cats and soft cushions in the daytime and see the roses in the garden, then stand up and watch the ocean, no worries, of course Grandma said that was no way to do your homework, there was a ladder in the room, and Mai would climb it with Augustino to get books off the shelves in the library, Grandmother thought every room should seem like an art gallery or an exhibition room, in Mai's room, against the beige wall, there was a framed black-and-white photo by Robert Mapplethorpe of a bouquet of dried flowers in a shaft of light, like the open window onto the rose garden, it looked as though someone could just part the flowers and attack you in your bed, there was nothing to it, but Mai believed it, the man who showed up the most was not a tangle of beard and hair, a funny, clean-shaven young man, sitting on the soft cushions of the window-seat, he said to Mai, don't tell anyone you saw me, they call me molester, rapist, and my picture's everywhere, at the town hall and the post office, then under my name they've written WANTED, but what for, I'm already in prison, you can see the fence of the state prison, they say watch out, behind my smooth exterior, sometimes it's the likeable ones, they say I exploited you, kidnapped you, but I'm just a respectable citizen like all the others, how would you like to go out for a walk with me, first take off your pyjamas and let's have a look at you, with her cats by her knees, Mai was not afraid of anything, the ray of light under Augustino's door was still there, you were supposed to fall asleep right away to the sound of the waves, Daddy and her grandmother said so. Here it is, nightime, Caroline said, and Harriet, Miss Désirée, half asleep in the armchair, what servitude she goes through with me, never loses patience, a good nurse for an old lady, can she sense it will soon be over, today I had a bit of tea so as not upset her as much by being finicky, when I think about Charles, I can see he needed to be in love, in love with Frédéric, in love with love, in love with Cyril, and the idea of fertile love for literary creativity, loving and passionate, that's what he said, or was it Frédéric, that the poet and writer's life was an act of love that consumed, even destroyed one, Charles' life should have been like François René de Chateaubriand's, a life of nothing but action, filled with pitfalls, sandbanks and reefs, action, travels, creation and a career as bursting with carnal intensity as scrapes in a very personal mysticism, for thus was written the unending *Mémoires d'outre-tombe* in a torrent of ardent living, powered by all its excess, some days Charles was the incarnation of the most turbulent poets, no less taken by love, he was Walt Whitman, a bard of liberalism who sang the praises of equality between men and women, the innocence of the body, love, his headlong passion fearless of words, this was the effect Cyril surely had, the praise of love received, and writing hundreds of poems, building so many *Leaves of Grass*, building a temple of meditation of ripened thoughts on life, death, and our eternal vagabond wanderings, Cyril listened and learned, the desire to love seeming so simple to him, so spontaneous, he recited for Charles from a memory which rarely faltered — a privilege of youth — the words of Raymond Radiguet, who like Charles, had written poetry at fifteen, "I burned, I hastened like those bound to die young," these words must have tortured Cyril, the typhoid fever that killed Radiguet shortly after this joyously pronounced premonition, or was it frivolously, what we now call viral pneumonia, let's lay out the real evil that will carry me away, thought Cyril, it wasn't there in the arms of a man that the ghost of fear slipped by, Cyril was burning up too fast, and in loving, Charles' gaze spread out, sudden and lonely, to those melancholy landscapes of his life where Jacques and Justin still called to him, the kingdom of death clinging to him by a mere thread of dew, it seemed, like the life of spiders, and the spouse still alive, Frédéric, his Frédéric, the most perfect of all, and the one who asked nothing except that Charles be happy, so delicate that Charles could sense his indignation, oh, if only the fascination and temptation were never to end before this poet's gaze, Cyril thought, and yet there he goes without saying a word to me, off to the ancient lands of his world, that's

what it was, completion of one another, however dissimilar
Charles and Frédéric were, they came together harmoniously,
these thoughts suddenly enraged Cyril with jealousy, their
geniuses completed one another with the extravagant diversity
of their gifts, between them, nothing was beyond their grasp:
painting, drawing, writing, and they were highly praised musicians as well, did Charles love Cyril or was he just the beautiful creature of an interlude, gifted actor that he was, he could
see in Charles' eyes, as though they had suddenly taken on an
amorous glimmer, what the entity of Charles and Frédéric was,
Charles thought of all the books he and Frédéric had written
together, and the ones for which Frédéric had done illustra-
tions, art books bound in night-blue, hands joined, Cyril
thought, what did Charles revisit while they played the piano
together? So many pictures, places and faces erupted from the
portfolio of their lives, an ethereal temple Frédéric had drawn
in Athens, so many portraits, though Frédéric was the painter
of dark tints unto which he infused lightness of being, his portraits were so real they seemed made of flesh and blood, the
peach colour in the cheeks and lips of a seventeen-year-old
Greek boy brought the freshness of the outside indoors, he
was sitting in a yellow armchair, and the model's head seemed
to be crowned with yellow and blue flowers, though the illusion was created by the mirrored reflection of the vase they
were placed in, that yellow, Charles said, how can you forget
that, it's as vehement as Van Gogh's, the colour of buckled
gold, Van Gogh's fist, painting his miners and paupers in a hal-
lucinatory state, the virulent yellow belonged even more to the
fields harvested with a scythe by the Greek boy now settled
into the armchair of the house Charles and Frédéric had
rented on one of the islands surrounded by the churning seas
where they had washed up sometime that August, Frédéric
suffering from seasickness, they had slept on straw in the barn
belonging to a family of peasants, and that morning at dawn,
Charles was soaking his face at the fountain with a towel

around his neck when the daughter of the house asked the stranger, who are you, or maybe she said in Greek, *eisai Kalos*, you're good-looking, feeling bashful for a long time, he had hesitated before finally answering *eisai Kalos*, both of them reddening, and you of inexpressible beauty, he had said, when the grandmother came and separated them, saying to Charles, you, stranger, move on, my granddaughter is not for some foreigner, a boat would be leaving for Athens at one o'clock, well, the critics should have mentioned it, Charles said, that Van Gogh's yellow was compassionate, that's the only way to describe it, the bitterness of that colour moderated by sympathy was the yellow of death, the virulent death of Jacques, whom Charles could not stop thinking about and would carry in his heart like a tombstone which weighed on his pleasure and his love, where is Tanjou, Jacques asked from the depths of his reincarnations, Tanjou, the unfinished book on Kafka, is this what we have inherited with Kafka's revelations, a bunch of malevolent demiurges running the world through their totalitarian regimes, ants that we are, insects crawling in moonlight to the labyrinths of the Castle where all are forbidden to lay their souls to rest, it is madness that Kafka wrote in the language of the enemy and lived in a country lent to them by the enemy, or had he already learned this frightening comedy in the ghettos, the writing hand caricaturing this pact with the enemy or resigning itself, this stone weighing on Charles' heart, heavy book, now Jacques' book was taking root in the very fibre of Charles' being and in his love, though disappointing for Cyril at times, the book that had reached fruition called out to Charles to be written, recount all of Kafka's humiliation, living and writing in the language of his persecutors, wouldn't it have been better to leave Prague for Vienna or Berlin, thus his presence would have been just one more shadow among others, a beggar, just as destitute, he was a beggar of cultural magnificence, of knowledge, his shadow pivoting on the fragile consciousness of an insect in the universities where he was initiated into the science of law, then, small as he was, he gazed up at the pillars of courts, all those emperors who for centuries had barred Jews from their territories, Kafka was born to a state of mourning, too sensitive to ignore past and future riots, synagogues had been vandalized for many years, attacks had occurred in the streets, store windows had been broken, archives had been plundered, and by writing fables and allegories, Kafka was displaying his ancestral anxiety, perhaps his father, a hard man, had shown the same heroic courage as the cockroach by stubbornly continuing to live in the hell of Prague, son of a butcher and meat merchant in peasant villages, this dominating and poorly educated father of Kafka's and his obsessive curse would turn the son against his meat-eating father and make him a vegetarian, excessively prudent about his health, till his pores and respiratory passages were infected by Koch's Bacilla, an infestation Kafka called the Animal, Jacques would have said that the Animal of Pain was his too, he would have begged his doctor, as Kafka did when they brought him comfort in the form of morphine, Kafka's irony would have been his, I'll be a rock in the face of the Animal, Jacques said, all the while he was writing, Jacques was confronted with a Trial he did not deserve, jurisprudence sneered at him, their tribulations were the same, the verdict would be pitiless, still Tanjou laid the balm of his caresses on Jacques' wounds, Charles reflected, Tanjou, about whom we knew nothing and who had fled inconsolable, they said he had rebuilt his life and was living in poverty in New York, having given up his dance company and his stripped-down choreographies to music by a Chinese composer, he wasn't the same Tanjou that Jacques had loved and stimulated, was he account-administrator in a less well-known dance company, was he a silhouette bent over files in a huge building, who knows, you had to take the chance of hastily formed relationships, adventures, thought Cyril, burn up before rows of coffins piled up on acres of greenery, speed up the pulse before the flu or yellow fever came back, despite the fact that this was the century of medical miracles, Cyril would have liked to rejuvenate the theatre, the century, and the metamorphosis of art, that could be done in a cave, an underground bomb shelter, there one would see a painfully modern Phaedra, as Cyril explained it to Charles with such ardour as he would have felt playing Hyppolitus armoured in leather, as a young prince more nihilist than punk, and with as many violent liaisons with Phaedra as with the rest of the world, the world as her country, her prince, like Hamlet, would be especially emotional beneath his angular armour, incapable of fighting the violence that had been bred in him, the bitter fruit of years of service in deserts of blood, his passion for Phaedra or hers for him would have been like Charles and Cyril, the sign of fate, an inevitable predestination, like in the dramas of Euripides, and Charles said the fate or predestination was null, though the presentation of Hyppolitus as someone violently aggressed by the world was interesting, Charles wondered why Cyril, so gentle-seeming, had always felt such repugnance for violence, scars of a disabused, sabotaged youth perhaps, he thought, he resolved to be more attentive and understanding; so it was that there grew up around Charles and Cyril, Charles and me, like in the plays of Euripides or Seneca, that vague something that appeared to be the workings of fate in each of us, and we did not know how to avoid it or defend ourselves from it. If planes took off from the kitchen table in Samuel's kitchen, he could also see very young people he'd never seen before from his window, clusters of adolescents, black and white, adhering to one another in airless half-smoke rooms, some passed out on the floor, cigarettes in their hands, motionless, as though having given in to exhaustion from a long dope session, others, barely worked up, looking fixedly in front of them, as though they'd seen Samuel without seeing him, a girl, a boy, or two girls and boys, in sloppy underwear, looking like little orphans wearing themselves out in deeply sensual postures they'd long been practising since their addiction to crack and cocaine, they were suspicious, Samuel thought, as troubling as the teenagers in photographs by Larry Clark, the debauchery and lasciviousness in unmade beds and dirty sheets seeming to limit themselves suddenly to hallucinogenic prowess, still Samuel would appear to have no control over them and their carousing, busy with their swapping, among his books, appearing to have no visitors, parents or guardians, spending entire days in blissful unawareness, always lumped together, wired to one another, and before them the monumental dream that life was not worth living, sex, stupor and being stoned, well yes, that was alright, all at once Samuel shut his eyes and saw them no more than he saw planes taking off from his kitchen table, was he dreaming or awake when he examined in detail faces and bodies in newspapers and magazines just in case Our Lady of the Bags was among them, one of the homeless that had made it through the earthquakes, along streets filled with debris, indescribable horrors reflected on their faces, in below-zero temperatures without tents or covers or food, under some ruin or other, at some level below a citadel, tower, or fortress of which the steel beams had melted in less than an hour, where had Our Lady of the Bags been sent, Samuel wondered, or maybe during reconstruction of the city, by an oversight she had been poured in cement and walled up with bricks where even dogs could not find her; a mute woman with pleated hair took Our Lady's place with dignity in that Manhattan park on South Avenue, and her eyes were sad, her face tense, as she sat upright drawing the attention of passers-by to a piece of cardboard on which she had written, *I can't speak, money or food*, it was as though she stood apart from any request, like Our Lady, all the more devastating because she was mute, Our Lady had no place to fall from, there was no precipice where she could twist her ankle, nor tip over her Bible on her chest, because where she solicited people for prayer, there was nothing to give altitude, and when she had to go from one place to another, it was always by lower passageways, flagstone walkways, asphalt passages sloping downwards to the innards of the subway, perhaps one would pick up her trail among the grey, gravelled, rock-strewn lots from a few definable objects — the comb she used to wave her hair in moments of vanity, or her Bible, or her plaited skirt, but so much dirt had been shovelled, a tide of pebbles, she would have found her home at last circled like grass around her compact grave, flagstoned, asphalted and well below the earth from which strange flowers would spring again, how evanescent this world was, didn't they always say that at bottom it was solid and material, all those office workers, bureaucrats, obscure secretaries dictating the order of things free of panic, evanescent this world now gone, Samuel thought, after morning coffee, men and women gathered together before reading the day's first e-mails, and before the cataclysm dispersed them in whirlwinds, in stairways, against window-bars, where all could see they were still alive, piled on one another, perhaps giving a last word of consolation, was Samuel asleep or in a highly agitated state of consciousness while he slept, from his window he could see the wall facing him brighten with autumn sunlight, endlessly replaying the act of falling, some as if with limbs as powdery as sugar, interwoven with one another, leg, head, arm glimpsed outside against the azure, spilling from concrete columns, characters in a tableau that had ground into motion, with nothing but emptiness for them to fall into, an arm, a leg, a head bursting forth with a white flag, the torch showing its colours, help us, they cried all together, their voices modulated like a choir, handkerchiefs, white flags, who could they save, or were these messages of farewell, others jumping solitary, a plunge that seemed infinitely long and deliberate, a fall whose stiffness, step and bend of the knee, Samuel had studied, the step between heaven and earth, already celestial, no longer that of someone

walking, will never walk again, moving in air, distancing themselves from bodies, ties, scarves, stoles whose flight became as
agile as doves, along this wall fell the solitary man with his
boots on, of whom Samuel thought, once a friend of the family, perhaps only ten years older than me, this is how he
looked when he was a dancer, Tanjou the student from
Pakistan, he who stumbled, finished, no future, smoke had
blackened his forehead, the lone falling man was him, Tanjou,
Samuel could have kept him from falling by stretching out his
hand and saying, let me take you home, you'll be safe, before
the rescue teams and paramedics arrive, but there hadn't been
time, the string of bodies from the sky went on, Tanjou
stopped a second in front of the window then continued far
below, if it was him, he was among that pile of legs, feet held
on by boots, an ear, that pile on the pyre over which a rescuer
had wept, saying how can I see this, and why didn't Samuel
run down into the street saying, this arm and foot, that's my
friend Tanjou, or is it someone else, after seeing all this and
examining the pictures, Samuel had figured out how to dance
Tanjou's last step, but at night on the opposite wall outside it
seemed like Samuel's set in the theatre and the planes circled
before landing on his kitchen table, an evanescent world now
disappeared during the coffee-break, Tanjou had read his first
e-mail of the morning, saying it was going to be a beautiful
day, he had on boots that had picked up red leaves in the
streets and avenues leading to work in that moderately cool
light of September-October, soon to begin fading, it seemed
like a leisurely stroll, it was his ultimate step, it was going to
be so nice today, not a cloud in the sky, Tanjou had mused, all
that was needed was for Samuel to open the window and stop
the solitary man from falling, before the boots disappeared
into night, where were they, Tanjou the Pakistani student he'd
met a while ago in Jacques' garden, the professor, Our Lady of
the Bags, where were they, then once Samuel thought he had
found her in a station or in an airport, she'd grown, she might

have been living with some ideologically oriented group in the terminus, a group of very young women kneeling in prayer, touching their Bibles compulsively, mumbling incoherent phrases, while their spiritual guide, an older man, the clown of the sect who knew the strength of his revelations to these women, standing among the kneeling women, gently nudging their heads close together, implanting the mark of servility in each one of them with the incompetence of his doctrine, I'll teach you how to survive the Apocalypse, he said, yes, my sisters and children, pray, pray, his voice was sententious and ordinary, one of them had raised her head, Our Lady of the Bags, she had asked, is it true, tell me the truth, where is my friend the Apostle, where am I, and the guide had replied, lower your head, obey, submit, her face, the face of she who was Our Lady of the Bags, still had its purity intact, her tone of voice was limpid and detached, but perhaps this voice had a higher timbre, her hair was no longer wavy but short, dogmatized, stigmatized, who was she really, and Samuel longed to say to her, so you're alive after all, can you find it in you to pardon me, then, like waking from a dream, he knew it was not her, but someone equally pure begging and praying, head bowed to the ground amid all these travellers passing by, tightly bound to her master and guide by that renegade force that is servility, and feverishly turning the pages of her Bible, unlearned and broken, just as Our Lady had been, for this is how her guide, the head of the sect, liked them, tamed and repressed, tossing and turning in her bed, Mai revisited her dream, possibly it was as real as the photo of a dark bouquet framed on the wall, there were oyster-fishermen on the wharf, enormous, she'd never seen men that corpulent all at work, like the fisherman in the blue boat on The-Island-Nobody-Owns, leaning over his molluscs till she stumbled on him and he said, come with me over to the Australian pines, she knew these men were a larger reproduction of the same man; beneath the oyster flesh was life, she

thought, the precious milky pearl he had spoken of, they were
all just common fishermen roughly manhandling this abundance from the gulf whose basin of troubled, muddy water
Mai could see and in the shells of which swam a lime-like substance which was life, shouldn't these men have been especially careful at every instant, for they were conceivers of life,
allowing reproduction and life, like them one entered the vast
cycle of birth and death, and that was the secret Mai had deci-
phered, knowing she would never tell anyone, for it was a fearful thing, attractive too, and thus one day she would yield to
the clean-shaven young man who came in her bedroom window or took out his pocket-knife and slashed the flowers in
the Robert Mapplethorpe photo, saying, here I am, I'm the one
they're looking for, can I sit on your bed, even if you can see
the fence of the state prison where they kept me, I've come
back, he'd say to her, I'm your father, and I've come to kidnap
you and take you far away from here, why not follow me,
Daniel and Mélanie aren't your real parents, I am, I followed
little Ambre who was nine on her bike in Texas, and they
found her body four days later in a thicket, and despite the
laws of about thirty states and counties, they're still looking for
me, look at that tender skin under my penknife, when they're
only six, like Adam and Ethan, grabbed and taken off from toy
stores in New York and Hollywood, their deflowered ghosts
wander and wander the canals and rivers, I love birthday
parties when parents put their kids to bed very late, then I
come in here through the open window and take them in
their sleep from beds perfumed with their own smells, still a
taste of chocolate on their lips, sweet breath, so who loves
you more than me, Daniel and Mélanie aren't your real parents, Mai, come with me, do you hear me there under the
sheets with your cats at your feet, oh I'll bring you back, just
like lots of others, and you won't say a word, and your parents
will say, what a miracle that she's back, she's so silent, won't
say a word, still just as normal as yesterday, her room a mess

as it was before, she's forgotten it all, our joy, our hope is home, and your black nanny will take you to school every morning again, and you'll keep up your cello lessons, then later on you'll go out dancing with boys, you'll be perfectly normal, even after months of privation and deflowering, and they'll go looking for me again, parents, psychiatrists, judges, I'll hold them all captive in their fearful unawareness, their apathetic bigotry which works on them like an anaesthetic, for they'd like to put me on trial for my offences, but they don't want to know about my inappropriate acts, they don't want you to talk, because you might upset their prudery, and you'll go to the prom, you'll be the hope of the family later on, but you won't tell them a thing, not your parents, not judges, during a trial they'll say, the predator, the one who called himself a prophet, was with a woman, a mistress, wasn't he, and they both abused you, and when you left the house that night, they dragged you along with them to their hangout in the mountain, you have to talk about what happened there, but I know you won't say anything, you'd rather let them think you're just the same as you were before you left and came back, obedient to your grandmother, normal, totally normal, you'll never mention the days without eating, just some water in a dirty cup, one week, two, when you were our prisoner below ground, then one morning you'll say to your father with no feeling at all, you know, Daddy, I've gone a week without eating, and he won't ask any questions, because he doesn't want to know what we do with our captives, all of them, year after year, in caves, underground hiding-places and hangouts, some of them we simply left to die of thirst, starvation, and the accomplice — wife or mistress — had doubts, I think I ought to go down in the basement and see what's happening, then gradually she gives up on it, I can numb her into anything, guilt becomes more and more dormant and sterile, your parents will say, no need to rush to trial, they just don't want to know, parents and psychologists, none of them want to know anything about those lower depths, maybe you remember those underground storage cellars for fruit, well, that's what we did with some of you, eight-to-twelve-year-old boys and girls, we kept all of you quiet in the cellars, petrified with hunger and exhaustion, our best fruit rotted one by one, then suddenly the woman would say, I can't go down there any-more, there are too many bodies under the stairs and under the earth, I can't, I won't, and we'd take off again, walking to different mountains, I don't know why we let you get away back home, but at least you've got to let me come and visit you every day, open the window onto the rose garden wide, then the day will come when you'll give in to me again, and now, as she sat on her bed, Mai saw a shape moving in her room, she thought it was him again, the same odd young man the police were looking for, but it was Marie-Sylvie, the nanny, hey, how come you're not asleep yet, and the light's on in Augustino's room, your parents won't be in till late, not before dawn I bet, because it's your grandmother's birthday, Mai heard Marie-Sylvie de Toussaint's impatient voice, back where I come from, you wouldn't have a roof over your head, not a bed, nothing, she said, then brusquely she laid Mai on her bed, wishing it was Vincent she needed to comfort and relieve of his nightime fears instead, Vincent was in a sanatorium for the summer, that's really what it was, they had talked about a summer school for bronchitic children, but sanatorium said it better, for two or three months, Mélanie had taken him away from her, Vincent was her own child since she looked after him, my brother's going crazy in that ghost-country, no house, no home on an island that didn't even export coffee or sugar anymore, she went on as she slid Mai between the covers, then one day they discovered the victims had turned into tor-turers and fled the country, whatever their crimes, good citi-zens, barbers, higher-ups who had tortured my brother, you'd never know them abroad in their disguises, these words ran like a litany, and Marie-Sylvie told Mai she had to sleep, she wasn't going to put out the lamp until Mai had her eyes closed, she'd got a letter from Jenny today, Mai didn't remember her, she was too small, when you close your eyes you forget everything, then with the first cooing of the doves in the garden, it would be dawn, Mai, like her brother Augustino, recognized bird-songs when the wind stirred the chimes in the doorways, what innocent happiness those moments were when Marie-Sylvie carried Vincent to bed, calling, my angel, murmuring in his ear that they would take to the sea in the *Southern Light*, but not to say anything to his parents, no, no, they laughed together, Vincent, her child to protect, defend and cure, above all to distract from his coughing bouts, both of them rocked by the calm sea, navigable in fine weather, *Southern Light, Southern Light*, and in the arbour, slightly heady from the perfume of African lilies, Mélanie told Olivier that, if that shameful segregation had gradually come to an end in restaurants, hotels, and theatres, everywhere the crime of segregation had been legalized for so many years, it was thanks to one woman aged forty-two, Rosa Parks, who refused to give up her seat on a bus to a white man, in forty-eight hours she had overthrown those inexorable laws, Rosa said, no, I'm not getting up, take my fingerprints, set on your fierce dogs, I'm not getting up, no white passenger is going to sit here in my place, because I'm tired standing up, arrest me, every bus in town will be boycotted, we're going to march, get our mules and horses out of the countryside, but I'm not getting up to give my seat to a white man, a young Baptist pastor called Martin Luther King heard the voice of the young woman with a defiant look, sharp under her thick glasses, was the hour approaching when men would be delivered from their chains? Send on your packs of dogs whose souls you've twisted, it isn't they who are biting our legs but you, their masters, those are your teeth we can feel in our flesh, Rosa Parks says she was not alone, completely calm in her white cotton dress, a black student with a binder under her arm, walking to

Little Rock Central High School, picking her way through a
hateful crowd, women insulting her, in the front row, imper-
turbable, she continued forward, she could not go back, but
only go on to college and university, send on your dogs, Rosa
said, point your garden hoses at us, I'm not getting up, a president sensitive to our oppression, seeing these images of violence on television, will say, that makes me sick, he ought to
have said sick with shame, that was it, a young woman with a
defiant look had changed the world, said Mélanie, this time it
seemed that Olivier had listened to her, still complaining that
Jermaine had turned up his music, what do you call this,
blues, rock, sometimes it even sounds like off-beat church
singing, my son really loves it, and he even got his mother to
dance with him, come on, let's join the others, Olivier said,
taking Mélanie's hand, we really shouldn't be so preoccupied,
look at my wife, she knows how to escape all these problems
with her joie de vivre, when they got near the pool, Mélanie
saw Chuan and her son Jermaine dancing to music that was
way too loud in the phosphorescent rays from the water under
a starry sky that was gradually getting paler and paler, come
on, said Chuan exuberantly, come and dance, my friends, a
group of young people, as colourful in their hairstyles and
clothes as the house was in Chuan's orange-and-pink walls,
bounced around her and Jermaine, Mélanie spotted her
mother looking concerned at this frenetic celebration which
she hadn't expected to be endless, really these young people
do go to bed late, or maybe they just didn't sleep at all, one
could see the tiredness etched into Mère's face, who was also
wondering how Chuan managed to get along with a misan-
thropic husband like Olivier, who hardly appreciated the qualities of a woman specializing in design, creating comfort and
beauty, Chuan said she had decorated the house pleasantly so
he would have peace to write in, but Olivier was a man
steeped in sadness, there he sat in his hut, compiling the political errors of the past century, the catastrophes that could have

plunged us into an apocalypse and were avoided by a hair's breadth, whether it be the Cuban missile crisis resolved by the voice of a head of state on Radio Moscow, or the memory of infamous assassination in Dallas, from October, 1962 to that day of November 22, 1963, in his articles, Olivier still felt disturbed by grief, yet all around him, Chuan, the good fairy of harmony in an unharmonious world, aimed at a form of weightlessness in industrial fashion design, whether she was decorating an ancestral home in New Orleans where she allied present to past, a multi-branched crystal chandelier with shaded candles to illuminate a stairway whose steps looked like sand-coloured velvet and made one feel as though they were flowing in a torrent of water in this decor, Mère thought, modernity or old-fashioned elegance with antique clocks over marble fireplaces, Chuan evoked shades of the sun going down or already set that were her own, writing in the red room, did Olivier notice the way the Chinese porcelaine pieces were placed in the alcove, or the gilded horse sculpture on the wall-shelves by the window, or the loggia with French doors where he came for a rest with a book in hand, not even the explosion of lunar and solar colours could assuage his eyes and heart, and that fruit, all of it brought in every morning, avocado, lemons, pineapples, brilliant daffodils, did he see the flowers arranged on the patio each day, did he breathe them in, he liked the circular pool that had a view of the dwarf palm trees and the sea, the turquoise sea and sky flowed together completely, suddenly he would be biting into some fruit, chewing the twig of a plant, vaguely remembering that Chuan had brought the silk for the curtains from Brazil and the porcelain pieces, slightly too exquisite for a man's room, from China, and why was this room as red as Chuan's dresses and shoes, then he stopped thinking about it, repeating what he often said to Jermaine, all I want, my dear son, is for you to love me, and even if he was always just as ill at ease with his thoughts of the evil century past, he admitted to the comfort of being loved by his wife and beloved son, if he'd been a little more reasonable, perhaps he would have been less tormented by the irreversible repetition of events he resented, this was how Mère imagined the particular understanding between Olivier and Chuan, wasn't every couple just as unique; those charming couples, Bernard, Valérie, Nora, and Christiansen were carrying on their conversations amid the noise, would Mère have a chance to know them better when her right hand hurt, our physical maladies tend to keep us apart from those we think in better health than ourselves, she thought, younger, stronger, and Caroline said, take this tray away, Harriett, Miss Désirée, this bread dipped in soup is for old people forgotten in homes, not for me, no bouillon, nothing, I don't want to be one of those animals they stuff before the slaughter, yes, a little more green tea, I'd like that, *I love you*, Charles had written to Fédéric in the years when their union was flourishing, I am your drawing and painting hand, you are my writing hand, even apart, we will always be together, we are already, aren't we, Frédéric had painted the walls of a spacious house they had lived in a sanguine pink, almost orange, and although the living room was empty, it seemed as though they were both still there under the domed lighting-fixture that hung from the wooden ceiling, reading, painting, writing, hands on the glass table, friends and lovers always, seeking each other out from time-to-time over the books and notes, when you're no longer there, I'll look for you and see you everywhere, even in the arms of strangers, and summer dappled on the windows through the acacia branches, I'll love you tomorrow and always, see you everywhere, and neither of them seemed to foresee the last glimmers of summertime and the return of winter's chilly light, still less the boundless love that Charles would feel for Cyril years later, when I think of that picture of Frédéric, I can still see and hear them in that huge house, I'm still there beside them taking pictures, Charles' refined head against Frédéric's athletic shoulder, hearing the ripple of water from the fountain in the garden, flowers crowding the window in summer, Charly and Cyril not even born yet, perhaps growing like embryos in our respective limbos, gnawing on us without our knowing it, Charles and Frédéric writing and painting a lot, in those days, my husband and I went deer-hunting, killing the deer, I remember the animal fallen on the tracks, and my daughter not a viable foetus, so unhealthy the world, I'll love you through all that I no longer possess, under the chandelier they write and paint in the New England woods, the deer at dawn are as free and happy as in the painting by Courbet in which they stretch out to reach the leaves, wild and free and happy, not knowing we exist, my husband and I, with our dogs and hunting rifles, the deer heft their weight upwards into the tree and its sweet fruit, stretching their bulk and shaking themselves; perhaps it's their voices I hear in the roomy house, back from Greece, what a grand and beautiful universe, while I'm taking their pictures I don't tell them I'm pregnant, nothing about the scarcely viable little girl, I'm just a woman with a husband she doesn't love, I'll take a lover, I think that Charles and Frédéric will always love one another, I tell them, sit quietly together so I can photograph you, Charles unbuttons his shirt-collar, he doesn't like having his picture taken, but he has to because it's for the cover of his book, Charles, Frédéric, and I make up an independent and solid trio, enthusiastic about the same sports, riding and tennis, Charles is amazed when I tell him I've flown a plane and got a diploma in architecture, he says, I'll introduce you to my friend Jean-Mathieu, this winter I'll have a lover, and it will be him, we're in the most torrid of regions, by the sea, I meet Jean-Mathieu in a sunny February, and we languish on the terrace under the sun, Jean-Mathieu is wearing classic Italian shoes with no socks, I spot a scorpion and kill it with a swift blow of my book before its venomous stinger can reach him, we should go to Italy, Jean-Mathieu says, that was a long time ago, Harriett, when my villa

was open to so many venerable friends, Jean-Mathieu, Adrien
and Suzanne, Charles and Frédéric, later the European writer-
painter couples, Bernard and Valérie, Nora and Christiensen,
it's a crying shame that I'm shut up like this, no villa, no
friends, no Jean-Mathieu by my side, can you tell me why
Harriett, why force-feed me when it's nightime, it is night, isn't
it, you'll panic Charly's cat, where is Charly, always out dancing and drinking in the discotheques till dawn, it's a crying
shame, where has my house gone, Ma'am, she squandered
your fortune, that Charly, a really nasty piece of work, Ma'am,
remember that gap between her teeth, degrading a lost tooth
like that, it was her, she got on your nerves so many times, so
much bad temper, it was nothing, said Caroline, it wasn't her,
it was the ecstasy, it wasn't her behaviour, my sweet child
would never do that, but she had to buy more and more
expensive drugs, I know it wasn't her, Caroline repeated, and
they say the motivation for his actions was racial hatred,
Olivier thought, that's what he would emphasize in his article,
hate had pushed the skinhead to kill a black girl driving her
white fiancé, they were both twenty, the skinhead had shot
from his car, five shots had been heard, some said a trucker
was about to pass both cars when he saw the racist, the
engaged couple were students at the Atlantic University of
Florida, adolescents in love, their killer was twenty as well,
hate, hate was still killing these days, the bullet had hit the
girl's temple, they had been waiting for the light at an intersec-
tion, and they were found still wrapped in each other's arms,
hate, hate, thought Olivier holed up in his office, he was waiting for the night to end, the contralto voice of Nina Simone in
his headphones revived his anger, *Mississsippi Goddam*, sang
the voice, liberated but so pained, so that's what it all comes
down to for us, passion and pain, Olivier thought, this music
was once banned in the southern states, still no matter, passion and pain have survived, you know, I don't regret a thing
I said or sang, said Nina Simone's contralto voice, nothing, I

don't regret a single word, might that voice have warded off the hatred of the skinhead, a killing in broad daylight from a grey convertible, *Mississippi Goddam*, cursed be you for killing the black fiancée of the white boy, you've killed love, destroyed two lives and more besides, cursed be you, whether free or in jail, may you never enter into the kingdom of men or of God, Olivier thought, for they had to be examined rather than cursed, what purpose did it serve, and did Olivier have the right to punish and hate when he had a wife and son who adored him, what is the point to our love and our tolerance and our pity, what point, for every day hate kills, hate kills, and Ari looked at his daughter as she slept with her toys all around her, she was already asleep on his shoulder when he walked to the car amid the rumbling of the waves and the wind on the beach, there were stains of brilliant colour on Lou's round fists, she so loved to cover herself in the gooey gouache in her father's studio, and it wouldn't come off with soap and water in the bath, it was even in her tangled hair, soon Ari would teach her to cut her own hair, essential lessons were the ones that taught autonomy, you need to have the courage to discover that you are practically alone in the world, even if you have parents, Lou would be able to muddle through, you have to be able to find your way out of any mess in life, even if you had good parents, Ari and Ingrid were, and before she was ever born they too had been abandoned, Ari said Chagall's lovers were flying up to a red sky holding one another in their arms, it now seemed to him that the reproduction was inappropriate for Marie-Louise's room, for the charming bodies, no longer feeling desire for one another, were not flying up to their charnel ascension anymore, as seen in the painting, drifting joyfully over the rooftops of the city into a red sky with unusual creatures orbiting around them, a man with a fish-head coming to offer them a bouquet of lilacs, a bird that ran but did not fly, this was the sweet story told by the Russian painter, Ari said, but life was very different, two lovers could suddenly find themselves waging interminable battles, hating one another, for love was also a world of pettiness, a terrain of rivalry, in his profound naïveté, the painter of fairy modernism had seen nothing of these base squabbles, in gentleness he had painted a world where order reigned, what would Chagall think of this order or communion between the animal world and God when he returned to his country torn by war and revolution, well, if Marie-Louise liked the painting, lovers in the red sky of revolution, he wouldn't take it from her, Daddy, Mama, she said, what was true yesterday is no longer so, fallen from their flight, her parents were separated and wounded, Ari thought, but Lou would be with him until Sunday, he was happy after all, and as soon as the winds calmed, the boat would be ready, he had explained to Lou that her first boat would be shaped like a ballet slipper with a reinforced toe, he'd call it *Lou's Slipper*, the boats and yachts were anchored in the marina of the sailing club, and that's where they'd go tomorrow, Ari had washed and polished the mahogany sides of her boat ceaselessly, on the water it was a marvel of agility, though for now, Lou wasn't sure she liked the sea and big waves that pushed at you all the time, and those noisy gulls everywhere, the pelicans gathered in so close to the fishermen's cabin, Lou's boat looked as though it would hold up well at sea, how pleasant it will be to live in our cabin at anchor, just the two of us under a perfect blue sky, father and daughter at work on their gouaches, today's conceptual artists are so entirely different from Chagall and his mystical thinking or his dreams of a Russia without madness, they're loaded down with instruments, videos, installations, sound effects and stimulation, sets of posters and collages, their voluntary distortion of painting, the life-shock of these contemporaries, how restful and fresh were Chagall's lovers in a red sky, what culture is it we're living in when we can't even recognize beauty, tomorrow Lou's boat would be ready, Ari was never through polishing the hull, it was for her, so beloved of her father, they'd have a little time, as long as the winds died down, and Julio thought that this night would be a memorable one; he'd seen them before the navy officers and Coast Guard, they were a woman, three children, and a few men, who had arrived, compass in hand, in a boat they had built themselves, a huge pile of wood and steel sixteen feet long that sank in the water before the officers on night patrol or the Coast Guard heard their cries, Julio had thought, those are my people, what storm with easterly winds had brought them here, are there broken bones, why no baggage, yet cards hanging like medallions from their necks with addresses of those they hoped to find almost erased and illegible, then an officer appeared on the scene saying, I'll translate for them, but they just looked at him, suddenly wordless and voiceless, the addresses and phone numbers were their families, but where were they, we don't know them, they were given blankets and energy drinks, they had to be identified, those who had made it to shore could stay, those caught at sea had no rights and would be sent back, what Atlantic storm brought them here on the easterly winds, and that was the end of a memorable night, Julio thought, among them a woman and children, no baggage, Ramon, Oreste, their mother, they'd been calling for help a long time in the night, then carrying blankets and sweet drinks to them, Julio said, don't be afraid, you've reached shore, I'm Julio, the one you're looking for, there's a house ready for you on the Island, you can rest at last, come, quietly stumbling, the survivors had followed Julio along the sandy paths between the pines to the house of refuge, and Marie-Sylvie was delighted that at last Mai had closed her eyes and seemed to be sleeping, now she'd stop asking for things, Marie-Sylvie left a small light on, she could read while she kept watch over this child her parents had spoiled too much, what wouldn't they buy for her, just as many electronic games as her brother Augustino, though their grandmother disapproved, a more rigorous upbringing would have been better, no one knew why such a little girl was always running away or why she still wet her bed, the pediatrician they went to spoke in veiled terms, it's true kids nowadays are sexually precocious, he'd added, fixing Mai in the ambiguity of her unease, who knows what, thought Marie-Sylvie, to whom all this concern seemed unnecessary, this pediatrician hadn't seen the kids in her country covered with flies, did he even know they existed, Marie-Sylvie was irritable around Mai, though she'd been her nanny ever since replacing Jenny in the household, she despised being in Mai's service without Vincent around to coddle, frail Vincent, but what an illusion it was that one could give love when it wasn't a choice, naturally, all others were just a burden, with Jenny's letter in her trembling hands, she thought, you left me alone Jenny, as soon as your studies in medicine were over, you left, Doctors Without Borders, when am I going to see you again, I know so much less than you do, I used to keep bony goats on a hillside with my brother, you Jenny, you're different, you have a destiny, we'll always be stripped of everything, poverty stricken, Jenny wrote, in this remote Chinese province we're living a hot, steamy, suffocating summer, just me and a few doctors, these poor farming areas are hit by an epidemic, a short while ago we weren't even allowed to name the sickness, everyone is masked, and there is a crisis in these mountainous areas that they would rather not know about, every day, we stop before huge granite blocks which stand as tombstones for those buried (names withheld) under the scrubby grass, no one has any respect for them, just humble villagers who received transfusions from an infected blood-bank, now they have no names or identity either, as though they had never existed, couples who had worked hard on this land for their children, worthy men and women worn down by farming soy and corn, even whole families disappeared, fathers, mothers, children, sometimes aged grandparents take care of the orphans, many thought they could cure their skin lesions with herbs without knowing what was wrong, someone told them medicines bought in Thailand would help, that a vaccine would save them, but help could not reach them from so far away, we went to the dangerous parts of town where young prostitutes die every day, like the heroine addicts that visit them, with our surgical masks on, who could we help with so little medication and vaccine, I am haunted by the tombstones with no names on them that spring up everywhere, even between hills, in valleys under the sun-scorched grass, an epidemic they long refused to name, yet the number of victims kept growing, it must be nice where you are, Marie-Sylvie, far from the sepulchres and this humid heat, how can I see the unbearable things I witness here every day, parents of decimated families too weak to walk, pushing their ten-year-old children before them in squeaking wooden wheelbarrows, packets of bones, fleshless arms on stretchers, how I envy you where you are with healthy children, and Marie-Sylvie thought, why doesn't she stop talking, I wish she'd stop writing, what's she doing in China when she ought to be here with me, all at once she had the impression Jenny was writing in order to crush her, grind her up, working her indignation like a woman subjected to the laws of the rich, of course Mélanie's children were healthy, well-loved, if love was that superabundance, excess of caresses from Mélanie on Mai's hair and forehead, kisses and cuddles that so annoyed Marie-Sylvie who had never had any of that, the little girl need only scrape her knee and her mother was down before her, weren't those three women — Esther, Mélanie, and Mai — more than blood relations, more like sharing a single wavelength, possessing the same certain-ties, and also gifts of sensibility as well as seductive qualities which made them disrespectful of a creature so undone and wounded as herself, thought Marie-Sylvie, born under a bad sign . . . didn't they all, Mélanie, Daniel, and Esther, try to detach her from the only one she loved, Vincent, taken away from her for the whole summer; her long silhouette curved towards Mai's bed, she thought of herself as a dried stem bending under every servitude, as though without Vincent, she was just another black servant, she heard Mai murmuring in her sleep, however imperceptible her moan, her mother would have heard right away, woken her daughter and asked, what is it sweetheart, another one of those nightmares, whereas Marie-Sylvie steeled herself and pretended not to hear, what could Mai be complaining about since she had everything, Marie-Sylvie touched Mai's brow with her finger-tips and said, it isn't day yet, you have to sleep, Mai trembled in her sleep, walking alone without Augustino, her parents had told her so many times not to go along the sea by the path to the stadium alone, where they practised team sports like football or beach hockey under the midday sun, there never seemed to be anyone in the bleachers or on the stands, nor on the pathway that Mai took alone with her skateboard under her arm, she could feel the silence dripping down into her footprints, nobody would find her here, there was a black telephone near the stands she'd rather not hear ring, might it be a connection to her parents, but she was a separate person from them and her brothers, wasn't she, and why was she strictly forbidden to come to the stadium alone, strange people went through there, her mother said, and especially Mai was not to talk to strangers and certainly not take it into her head to follow them, you never knew what to expect with Mai, said Marie-Sylvie de la Toussaint, Mama kissed her in the morning and said, Mai dear, today try not to upset me the way you did yesterday, you wouldn't answer when I called, how am I to know where you are when you won't answer my call, if she were a boy, they'd have more respect for her, for several minutes no one showed up, and Mai didn't hear a sound, it was as though the grass-lined road beyond the stadium was being petrified in the sun, there wasn't even an occasional lost egret or heron to be seen, but someone had whispered and laughed, and this eruption of voices in the all-enveloping stillness had made her start from the highest platform, she'd seen him and her, but they hadn't seen her, a very young couple, the boy was pulling the girl's hair, Mai couldn't tell if this game was playful or nasty, but she didn't like hearing them quarrel, then all of a sudden, the girl didn't seem to be laughing anymore, but shouting and weeping, Mai was far enough away that they could not see her, was he teasing the girl or bullying her violently, she couldn't tell, although the girl stopped crying after a few moments, they were haranguing and tormenting each other now, her mother was right, you did see some weird people here, if she were asleep and this were a dream, she would wake up from this painful dream and not hear the screams of the girl being beaten by the boy anymore, was he beating her, or was it a game like when she had let him pull her hair and laughed, about-facing in an instant, Mai couldn't really tell who these adolescents were, the way their shadows flailed about on the stands, or if the boy was beating the girl, oh why didn't her nanny wake her up, Mai should never have come to the stadium, and Marie-Sylvie saw Mai tremble in her sleep, touched her forehead and said, it's nothing, just a nightmare, I'm putting the light out and going to my room now, as Mai half opened her eyelids, she saw the silhouette of Marie-Sylvie disappear down the hallway, where is Mama, she asked, but got no answer and so went back to sleep, the cries had stopped now, and Caroline repeated, Harriett, Miss Désirée, all this degradation isn't the fault of Charly but those young people she hangs out with in bars and discotheques, she comes back to me at dawn looking devastated and tottering, doesn't even recognize me, as though all at once she doesn't know who I am, this degradation, this being shut up with you in this house, Harriett, meanwhile an exhibition of my photography is touring the world, London, Paris, here you are treating me like a retarded old woman, when my mind is clear as it's ever been, this is not all Charly's fault, it's fate that caused us to meet, just as surely as it did Charles and Cyril, and whether that's sad or happy, it's our fate, even as a child, I knew nothing could be done about that, on beautiful days by the sea, when my mother had appointments to go to, her lover used to beckon me into his room, sat me down beside him and said, my, how you're growing, come over to the bed (their bed), and even as he was stroking my hair, I could see outside the window my cousin on his pony saying in his child's voice, Caroline, come and play with me, the man's hand slid along my back, hmmm it's rounded-in here, he said at the start of my waist, when a servant approached, he said in a low voice, you absolutely must not say anything about this, it's between us, isn't it now, let's just keep quiet about it, I kept quiet, complicit in the fate that gives each one of us our share of experience, intrigues and ruses, do we have any choice, running headlong over myself to perdition, as I ran to the man whenever my mother went out, the lovers' bedchamber, their love and pleasure, the man opened his arms to me, I was an accomplice in their affair, this conspiracy of the flesh they kept up night and day under sheets washed and ironed by the servants, my mother was not aware of my carryings-on with the man and his too-intimate kisses, of him, of us, of our silence, he said come, and there I was, what should we go discover this long afternoon, my cousin asked wandering through the dunes on his pony, I lost no time in joining him, slowly, gently, showing him how to bridle our skittish pony, my cousin was so naïve, he knew nothing about man or woman, and my sweet afternoon indulgences with my mother's lover who derived a special pleasure from picking up little girls, I loved the fact that this man was destined for me, because it was something forbidden, unimaginable, and that's how destiny got its claws into me, close against one another, my cousin and I went down to the dunes on our pony to where the waves broke, he candid, me uncontrollable, because I wanted to know everything about life, just as well you aren't listening to me Désirée, for you life is simple, you have God, I don't want this bouillon you've brought me, I don't want anything, you look on me with kindness and take my hand, I'm telling you I don't like the smell of that soup, I can't eat it, your black hand in mine, a union of pity or desolation, here we are the two of us, the way we used to be in my parents' house when you used to tell me to say my prayers and I wouldn't listen, uncontrollable, uncontrollable, you said, Harriett, Miss Désirée, in your hand I see a vigorous nobility, mine, well look at these fingers that drop everything, no longer agile, these knotted joints, this isn't me anymore, these are the hands of blind people I photographed, frozen still on a white page, but remember, it was only for an instant while they groped their way in the night, suddenly these hands were sighted and as light as Charles' fingers on the piano, he was so young and prodigious then, I remember how they all looked, and what surprises me even more is that I loved it when models some-times had their lips half open, it was as though they were all going to be speaking to us long after they had disappeared and only then betray the secret of their voluptuous living by spilling a few words, your hand in mine, you patiently suggest that I sleep, give me a sleeping pill that I turn down, annoyed, and say Harriett, Miss Désirée, leave me be, you're always watching over me, you obey, you're never far off, when I start to feel sleepy, I can feel you behind me, like the flinch of an animal, all those portraits I've done, all imprinted in the mem-ory of my eye, it's an unending photogravure, too many images and faithful reproductions, I always go back to my mother's lover in the bedroom, or my cousin in the woods on the pony in autumn, he who knows nothing about me, this plate is engraved and can never be effaced, not a word, not a gesture, an exasperating image because it endures forever, whether disorganized or not, it lasts, etched in the phospho-rescence of the past, as though present, it sees me with preci-sion as I see it, my models' mouths half open to say, today I live and tomorrow I die, whether it's Charles, Frédéric,

Suzanne or Adrien, they all say it, the young Caroline is busy
elsewhere in the half-shadow of the afternoon bedroom, when
she hears her cousin's voice, oh, when are you going to come
and play with me, the pony's getting nervous, then she hears
rumours of war being declared, and her parents send her
away to elite colleges and universities, she'll become an architect, she tells her classmates as she photographs them in studied, stilted poses in luxuriant gardens on campus, then all this
carefree happiness ends, and the skies bursts into flame, the
elegant world she lives in will no longer exist, she is afraid
when she takes her first flying lessons, but still she wants to fly
solo once, just once, and now here I am alone, high in the sky
with no visibility, solitary, just as I wanted with all my preoccupations elsewhere, young Caroline learns to fly with the
man who will become her first fiancé, her first death, hero or
angel thrown from a flaming heaven, here is the fiancé, the
uniformed lieutenant in his flying-suit, my first death, heroic,
no time to think about it as I have, in battle, one doesn't think,
one dies, maybe even without knowing fear, young people
give their lives without holding back, bravery is not an act of
reflection, thought does not hang on, one just dies, I received
the telegram, it might have been the same day I learned to use
a hunting rifle and gathered up a young pheasant whose
plumage had dripped blood all over my hand, perhaps the
day I remember my grandfather's words, don't point your
weapon upwards to the sky, that will bring out your determination to kill, the plumage with iris-like glints, plumage of
a bird fallen on the same day as he did. I could do nothing
about it then, Désirée, nor now. You have your God, I have
what was mine, and Samuel, working out at the bar, heard his
teacher Arnie's voice urging him to the lightness of Japanese
masters Samuel had seen dancing in the interpretation work-
shops that had so disoriented him, these masters were able
to show our western world the refinement of dance so slow
and other-worldly, when the body evolves into serenity, but

the relentless atmosphere of the world heralded to Samuel a
heavy footfall, no longer capable of slowing down, whose
echo he heard under his window at night, if he wanted others
to understand what he was feeling, he would have to dance
wearing fibres with the texture of flexible metal, like the
biological suits worn by hazardous-materials teams in post
offices or any strategic point where a troublesome bacterium
might have insinuated itself beneath a stamp or onto letter-
paper, living in symbiosis with the written word and travelling
with the letter, this bacterium would distance itself from its
host organism and any other secret information, these trackers
would spray the area with antibiotic powder, cleansing one
hand after the other of typhoid and diphtheria, Samuel would
dance through the streets of New York with a disturbing dressing over his mouth, held over his nose by two threads around
his ears, he'd wear the outfit he had just learned the term for,
Tyvek, which would be needed for his safety tomorrow, like
those worn by rescue teams in the worst epidemics, dancer or
mailman, he would be ready to resist infection, from the
minute he got up in the morning, he'd remember that even his
own shower could produce contamination, who knows what
harmful substance ran into the wells and seas and rivers, especially if an envelope holding a card or letter could propagate
pustules of smallpox or traces of chicken-pox, even more insid-
iously, the postal worker might contract something as harmless
as a cold, plan a picnic on Sunday with his family, being a
health enthusiast, drink eight glasses of water a day and stay
away from communion wine, Samuel too would be kept in
this trap of healthy living and false security, and wouldn't even
know what was ailing him, colic or nausea, he'd go to class
and be found at noon the next day lying on the bathroom
tiles, not breathing, or again he might be exercizing on the
bars, a butterfly of a dancer as light as he was graceful at one
instant, thinking of unencumbered grace, free of ornamenta-
tion, of the Japanese dancers, or the unclean cast out by all,

quarantined like so many others, whichever way it was to be, he had to live cautiously, especially being Samuel, it meant that his life and growth would forever be punctured, yet still he would be determined to live well, like his father and grandfather, thus it was with his home computer, Samuel thought, he communicated daily with his friends, and like him, they tried wriggle out from under the conformity of fear that could have destroyed the will to live in each of them, one poet from Argentina wrote that lately he couldn't sleep at night, a visual artist in India did a gouache of a lion emerging from a man's head, from Uruguay came red circles on the glass page of the computer, a composer in South Africa sent the opening pages of a piece with notes so tightly squeezed they seemed illegible, the art of combining sounds had also become the art of being seen and heard, however unmusical the combination of signs and notes might be, art put all its urgent preoccupations out there, as though a hand of iron had written in the sky over a calm countryside of mountains and hills, beware, can you not see me coming, and it was the voice of the red tumult heard by them all, thought Samuel, his musician friend wrote that his piece for violin and orchestra was to remind people of a lost perfume, a brief sparkle of light through a crystal, like us and our history, and as Samuel listened, it seemed that the crystal was odd and tarnished, in this light emerging from the earth in cacophonic music and videos — sometimes highlighting a scene from a past in conflagration — Samuel had the impression his friends saw the world as from a flying saucer where nothing could be pinpointed, it could not be labelled archival or propagandistic, was this a Vietnamese village, the morning after a deep night with all the villagers fled, the green smoke of a raid in Rwanda after a genocide in which even the children they carried on their backs were killed, mothers still alive then finished off with a machete as they ran with the little ones one their backs, this mother's race had been revived in the unvoiced terror of all mothers whose panting and running feet only could be heard, the race form all misfortunes in the shadows, but which ones, all terrible, all nameless, gliding towards the abyss, the killing-fields with millions of crushed skulls, so many fields on fields that no one knew who was in which, men or animals, so many genocides that they had no names or graves, and henceforth no commemoration, an occasional trial or improvised tribunal, perhaps, would underline the assassins' actions, but neither killer nor victim actually put in an appearance, no commemoration or jurisdiction, Samuel thought, just evanescence and smoke, the world as the artist discerned it on his radar, you could only go on as though this world was ours and go forever forward, but what kind of progress or advance was it for the artist, knowing how to paint a grey pigeon lying dead in an alley among the garbage, that abandoned bird would show our lack of respect for life and our obsession with death, a charcoal drawing of a fan on a table, as though the pigeon or the fan had provided the same purposeless energy, both mistreated and misused, tossed in a corner amid a limitless choice of objects, Samuel and his friends no longer knew what to remote-control, the almost weightless portable phone with a memory, or some other compact digital instrument, or the remote with pre-programmed keys, the only energy came from these tools, as easily tuned to us as we to them, comfortable, pleasing in format, easy to sip into a coat pocket, useful as a deliberate distraction, the stubborn determination to cut oneself off from whatever was happening out there, thought Samuel, every evocation of places where torture reigned over the lives of women and men was wiped out by the Leviathan authority of a VCS or a DVD, who wanted his Samsung SCH-i600 phone whose digital code, so new, so mysterious, with instant messaging, he thought, a whole range of virtuoso phones he'd have liked to own, though his father kept saying one was enough, he'd have liked to see on the diaphanous blue screen, not today's messages, often love-letters from the several women he loved at one time, he didn't seem to have time to get attached to just one since he'd broken off with Veronica, but what was happening in those forbidden hidden places his father wrote about, the gulags, the re-education camps, maybe it would have been too troubling to know so much about these catastrophic realities, sure they still happened, but it was so far away in North Korea or China, Hitlerian or Stalinist regimes where men and women took pleasure in torturing one another, they even said they enjoyed torturing children, women and men wherever this duty was required by their superiors, jailers who coldly used choking gas on those they called opponents or had carried out chemical tests, who would want to know all these macabre details on opening their e-mail, better maybe to forget all about this great terror machine and be a dancer-choreographer like Arnie Graal, possibly the real manifesto was in this staging, and you had to serve your art with rigour, the silent rigour that took time for love away from a young man, yes, said Caroline, my soldier fiancé was my first death, then the sadness fades till one feels nothing, but it was never like that for Charles, I can still see him when he returned from India, he came to see me in my villa by the sea, before this censorship that kept my friends from visiting, I'm no fool, I never was, as soon as Charly came into the house, people stopped seeing or phoning me, even dear Jean-Mathieu, I know Harriett, you'll say it was her all along, I don't know what Charly did to keep me apart from Jean-Mathieu, she may not fool me, but I can't hate her for it, sure poor Charles was in tears, but for all his pitiful air he never wrote so well, he paid for his genius in tears, so my dear Caroline, what do you think of this, Cyril likes promiscuity, hanging out with scum, I can't put up with it, what's going to happen to us, does he even realize what kind of world we're living in, I've never been so worried about any of my partners before, a friend who has contempt for any and all rules, what can you do, I told him, unaware that I too would

have to undergo this same promiscuity and disregard for any
rule one day, he is young and sensuous, that's all, isn't it more
like debauchery, said Charles, these words, debauchery and
sexual promiscuity, were as foreign to him as to me, so long
had we observed the world from our ivory tower, so honest,
so perfect before the temptation that overflows the bounds of
respectability, nor taking account of the fact that Cyril's flaunt-
ing our relationship everywhere hurts Frédéric, Charles went
on, I took his sweet, delicate head in my hands and comforted
him, what you're going through, Charles, may hurt you, but it
feeds your work, so you needn't be so unhappy, oh what
should I do, he asked, love him more or less, more, I told him,
always more, what I believed was that Charles, being a spiritual creature, ought to become more of this earth and learn,
like all of us, the implacable lesson of modesty in love, and
this is just what Cyril was forcing him to do, Charles' fleshly
rebirth was happening before my eyes, he loved, he cried,
another man entirely, through all this very palpable turbulence
of love, which humbles even the proudest and breaks the
spirit, I watched him grow, Cyril forces me to anger, oh why
did I ever meet him, and instead of taking that trip to India, I
should have taken care of Frédéric instead of leaving him to
others, though there were some angelic people looking after
him, besides I'm too old for Cyril, young people should be
with their own, what bothers me the most is that Cyril wants it
all and despises my attachment to Frédéric, in fact he begs me
not to see him anymore, can you imagine that, dear Caroline,
not see Frédéric anymore, never have him to go back to, and
when you think about it, we've never been able to live without one another, really a brilliant marriage, I told him, a very
successful one you had, until Frédéric began to go downhill,
Charles said, until we both realized our own mortality, that
day that Frédéric fell by the pool and he began to suffer memory loss, that was intolerable, and then along came Cyril, the
demon of youth and dark light, what could I do, and now it's

too late, I'm in to stay, so all I can do is love even more, as you say, they had had this conversation a long time ago, I was feeling strong in those days, it was not yet that fateful time when I was no longer to see Jean-Mathieu, on his return from Italy from which there was no return, ever, it wasn't yet the time of scattered ashes off The-Island-Nobody-Owns, I went out in the evening arm-in-arm with Jean-Mathieu, sometimes his tone held a note of reproach, he said I was too proud, maybe it was an air of patriotic arrogance that he had always disliked, we were from different social classes and different countries, you can't build a country on servitude or the enslavement of some for the shameless profit of those who have the upper hand and hold them down, Jean-Mathieu was one of those thousands of child labourers exploited in a period from which I'd collected photographs, I couldn't help feeling shame at seeing those kids in black boots carrying heavy loads, just like in Dickens' time, a curse on us who allowed it, I said to myself, knowing that it was not just my ancestors who needed to be judged, but all of them, was it my fault if Jean-Mathieu was so vulnerable sometimes and compared himself to those sons of immigrant farmers living in a nameless misery, that tone of his upset me, and yet I felt no bitterness, Jean-Mathieu always seemed ready to pardon me without being patronizing, but I hear his voice in my ear, so close it's as though he's here in this room where you're keeping me captive, all of them, I can hear all their voices, Charles' is melodious, and Frédéric's, Suzanne's laughter, you never die, she says, they just tell us we do, hey, courage Caroline, come back and join us, what are you doing with that black nurse, you've bored the poor woman with all your stories and now she's asleep in her armchair, you mustn't refuse to eat, that could be bad for you, come back to us, Caroline, let's go out to the tennis court at dawn, I'll expect you there tomorrow, it will soon be day, Caroline, or is it the voice of my cousin telling me the pony is shying at the fence, we'll soon be trundling down the dunes and the grass, the sand will still be wet, I'll say shivering in warm daylight, maybe I'll keep quiet, or maybe I'll say, listen, dear cousin, this is my secret, I was with a man, my mother's lover yesterday afternoon; maybe I'll see a line of all those poets I've photographed coming towards me pushing aside the leaves in an arbour, and they'll say to me, prepare to follow us, and one says, the thing I regret the most is the night I left at age thirty-nine, I had drunk so much I don't even know how it happened, just a stupid mistake, I wish I were still there with my wife and children, especially the youngest whom I haven't seen growing up, a mistake that can't be fixed; the young painter from London, still shadowy and desolate, says, yes, it was an absurd suicide, remember, a few days after we met in London, I said goodbye to the earth, you took a picture of my hands clenched around the pencil, one must never say goodbye to the earth, because the earth reclaims us, all of them, I can see and hear all of them, that laugh of Suzanne's that her husband never was able to tame, a laughter so fresh it just might convince me, we're having a party for Esther's eightieth, do please come with us, Caroline, but I have to tell her I haven't got a dress or shoes anymore, just that ridiculous hospital gown I can't go out in, and my hat, I've asked Harriett, my servant, over and over where she's put my hat and gloves, but she's just a servant, Charly would have scolded me soundly, Harriett was my nurse's name, not a servant anymore, I'm your friend says Miss Désirée, and that is God's will, not mine, now Harriett's gone without telling me where she's put my hat and gloves, my cousin and I have a beautiful pony, his name's Beauty, but has the hour struck when the falcons fly to their prey, no, I don't think so, it's not yet dawn, though the sun is pale, the falconers have pitched their tents in the desert and lit the braziers, the deer have heard the dogs barking in their sleep, and the gazelles tremble when they hear the squeal of tires on the country road, they can sense us coming, my

husband and I, and our accurate shooting from the convertible, we're afraid of nothing; my mother was a rebel, when we
have our picture taken together, she wants me to sit next to
her on the lawn in front of the entrance to a grand hotel, she
looks sleepy, and so do I, she is distracted as she'll often be,
perhaps she's thinking of her nightime lover and his charming
smile, she seems to be saying, like a woman use to luxury, listen my dear, I'll never be a submissive woman, nor the kind of
mother you might want me to be, no, I move with a kind of
magnificence that makes me unapproachable, that, no doubt,
is why she left me from birth in the care of her servants, of
aunts and uncles whose houses were often filled, tender
uncles filled with goodwill who rape their nieces when the
mothers are away, is it time for the falconers to urge their
rapacious hawks to the skies . . . already? A star glitters in the
paling sky, Harriett is sleeping noisily, head on chest, it really
is the time when there is no one around, even vigilance
sleeps, and my mother has brought a more-than-viable girl
into the world, hard and conquering, the hardiness and
courage were hers, I didn't want a merely viable daughter, for
she would hardly have survived our massive insanity, barely
more than few years, like the brothers and sisters in one family who were slaughtered slowly by the Red Guard after their
father had been fired, humiliated in front of a crowd, a time of
dissoluteness and madness, or perhaps I'm wrong, maybe she
would have fought like me, one of the first to do so, she
would have been a friend and ally, not that vain and cruel
Charly who hurt me so badly, please realize she is not the
main cause of the catastrophes in my life, no, she would have
been the non-viable daughter, the first surgeon as good at
heart transplants as any man she admired, an enthusiast, an
astronaut, her footprint venerated, honoured in twenty-two
countries, would she be repudiated in her dazzling abilities on
unknown planets as she had been on the one she knew so
well, would she still be that question mark in one world and

another, in the reign of mass insanity, or taking the first invincible step of man on the moon, or flying one-by-one to the other planets, then would she still be marginally viable? She'd have fought as I did, for the right to legal abortion, been excluded amid controversy like Norma McCorvey as she overthrew the outdated laws of Texas that January Monday in 1973, she'd have lived in a time of exiled prophets, miracle babies fertilized in test tubes, sidestepped the laws of our species, committed the bold strokes and dangers of freedom before ever being born, viable to see so much, belonged to so many alliances, witnessed the falling of walls as well as the erecting of new ramparts to separate nations, been on the other side of the barbed wire in Berlin with no one to hear her name, been an activist with a gas mask, shouted, been viable and alive, mine, my child, my daughter, if I had never felt so strongly in the time of hostilities that she could never be born of a woman, scarcely viable. Timidly affable, Mère had approached Nora and her husband Christiansen, shaking hands with them, she'd said how much she wanted to get to know them better, but when would that music Chuan's son had chosen be over with, these young people, she thought, do they always have to hammer our ears with those loud noises, soon this night would be over and she wouldn't have anything to complain about, in this evening scented with jasmine and frangipani, Nora's face, thinned since her return from Africa, expressed the same sudden fatigue as Mère's, so it wasn't age, Mère observed, but an ascetic way of life Nora had adopted in Africa: a sort of moral exhaustion, Nora looked around her, wondering if this was a celebration or something else in a disgraced and ruined country, there are birthdays and anniversaries for people, but not many for tragedies that have shaken the world, Nora thought, victims don't speak, we treat them as voiceless, forgetfulness or silence, what point was a tormented conscience, maybe Nora should have listened to her children and not left, while her husband Christiansen had strongly advised going back there, how edgy it was with your father already doing medicine in the bush, but now the soil of Rwanda was so weighed down with the dead — although the newspapers and TV rarely talked about it, about Tutsi children killed by the thousands — who would Nora be tomorrow, the same person or someone else, it was so easy to get comfortable again and forget what she had seen and smelt, the intoxicating perfume of jasmine, the burning brush, landing in Kinshasa with lights on in the rain, seeing the southern Sahara again from the window, an expanse of white sand I'd have liked to go running in, the smell of smoke so close choked me, was it a gold-coloured or a whitish sea that blinded me, a chauffeur and a porter asked me if I was the nurse they'd been expecting for days, no, I said, I was just there to revisit the country, but I was available if they needed me, I had no particular role, mother, artist, how could I explain to them who I was, Nora, I am Nora, coming back to a disgraced and ruined country, there were so many people around me, so many kilometres from town, the smoky smell was from all the votive candles that had been lit, merchants and vendors sitting on chairs along the road, all of them with ridiculous things to sell, since we're travelling by car, there are checkpoints everywhere, one truck is piled high with huge sacks of rice, children with their mothers, hunger in those eyes feverishly staring at us, should I stay or go, the girls said, don't leave tomorrow, have you forgotten that at fifty you need to accept the state of the world as it is, wasn't it a sneaky manœuvre for the girls always to keep her close to them, Nora thought, maybe just a form of legitimate self-concern, for what else can they do, even as we grow old and suddenly feel unable to offer them what they demand of us, they still do, yet we can offer it to others, we'd like to give whatever is left to those kids crouching over sacks of food that thieves will come and steal from them before they get to town, stay or go, a grandson was on the way, and Nora had thought long and hard about them at night in Kinshasa, her three daughters and two sons, having a light dinner of samosas by the hotel pool, tomorrow Nora would be knocking on a schoolroom door, she knew people thanks to her diplomat husband who had often stayed in the region before, no, it would be better to act alone, already there in the deserted hotel, she'd written to them, my angels, each one of you is unique, tonight I'm sending you these few words, I love you, Dad must not forget to transfer some money, please believe, all of you, that I am serene and happy, your were all together for Thanksgiving, all my love, Christiansen, you who often understand better than I do myself the overall direction my life must take, if I myself have any doubt, dear Christiansen, it is that am afraid your limitless confidence in me might be disappointed, then I would falter, yes, I'll go to the African party at your friends', I hug and kiss you my unique children, stay or go, it was dizzying, Nora explained to Mère, I didn't know what to decide, look at that heat-mist over the sea, and those purple-and-pink waves which will soon wash away the night, that smell of smoke and water, like the brush fires of my childhood, we used to have a couple of little monkeys, then one night they disappeared, my brother was devastated, my father said owning toys was a frivolous thing anyway, he was on call night and day and didn't have much time for my mother and us, and Mère told Nora, it has been a long night, I was going to ask my daughter if I could excuse myself and go to bed, but listening to you now, Nora, I don't feel like sleeping, at last they've turned that music down, the malaria has weakened you quite a bit, you must take good care of yourself, Mère said recovering her maternal instincts with Nora as if she'd been talking to Mélanie, my poor girl, women seem so brave, stay or go, Nora shouldn't have come back, she should have taken time there to get better, why did her daughters get worried so quickly, there was an African party where they had spent all day making chicken in peanut sauce, fish in manioc leaves, lots of music and tons to drink, some drinking themselves into a stupor and dancing, do white women come here with their husbands and drink and dance this much so as to forget the country's devastation and the mute pain of their African servants? What was that awful malaise I'd already started to feel myself those first days and nights, Mère said, I'd be very sad too if someone had taken away the little monkey or lion-cub who kept me company during the night without my knowing why, growing up alone like that, one certainly can be inconsolable, how can one imagine it, Nora said, going to school meant a boat-trip for days and unstable planes, my brother and I went away for months, far from our family, he was six, and I was eight, he started throwing up and wouldn't stop crying, he was so afraid, hand-in-hand we spent Christmas holidays with the nuns, all of them very loving to us, when are Mummy and Daddy coming to get us, soon, the nuns said, when the school year is over, patience my treasures, patience, your parents will be back, oh how sad you are, come on now, be brave, blow your nose, big boys don't cry, they said to my brother, and he was always crying, they'd taken our monkeys away a long time ago, a roving hyena had eaten them during the night, we'd heard strange noises on the mosquito-screen, Mummy had said not to get up, kids can feel such awful things, Mère said, I had a French nanny I adored, and when I came back from Europe — I remember a huge luxury liner and being seasick — the French nanny wasn't at home, I never saw her again, I don't know what kind of plotting or manoeuvring my parents had done to take her away from me, I never did find out, Mère became morose as she reflected on it, this first betrayal was to be followed by many others, she admitted, oh well, such is life, I wanted to work with street-kids in Kinshasa, Nora said, I felt guilty when I read my daughter's e-mails, and what about us, Mama, couldn't you take care of us, we need you here at home, I'm expecting a baby, Mama, and the waiting is awful, why can't you be here

with me, Mama dear, we are women, Mère said, and sometimes I feel it's a sort of curse, I love all my grandchildren, but
I'd so have liked it if Mélanie had only her career to think of,
that would be quite enough, Nora said, this is where I have so
much to do, that's what I said to my daughter Greta, my dear,
my only, believe me, I don't think any of my letters and calls
from town reached them for a long time, my darlings that I'd
willingly left behind, even the one in which I told Greta, I'm
flying to Gemena, Kindu, tomorrow, it's a reconnaissance mission to assess needs in orphanages, maternity clinics, lack of
support, prevention, and you know, Greta, how I'm thinking
of you every day in this difficult pregnancy, what I mean, my
sweet, is that every one is difficult, when it was you, I was too
nervous with anticipation, and despite what I thought, there
were no complications, conceived in Africa during one of your
father's missions, there you were, beautiful and blonde, and
Dad said, this will be my little Norwegian, I've got to meet the
experts, doctors especially, I'll be living in a guest-house with
four rooms and a shared kitchen and bathroom, that is why I
have left, dearest, we've got to the point where two or three
bathrooms are essential, more than one car too, we could live
with so much less, especially the things we have in duplicate,
and even so, I'm so sorry about leaving you feeling hurt, but
we will have central air conditioning and filtered water, I've
bought a chair and a hot-plate, but I'm afraid I'm boring you
with all these details, my treasure, kiss Dad for me, your
father's a model, my dear, the directress is lending me a table
and a foam mattress that will just go on the ground, think of
all those rooms and beds we have in the house, we really are
spoiled, as Dad often says, after seeing so many sad things in
his work overseas, has he transferred the money, I've had no
news from any of you for days, I'd really like to have that
money for the orphans' Christmas, I know your father will be
in touch with the charitable organizations right away, my
kisses to you all as I eat my first African corn right here in the

street, I used to feel that my childhood shared with my brother gave me all possible happiness, it was just for an instant, that school you visited in the bush, what was it like, Mère asked, her gaze riveted on Nora's intense expression, and I couldn't believe it, she replied, all those groups of kids and only two teachers, now my kids have all been to private schools where they had plenty of space and attention, how moving they were those hundred-and-fifty children, all so hungry to learn despite the awful conditions, in a hut made of *matiti*, manioc-stalks, with a roof of palm-branches covered with a tarp, a school in the savannah, the soldiers have taken a part of the roof, so when it rained there was no school, the families pay for school uniforms, as well as books and exercise-books, which is a lot for them, but still it's the least every schoolchild must have, I don't think I even gave a thought to the cost of uniforms and notebooks before I came to Africa. Never, that's the truth, so many things I didn't know or just forgot, like the teacher taking the blackboard with him after class so it won't be stolen. I thought of my own kids, each with his or her own desk, table and board . . . benches for these children are just planks nailed to uprights, Mama how can you go on making comparisons all the time, Greta wrote me, come home for Christmas, my dearest, every day I worry about the baby, is it normal to be this way, come home, we're waiting for you, Nora was thinking that she had not yielded to Greta's demands, nor any other, that might have distracted her from her goal, after the school in the bush, she'd visited a hospital, and there, she wrote Christiansen, we've got about sixty beds, almost all with no mattresses or covers, one clean operating-room, only one maternity room, and it was also used for patients with sleeping-sickness, mentioning only the ways in which she felt well off and serene, Nora did not say she was beginning to feel the vague effects of paludism, of course malaria was very common here, and Nora wrote to her hus-band that she had been especially moved by a patient who ran towards her with a foam of blood on his lips, begging her for money to buy medication, this scene often came back to haunt her dreams in endless torment, she felt disgusted by the twenty-five-dollar donation she'd made to the doctor on the ward, and if she couldn't do anything remotely helpful here, she'd go to Mount Ngafula and help out with the orphans, lots of abandoned babies, this was the only place where she had felt fulfillment and joy, giving the bottle to a couple of the newborns found during the night at the door of this refuge for abandoned children, she'd at once written to Greta, you know, my dear, everything's going to be fine for your baby, and it's perfectly normal to feel the way you do, what was stupid of me was not to have brought the candies the older ones asked for, oh, if only you saw these kids with nothing, so tiny, playing in the dirt, and through it all, still able to laugh, I'll say it again, you have nothing to worry about Greta, everything will go just fine, it's often like this the first time, when I was expecting your brother Hans, I was just like you, and now look at him, he's a flight-attendant, already a man, oh the older ones in Room 8 held on to me, asking, where are the candies, how stupid I felt, how worthless, I was the volunteer in the shelter run by an Italian doctor-priest, I learned how to give a blood transfusion to a three-year-old boy, so underdeveloped he hardly looked two, no running water in this hospital, it has to be brought in by tanker-truck, the volunteer I replaced had malaria, then typhoid, and wouldn't be able to work again for several weeks, Nora did not tell her daughters nor her husband about the skin-inflammation at night that felt like worms crawling around underneath the surface, she'd have been self-indulgent to complain, these infections came from washing the bodies of kids found lying on piles of filth, then reanimating and feeding them, pathetic little creatures so quick to come back to life, that was the miracle, every day we saved some, all of a sudden the child would be healthy and happy, the little girls are often adorable, Nora cared for them so much she'd have liked to adopt them right away, while the inflammation or nest of worms under the skin continued, she wasn't sure which it was, the volunteer wanted to adopt one of the little girls as soon as she was better, the miracle was that joy in their eyes, were her letters and faxes getting through to her husband and children, alone with the magnificent sunsets, Nora waited in silence, suddenly startled by the song of the toads, this was when she missed her family most and reminded herself this was where she was meant to be, Christiansen supported her when the work was most dangerous, how she would have liked to feel his hands on her shoulders, when would she see him again, would she leave these tropical swamps intact or with jaundice, no, this was where she was meant to be, that was certain: the nights were warm, and she was behind window-bars and locked doors, under mosquito-netting, when she would rather have slept with windows open onto the valley, this same song of the bull-toads she'd heard before in her parents' house when they'd left her brother's monkey outside, her mother saying the air was less oppressive for monkeys when they spent the night outside, and Nora always added at the end of her letters how much she was with her children in thought, never forgetting them, it had rained for several days, she wrote, and on her way to the post office in Kinshasa the roads had turned to mud, beggars emerged from everywhere, grabbing hold of the truck, but the driver had said, we're not stopping, it was only an impression perhaps, but there was such ruin and dilapidation in the streets of Kinshasa, it is said that malaria grows here in drains buried under garbage and filthy water, it certainly didn't spare the eight-year-olds working in the streets like adults selling cans of oil, there are also traffickers who take advantage of them, beggars and children crying out with hands reaching for our truck, Nora was afraid one of them might get run over as the driver kept saying, faster, we can't stop, Mère said, I think you must have felt joy and even fulfilment, Nora my dear, in Kinshasa you were in charge of your own destiny, that's a great delight for a woman, perhaps, Nora had allowed, but a mother who really is a mother as I am can never feel that kind of satisfaction away from her husband and children, there was always that shadow, Nora said, and her eyes darkened as she began to see herself as Ibsen's Nora, torn between an almost-primitive longing for freedom and a conventional set of familial attachments that had prevented it; furthermore, unlike Nora Helmer in *A Doll's House*, she could not blame her husband for any masculine egotism, she thought, Christiansen loved her free and even more self-affirming in her convictions of freedom than she actually was, and she told herself that any selfishness was probably her own in the unrealistic expectation of combining her family life and household with her bohemian life of humanitarianism, still nothing can ever be full harmonized for us women, Mère said, and here come the first rays of sun on the ocean, Nora remarked, and there was a smell of fried plantain and smoke over the water, no doubt Jermain and his friends had decided to have breakfast by the pool after a night of dancing, at last the music had died down to a vague rumble, Mère said, we can hear each other talk, it's going to be a hazy sun in that heat today, Nora went on, I was independent, I had a place to live while I was working in the daytime, I asked nothing of anybody, except to be allowed to volunteer, the feeling of freedom and fulfillment was delicious, I'm sure it was, said Mère, so many authoritarian attitudes made me feel hemmed in, Nora replied, like when I was kid, the way foreigners — whether black or white — talked to servants was unbearable, they had to be venerated and obeyed, especially those with high positions in embassies, and I suppose nothing has changed since those days, eh? I'm afraid nothing has changed the way we wanted it to, said Mère, her right hand apparently trembling more since she'd been talking to Nora, maybe paying so much attention to what she said had exacerbated it, she was sorry now to see daylight after finding

the night so long, I love listening to you, Nora, she said, it's as
though your busy life and commitment underline how inactive
mine is, except with my family of course, now why didn't I set
up hospitals like your friends, the women doctors who rescue
children and the handicapped from the streets where they
have nothing but awnings for shelter in the rainy season, all I
do is bring up my grandchildren, oh I've been cultural director
of some museums, but it's not much, Mère's cheeks reddened,
she was proud all of a sudden, of herself and Nora, women
often being strong and loyal, her life would be prolonged by
Mélanie and Nora, for what was a successful life if not a
serene extension into the lives of others, since all things came
to an end, and one has to resign oneself to that without a
struggle, seeing churches bothered me just as it did when I
was a child, said Nora, a shameful abuse of a credulous populace too poor to fend off the hold of religion on their lives, as
long as they pray they don't rebel, instead of giving out bread
and rocks and cement to rebuild the roads, instead of recovering a little dignity through work and education, it's anaesthesia
through prayer and hymns, Nora fell silent, afraid of boring
Mère with her laconic remarks, how could Nora judge the
power of hymn-singing after making friends with a doctor-
priest in Kinshasa, only too happy to load the trunk of the car
with powdered milk, candy, cocoa, marmalade and cookies
for the kids with tuberculosis in one of the hospital wards,
when every piece of bread and every drop was so precious,
the least effort by a woman or a priest, however small it might
be, had meaning, Nora thought, you couldn't really measure
their value, and after the party was over in the tubercular
ward, she followed the doctor-priest into Room 6, for which
she would be responsible, they had assigned her a sixteen-
month-old baby with AIDS and weighing so little it seemed
almost weightless in her arms, no longer really a baby, she
said to Mère, just a small thing with skin that seemed to be
eaten away with scabs and fleas, so tell me, where is God in

all this misery, I asked the priest, he didn't answer, what's the point in this epidemic of churches springing up everywhere, Nora had brought her own children up in atheism and certainly didn't regret it, she said to Esther, and Mère felt in her that fierce will not to depend on any phoney spirituality, though it seemed amazing when Nora had self-doubts and needed that faith, or at least that hope from which she distanced herself, they had to look to the management of things, and in the evening, older orphans in Room 12 who were taken to school several kilometres from the hospital, another mission run by nuns, and without these stalwart women there would be no schooling, said Nora, when they lent me the jeep, the kids would not have to walk home from school in the afternoon, I'd buy some dried fish and some sugar, always berating myself for things not done, so why were there no young idealists here, engineers and doctors, it's as though I'd never brought it up with our influential friends, the hospital was on the side of a mountain and something had to be done to stop the erosion in the rainy season, rainwater collected in gutters would have irrigated the vegetable garden and the orchard instead of ruining what was once a beautiful country, all that corruption, individuals as well as fraudulent organizations, multinational corporations and politicians, angry words that Nora wrote to Christiansen every night from her locked room, reminding him how much she loved him, restraining her anxiousness to see him again, underlining how much farther she wanted to go, you know, Christiansen, this country's so divided you need permits to get to the Equator — Ituri, Maniema, Kivu or Shaba, kiss all the kids for me, dear Christiansen, and tell each of them how much they mean to me, and please tell Greta to have more trust in the future, we're going to have a wonderful grandson, you must reassure her, dear, because you're there with her, as I promised you all, I hope to be there in time for the birth, but, thought Nora, what exactly was that promise but the expression of a visceral doubt, she wouldn't have promised anything if she'd been in less doubt about the genuineness of her volunteer work in Africa, she who so wanted to be free and unattached, she always had to go and contradict herself, no doubt because she never had enough patience and plunged hastily into way too many life contests, always wanting to outdo herself, while for many life was a slow and much-delayed process, Nora could not wait, no, she told Esther, it's a serious failing, I have no patience, mission mandates arrived slowly, meanwhile people died because of me, those handicapped from war and babies I'd held in my arms, they said every mission was too danger-ous for me, whether in hospitals or the bush, but nothing was, none of it, and as a heat-haze blotted out the horizon over the sea, now turning mauve in the dawn, Nora felt herself vacillat-ing and stunned, it was the smell of smoke and jasmine per-haps, when her mind overflowed with so many images and memories, like white and orange frangipanis bent under the weight of their brilliant branches, she no longer knew if she was in Chuan and Olivier's garden or back there with the doc-tor-priest who was saying, oh if only you'd seen what I saw in the war-zones, everything destroyed with machetes and burnt, the malnutrition is even more widespread, if you knew, the priest's voice saddened her the way her father's had done before when he said there were so many lepers and so few doctors with him in the bush, and now here was Nora spend-ing the night out joyfully celebrating Esther's birthday with Christiansen, as though of a sudden she'd been relieved of any perception she had of the suffering, so close up, like her father before her; the red-eyed turtle-doves could be heard cooing, and she again saw the grey or Gabon parrots flying over Kinshasa, she thought she heard their whistling imitation of other birds, that is where her home was, she thought, she had to go back, if her father was the saint they said he was, why was he so intolerant with his wife and children at home, God was no more present in his thoughts than in Nora's, but he shared his daughter's failing of impatience, always pressed by work, he ordered them to do everything instantly, meals, sleep, what was this laziness of the kids who didn't always get top marks at school, his wife and nursing-aide was never appreciated, Mama worked so hard for that man, Nora thought, sometimes said, my life will be a failure because of that man, I'll avenge you, Mama, I used to tell her, but she quickly smoothed it over, you know Nora, I love your father, I'd just like to do better, that's all, and that's what Nora wished for, a productive ability to cure, now where had she got to, once back from Africa, she had spent too much on clothes, this was her particular way of dressing, and there was nothing she could do about it, Christiansen liked her looking this way, sweet and ravishing, her ribbonned straw halt tilted forward over her forehead, a slightly androgynous touch to her very feminine outfits, that was Nora, not saintly like her father, nor exuberant and rational like her husband, complex, disturbing, she had to live fast, paint everything she saw with the same vivid alertness, love everything with an ever-more-lively passion, she thought, how disappointed she'd been when she found out that her mission to Kindu had been cancelled, the departure for Lubumbashi with an ambassador friend delayed, too much time wasted on discussions of protocol, she'd written to Christiansen, still nothing from you, my darlings, I'll try for the plateau where perhaps you could wait for me, waiting for a mission is so very lonely, I'm thinking of each one of you, my darlings, Greta, do be careful, on the local TV I saw an unscrupulous bishop tell his flock about damnation from his ecclesiastical throne on high, I know what you're thinking dear, I'm just the same as I always was, these shameless preachers still make me so enraged and cynical, as I write this, I can see a cloud of hummingbirds enjoying the nectar from the flowers, and every day outside my window, I can see my passeriformes suspended in flight, motionless in this palpably humid air, I was able to draw a few of them for an African tableau I started before I left, remember Christiansen, I only like painting outside, and I'd forgotten it in the garden during the rain, it was you that brought it in and said I'd been careless, and why was I, maybe because I didn't really take my talent as a painter seriously, so when am I going to be able to convince you how little confidence I have in myself, not in you, my dear ones, in me, I paint outside so I can be surrounded by light, everything's beautiful then, but I am glad you saved it from the rain and that you like it, sweetheart, I'm afraid to return to what once was my homeland, now a dying one, I can't yet leave it because of that, now the sweet nectar that delighted the hummingbirds was intoxicating the air that Nora breathed from Chuan's garden, and this is what made her tipsy, wobbly on her feet like when she'd shared a hash joint with Bernard and taken on a daring air for one who'd never even had cannabis before, you'll see, Bernard, I won't even get high, these artificial paradises are just an illusion, and just as she said this, she had almost fainted onto the garden fence amid the perfume of acacias, so quickly had the intoxication overcome the resistance of her brain, and Bernard had laughed and taken her in his arms before she fell, a benevolent and tender laugh she remembered, and she was amazed at her body's being so rubbery all of a sudden, a slow elasticity that altered the collapse of her limbs onto the grass, oh what a sudden and unpleasant feeling of emptiness, Valérie disapproved of this habit her husband Bernard had of giving joints to his friends following an after-dinner cognac, she was afraid they'd have to bicycle home wavering and euphoric, the way Bernard sometimes arrived home, head in the clouds, hands barely touching the handlebars, you're not supposed to do that at our age, she told him sternly, but he wasn't listening, a complicit smile on his lips for Nora whom he'd helped out of the acacia bush saying, here, Nora dear, let me drive you home, Christiansen's been gone to the Niger Republic for weeks, don't stay on your own, come and see us, it may have been at that instant she had thought about the monkeys stolen by thieves or killed by hyenas during the long African nights a while ago, as Bernard guided her through the night arm-in-arm, she had the impression she had mumbled confusedly about how much she loved his books, but wasn't sure he heard, Nora was not a creature of civilization like him or Valérie or all the others, not regimented or gifted by the touch of civilization, she had only come to know Europe when her parents had sent her to school in France, but maybe it was too late by then, a child of Africa, she could not be reborn elsewhere in a web of societies where she would always be an outsider, in that rapid euphoria she'd known while talking to Mère, and still stunned by the weakness of her body after overcoming tropical diseases, Nora wondered, is it true, one day will I too belong to civilization or at least be accepted in it, no, I can't, I'm too wild, when will I see my country again, I wonder if my kids will let me leave again, and Marie-Sylvie heard the cock-crow in her sleep, when the first was over, others echoed it in reply, she was with Jenny in the Chinese province where the hills rose in a choking mist, pushing the wheelbarrow her brother, He-who-never-sleeps, was struggling to get out of, you can't bury me, he was yelling in his insane voice, I'm still alive, Marie-Sylvie would have liked to bury him under one of those stones that lay over so many anonymous coffins, but there was too much mist, a sulphurous mist that stuck to your skin, no, you can't, you can't, he screamed just as Marie-Sylvie awoke and cursed the crowing cocks, she was covered in sweat, these regions of the dead that Jenny had told her about were terrifying, why would she abandon her brother here, you could even smell the dead who'd been buried in a rush, soon it would be daylight and still Daniel, Mélanie, and Esther weren't back, the light still shone from under Augustino's door, Marie-Sylvie was going to chase those cocks out of the courtyard, they were the neighbour's, and Daniel put up with them, but he was too tolerant, she thought, hens and cocks in the yard at all times, like Augustino's parrots and parakeets that also made a racket in the garden, and those cats that slept with Mai, now how could you keep the house clean when you had to give in to everyone's whims, even in the nightmare she'd just awoken from feeling agitated, He-who-never-sleeps had seemed far too much alive, in a pile, arms and legs swung out from the wheelbarrow, around his mouth and eyes — one of them partly open and glassy — a thick coating of flies like those she'd often seen on children's face in the Cité du Soleil, surrounding their eyes and mouths drooling black saliva, doing who-knows-what damage to their skin, or was that just something sulphurous sticking to their skin, in Marie-Sylvie's dream, these flies were so close to the tongues and lips that the kids couldn't even spit anymore, they were so close to the whites of their eyes that they couldn't close their eyelids anymore, this cock-crowing would just not let up, while Marie-Sylvie washed her face and eyes, she kept wondering, where can he be hiding, why does he have to persecute me that miserable brother of mine, He-who-never-sleeps, I can't stand to see him, the hospitals in Port-au-Prince were overflowing with kids just like him, why does he go on haunting me? The funny, clean-shaven young man was there again, in Mai's room, his head a dark shadow against the rows of bookshelves, once more he'd managed to get in through the window, taking out the screen with his knife, getting slowly closer to Mai's bed, I'm here, he said in his smooth voice, even if you're asleep, don't pretend you can't hear my voice, I've come to get you for Colombia, for the Cause, the one and only, you've got to get dressed and come with me because we really need little girls like you, headstrong child, you can't be locked up in your parents' house with a nanny who doesn't even like you, you'll have your own gun and be able to work like all my other recruits, your own group, your own unit, you'll be queen of the mine-fields, the younger girls will follow your orders for the Cause, the one and only, I'm not just a predator, I'm a fighter bringing along the youth, and what could be more tender and youthful than you, you can be ready and useful for all kinds of kinds of expeditions, you open the way to fields men fear to die in, there's nothing you won't do because you have no idea yet what you'll be forced to do, we used to take only boys, and that was a mistake, we need girls in our groups too, come on, wake up, please, we've got to leave for Colombia, they're waiting for us, your gun will take care of you, even defend you against rape, you'll be completely unaware of explosive charges under the earth and follow the paths where antipersonnel mines sleep waiting for your step, Mai, I'm waiting for you to open your eyes and see me, my head's shadowed against the bookshelves, I cut through the mosquito-net with my pocket knife, I don't like screens and curtains they sometimes put around kids' beds, anytime now your nanny will come in and chase me away, please Mai, I've come to take you to Colombia, there are so many countries where thousands of little girls fight with cool calm, they're every bit as good as boys, come on, let's go to the minefields, the sky is grey right now, but I can see dawn beginning to show, Caroline said, Harriett, Miss Désirée, time to wake up, let's go down to the port and look for the first glint of day on the water, my father's down there with one of his many wives, elegantly dressed, glass in hand, he's still actually a colonel, but they call him Captain, always navigating to his pleasure-spots, his home in the Bahamas, with servants, a cabin under the palms, he's a man of the world who sometimes likes to be a hermit, fishing alone on his island, suddenly disappearing for months, I wonder if the wind will whip the waves up to the windows today, splashing against the glass, the tide is up, way up, into the doorways and windows, cracking like whips at windows, shutters, masts on yachts dipping into the ocean, each time my parents got married I wondered who would adopt me, would it be you, Harriett, they said, or an aunt or a grandfather, what do we do with the little one, you say you're the one, Harriett, you'll keep me close, I'll take care of her, you say, it is God's will, you go on and on about it's being God's will that I be with you, there's still a crescent moon in the sky, and the sea will calm down, these lashing winds in December, like all men of his class, my father wears white pants and a blazer, I hide behind you while you serve cocktails, what will we do with the little one, this crescent moon can drive women out of their heads, women like me who ask this grey hour why they are here, one is a great sculptress and remembers the name of her master better than her own, was she drugged or poisoned so she no longer knows who she is, or why she is in this asylum in Montdevergues, she remembers her fingers getting worn on some sharp, rocky substance, but what is she doing here, she has been poisoned by the bitterness of betrayal, everyone remembers her master better than her own name, one of them recalls a brother-in-law called Manet, she herself has the merest shadowy recollection of him, that's right, she was an impressionist painter, yes, betrayed perhaps, locked up here with me, she doesn't know how or when she'll get out, and the sea continues to rise, cottages and houses lose their roofs in the violent winds, fleeing the coast and going upstream on the boiling rivers, the gulls and seagulls, all the marine birds have gradually deserted the shores, and from my window, I photograph the sky and the waters, I would so like to go out in this weather, Harriett, instead of being shut up here with these moaning, visionary women, one futilely hooking her nails onto a block of marble, where are my sculptures, she asks me, where are my children, what treachery was used to take them away from me, and if they're visionaries the way I once was, why weren't they able to survive, as I did, by avoiding all sentimentality in my relations with men, I wouldn't associate with them except as an equal, perhaps they said I was seductive but hard, but what else could I do, if they moan and cry, it's because they were forced to silence for a long time, the one whose brother-in-law Manet never commented on her work, even though she was an essential member of the Impressionist movement, well maybe, he observed condescendingly, Berthe, my sister-in-law Berthe Morisot, can paint, sure, but she's still just a woman, it may not have been said, but Berthe heard it anyway, just the murmur of a suspicion, but audible to her nevertheless, a murmur and thus a defeat, another, an American artist who had lived all her life in Paris, apparently painting the joys of serene motherhood, still nothing was more troubling than that appearance over submerged, shifting, burning floes of ice, this painter had been advised by Degas, but in what manner, friendly or authoritarian, and how had she received it, no one knows, only maternal happiness seems to have made a lasting impression and set limits on the self-expression of this genius, a woman knowing how to paint the exclusive and fleeting happiness of motherhood, just this, portraitist of mothers with pink-skinned children, they don't say who this woman was, Mary Cassatt born in Pennsylvania in 1844, a master of chalk and pastel drawing, that much perhaps is said, all the pastel drawings laying bare the clear, pink skin of the faces, critics praised her work, adding treacherously, it is too bad that such a remarkable artist, with such mastery of colour and supple technique, too bad that she became blind after a botched operation on her eyes, she might have overcome the fact that her work bore too much resemblance to Degas, those last pastels of his, free and tormented at the same time, so it was not enough to be a master colourist, even blind, her eyes mutilated by bad surgery, Mary Cassatt had to be the perfect pupil to Degas, otherwise insignificant in a style limited to her experience as a woman and mother, shouldn't she just be contented with that, her expression, perhaps inwardly tormented, looked like Degas, so what did the work of a woman born in hostile times amount to, the waves on the ocean continued to rise with no let-up, the masts on yachts bending and curving in the wind, Harriett, you say I can't go out, it wouldn't be a good idea, so here I sit and wait in my chair in the portico near the bay window, Adrien and Suzanne are coming for dinner tonight, have you ironed the black outfit you're going to put on me, I don't want any tea or bouillon, nothing at all, I loved the English poets I photographed, Jean-Mathieu wrote their stories next to me, travelled with me, two painters of souls and the landscapes their bodies were going to, so beloved that I felt the inexpressible thoughts and desires of these poets were my own as well, one day in the exaltation of being alive, the next with despair tightening one's throat, was it them or was it me, I was the pet dog that consoled them, the woman who took them in her arms, I was also Jean-Mathieu reading their thoughts, just as he was the photographer of their disordered poses as well as their real lives, and the branches entwined about their chests, crucifying them all, men with no future, their houseboats built on fragile rocks and slipping into the waves at Laugharne, the poet sends out a lifeboat, I recognize it, no wine glass, no bunch of blue grapes, take nothing that is offered, for it will be poison, I tell her, and Harriett stupidly says that it was Charly that offered me the glass that I drank from without any fear, Harriett said, that was your downfall, having her in your house, or perhaps it goes back even further, with its roots in Jamaica, where Charly herself decided to follow me and be my chauffeur, after all those hours in the darkroom, I couldn't see well and had to give up driving, but the real truth is that, whether it be Charly or Cyril, fate knocked on my door as usual, and there was nothing I could do, not a thing. Mère noticed Nora was walking more quickly, racing along, which showed her impatience, outside the house and along the path that Chuan had decorated with bouquets of red roses in glass vases, she walked towards the sea saying to Esther, come on, come on, look at that flame of colour under the fog, Mère was thinking and walking slowly towards the beach path, turning to listen to

Jermaine talk to his friends, to her the voices of all these young people sounded like a nearly incomprehensible choir, for she didn't really know what they were talking about so fervently after dancing all night, it's my world, he or one of his friends was saying, electronic music, DJ-ing, that's my thing, first you mix the styles and rhythms, then bang, no need for words, words are my father's thing . . . he writes, electronic music for raves doesn't need words or hot melodies, it's a question of technique, especially for dancefloors, and bang, hey let's wake up the sleepers, even electro will soon be out of date, keyboards, synthesizers, all that can be junked with the past, who's going to want to remember the 2000s, even electro music, all of it gone, listen to me, we'll have walked on the Red Planet and be living there, just like on earth, maybe things will be just as bad as here, you are totally the best DJ in the club, bang, no words — that verbal stuff that sticks you with a way of seeing things, raves, all-nighters, that's a cacophonic language like the music Samuel listened to when he was with us, Mère thought, deplorable, that's what it is, still Jermaine is a good son, certainly his parents' pride and joy whatever his language, they're good kids, as Jermaine and his friends passed by her on their way to the beach, he greeted her with respect, happy birthday, he said optimistically from a way off, and she responded with a nod of her head, as if to say, why are you pretending to be polite, as though I were an old lady, which I am not, then she pressed on to catch up with Nora on the beach, happy and encouraged at the thought of talking with her, so Nora, you finally got authorization to go to Lubumbashi, you can see the river the second you step off the plane, Nora said, so much mist on the water, just like today, I saw the same hills again, the river widening and then narrowing again, those red waters you see all over equatorial Africa, I was home, then came the sadness of areas of Lubumbashi where I again saw orphans in the camps for war refugees, there were some representatives of donor countries with me, I am ashamed as I say this, of course they say they're helping the displaced population, but do they really, or is it just official posturing, they were amazed when they saw kids in schools and maternity wards dancing and singing to the drums for them, I just wanted to weep, even at that well-kept Methodist orphanage with freshly repainted walls, where teenagers sang in long robes, I wanted to cry, saying to myself, what's going to happen to these refugee kids, when I went to the delivery-rooms in a hospital, I asked, why can't I come work here right away, the tables were rusted, why no linen in the cribs, they said, yes, you can stay till tomorrow and help our nurses, I didn't want to go back to the hotel with the others nor have the evening buffet, no, all of a sudden, in the middle of the day, I saw an ibis running across the light, a sacred ibis, I couldn't believe it, I really was there, I had to be, I told myself, it was a miraculous vision, why did I have to feel so badly when my daughter Greta wrote me, what are you fighting for, Mama, and against whom, dear Don Quixote, tilting at wind-mills when you ought to be with us, your family and kids, Dad hasn't got much time for us, his work in New York takes up nearly all his time, besides it's not the same, he's not a woman, Mama, come home, Esther, was it selfishness for me to want to scream at my daughter whom I love so much, don't write to me anymore, leave me alone, all I want is to be here alone without you, let me live these private moments of mine, life is so short, do we really have the time we need to better know humanity and all it suffers from, of course not, no, said Mère there was no selfish complacency on your part, it's intelligent to want to understand in a world like ours, that's all, your daughter was wrong about you, it often happens, sometimes our children really don't know us well at all, but she was care-ful not to mention her sons to Nora, she immediately added, with the privileged feelings she had for Mélanie, I don't mean to be unjust, but my daughter is so intuitive she knows a little too much about me, and I can't blame her, it seemed as though Nora was not listening but just looking at the sky, I was able to go back to the bush in the Lower Congo, she said at once, I was being stubborn after what Greta had said about the absurdity of my battle, I'm sure I did resemble that ridiculous Don Quixote, but that was who I was after all, Nora felt so mortified by the memory of Greta's words that she longed to rest her head in Christiansen's arms, as she often did in a silent gesture of confidence, and he would write or read with her nearby, a bird in its nest, he felt less stricken by the report or exposé he was working on when Nora was near, then, once calmed, she would take flight again, she had three paintings to work on outside under the eucalyptus leaves where she painted all morning, three pictures before the town bell rang noon, because the afternoon would be taken up with shopping for her future grandson and getting surprise meals ready for the beach-wanderers, what did Christiansen think of the African painting still outside after two storms, that was clumsy, I may have to start it again for a third time, only then did her husband lose patience, I've already told you how much I liked that picture, don't touch it, you don't want to say so, she said with her usual self-doubt, but that gold on a black sky is overdone, isn't it, oh sweetheart, are you really sure you like it, I really am an awkward woman, how can you possibly love me, that was who she was, Nora, it couldn't be any other way, she thought, the child on whom her father had impressed doubt and clumsiness forever, when I needed to win the right to feel at ease each morning, my dream was to revisit all those places we had lived in, my brother and I, the way you do in a picture when you paint those subconscious regions from the past, but it seemed even more important to revisit the tubercular children's ward where I might be of some help, Nora said, because you have to do what you can, however little, even if it has no impact, that meagre contribution is what gives life its value, how else can we know who we are, Mère felt Nora was asking these questions of herself alone, for a long time I was with the kids in Building 8, Nora went on, I bathed them early in the morning, they told me to do it in cold water, but I heated the water when no one was looking, these poor little things should have been in incubators, all of them premature, often their mothers had died a few hours after giving birth, their fathers left them at the hospital entrance, I often had one of the babies in my arms, because in the cradle their atrophied limbs could not stretch out, and they suffered from scoliosis, I can still see those tiny thin limbs, Hugo his name was, I finally found him an orthopedist, though there's little hope he's still alive, the soldiers had found him on a garbage can, he was eight days old then, you can't imagine how these little kids suffer, another newborn I was changing was so lacking in vitamin A that his skin was raw in places, you can't imagine, I wrote to all my kids, though I didn't tell them how revivifying it was for me to be mother to a second family, Hugo or Garcia, I loved them like my own children, and nothing seemed more natural, Garcia, my orphan suffering from tuberculosis of the bone, he had to stay lying down, held to a board with straps, we got him to smile, though I knew his heart would eventually stifle his lungs, as the doctor explained it to me, death was everywhere, waiting, the only thing was life, everything to hold onto it, there was still the smile of life on Garcia's dry lips, though I did feel terribly cut off from the world, alone with my distressed kids, now I am far from Garcia and Hugo, once again in the social whirl, the hospital kitchen was a rudimentary shelter with a corrugated tin roof, no light and very little food, worn out as we were, the evening meal of beans and cold noodles seemed like a feast, and I just can't say how happy I am to be with you all again, Esther, how do you account for such contradictions, probably because we're children at heart, and we adapt easily to sadness and to joy, still I wish I could have contributed, just a little, and then, as though embarrassed by having confided too much in Mère, Nora walked faster in the direction of the sea to put distance between them, pelicans were diving headlong into the waves, putting her cell phone to her ear, she thought all of a sudden she heard her son's voice, Mum, it's me, Hans, sounding lost, Nora could hear his laboured, staccato breathing, Mum, our plane's been hijacked around Ohio, I don't know where exactly, it's nearly eight in the morning, can you hear me, the other flight attendants and me, Mum, can you hear me, I don't know what direction we're going in now, a bump, another bump in all this fog, we're going down, we can't descend any farther, we served breakfast the way we always do on this morning flight, everything as usual, listen, Mum, kids are sleeping in their mothers' arms, and we can't say anything yet, especially not now, because it's too soon, I'm sure, our plane, Mum, hug Dad and my sisters for me, they're wolves in sheep's clothing, we were fooled, I'm not saying everything's gone bad for us on Flight 88, but listen, above all, don't panic, just listen, first, you're going to need to be very patient, and you aren't, you know that, don't let your pain and grief and impatience get the better of you, Mum, I'll always be your son, whatever happens today, we're not over Ohio anymore, those are shouts you hear from the back of the plane, we're going to reassure the passengers, none of us can be afraid, only brave, I always told you I wanted to be a hero, didn't I, well now's the time, we're going down, we're going to fight and defend the passengers, all those fields in the fog, we can still avoid cities, going down, yes, we really want to pull this off, no shouts, now, Mum, nothing, just something like a prayer, I don't know how to do that, because you never showed me, not shouts, something like a prayer that says, above all, Mum, don't lose patience, I know what you're like, you know, darling Mum, they're not screaming anymore, they're singing, listen Mum, kids are waking up and asking why, they're not screaming anymore, they're singing, listen Mum, they're saying, we're going through the valley of the shadow, be not afraid, we have noth-

ing to fear, can you hear me Mum, it's me, Hans, your son,
we're coming down to the fields, the valley of the shadow,
they're saying, it's me, Hans, we're landing on time, we won't
be late, Mum, on time, either with an irreversible slowness or
a deafening noise, I can't hear anything anymore, Mum, breakfast has been served, hijacked to where, I don't know, I don't
know anything anymore, that's what we had to do, serve
breakfast, a razor blade to the pilot's throat, breakfast, all
polite, that's what we have to do, we already knew about the
pilot, we knew, what you're hearing, Mum, aren't shouts,
those have stopped, it's more like a prayer, the Lord is my
shepherd, that's what they're singing in those heartbreaking
voices, I go on working, that's what you asked of me, they'll
tell you I was a hero, freeing the pilot too late, taken hostage,
Mum, all of the others are heroes too, even the little kids who
don't know what's going on, every one, where is the valley of
the shadow of death, we're flying low over it, so low we can
see the grass and raspberry fields, low without wanting to,
we've lost all control, the real hero was Dad, a child resistance-fighter in Norway under siege, and you, Mum, sacrificing
your art for us, first prize at the School of Fine Art, for us, just
us, please be patient, we'll make it, soft green and dirt-yellow
fields all around us, the sky's gone white all of a sudden, state
of siege here, like in Dad's time, heroes, everyone here praying, me last of all, the man you gave birth to is no hero, just a
man, what was it Dad said that evening when we were all
together in New York, Dad said that one day there was an
awful, dark moment in our history, we were with him after he
came back from Jordan — he's been all over, more than seventy-five countries, he said — and what was that dark moment
in your country's history, I asked him, nothing specific, he
said, but I picture myself as a little boy running with evil joy
behind trucks with crying women whose heads were shaved,
a terribly dark moment, and so you commit your first act of
cruelty, Dad said, I didn't know then that all the children born

of those who had collaborated would undergo the same fate
as their mothers and be punished forever, I knew none of that
running happily behind the trucks that way, no, I wanted to
be a hero like Dad, although he said he never was because of
that terrible, dark moment, and you'll see, Mum, everyone
here is a hero without knowing it, it seems like the valley of
death we are in, but don't you believe it, there's nothing else
we can do, Mum, I'll be on time, but don't wait for me at the
airport the way you usually do, our crew's courageous and
will go on that way, we're going down, I'm kissing you, Mum,
how green the fields are, how green the autumn is, Mum, but
hearing only the song of the waves, Nora put her cell phone
away in its case, thinking, of course Hans will be on time at
the airport, unless there's turbulence from the fog, no storms
are expected, and Mère plodded on in Nora's direction, a little
out of breath and tempted to take her shoes off too, but she
didn't, it was more appropriate for Nora, who was still young,
svelte and a bit tomboy, maybe a veneer of upbringing she
had missed, Mère thought without judging her, for Mère
admired her primal instinct for freedom, then Mère thought
about all the money this birthday party of hers had cost, it
must surely have cost Chuan and Olivier thousands of dollars
for such a fabulous party and banquet, she thought, too much,
too bad Mère had not thought of this before this conversation
with Nora that changed her view of everything, even the cost
of her celebration, maybe she should have turned it down,
and why had she willed so much money to museums and cultural institutions, when the African hospitals . . . oh, what's the
point, she thought, as she saw her right hand trembling, it
must be too late, this stupid tremor, when you think about it,
she'd done what she had to do, and Mère thought back to the
boy Chuan called Lazaro, almost a second son to her, the
caterer who often went out fishing with the men for months at
a time, with what heavy resentment he had dumped the tray
of seafood on the kitchen table, he seemed sinister in his

white apron, there was no mistaking the look of hate on his face, and why was that, since Chuan welcomed into her house like a son and was friends with his mother Caridad, bought handicrafts from her, knowing she often cried, saying she had lost her son, he'd lost his way, his hostile face confronted Mère and seemed to say, you ought to be ashamed of all this money spent on your celebration, you'll repent this, on Bahama and Esmerelda Streets, we've got our gangs about which you know nothing, nor about us, I, Lazaro, am not alone on Bahama and Esmerelda, then Mère dismissed this concern, for that's all it was, her friends had fêted her, and she was happy, even if this tremor in her right hand worried her constantly, Nora came back up from the beach, smiling, you know what Bernard says, that we can't be responsible for everything that happens, it's already commendable to look out for friends and relatives, she said, and for Bernard, friends means writers, which is why he's so generous to colleagues of his all round the world, that's pretty wise, I wish I were like that, it's the sort of thing a man would think, said Mère, Bernard is a man who's more sure of his qualities than you or I, Nora, and his wife Valérie too, she's more like us as far as that goes, sometimes I wish I were him, she continued, I'd own a few more certainties, but I don't want to be him, because he either negates or downplays the number of women philosophers, fortunately Valérie stands up to him on that, I mean, women writers and philosophers have always existed and always will, whatever our delicious friend Bernard thinks, the most learned among us, but did you know I can beat him at poker, she said, thinking that the tremor was fairly slight after all, no one, except Mélanie perhaps, had noticed it, and why had critics not attentively considered that Valérie's novels were essentially philosophical, the work of a moralist rigorously examining the drama of individual responsibility, all they ever talked about was the ambivalence of her characters without getting through to their motivation, be they cowardly or destined to contempt and condemnation, Valérie had written that crimes of cowardice were human too, and why did she frequently get up at four in the morning, sneak out of the house, and stand alone at the far end of the beaches, where, she said, the structure of her books was developed gradually a hundred times over and synthesized in a thousand details, in the calm of dawn by the ocean, and in a mind no longer agitated, it was that philosopher's thought that took flight like an incantation that would give shape to her novels, who should be held to account in this drama of responsibility which everyone shared, it was wrong, Mère thought, that Bernard and his friends rarely let women play poker with them, they were wrong to think that a new Descartes might spring from the mind of a woman, Valérie was not a mathematician or physicist like Descartes, and she never claimed to have reconstituted the foundations of learning, as a woman she would never have a notion of absolute certitude, but her humanity was her science and her field of inquiry and reflection, she often woke up by Bernard's side, heart beating wildly, she said, that's when she had to go and quietly get her bike from the garden, followed by her cat, how precious that solitude by the sea with no one to see her, and the illumination of thought took on solid form in the last traces of night trailing away on the water, instead of seeing Valérie as a writer unconcerned with praise, as an unpretentious philosopher, Bernard's friends surely only saw in her the dark-haired woman who might have been one of Goya's models, someone they ran into early each morning during their workout, a great companion for men and women doing their workout or aerobic dance, Valérie, whose joie de vivre, better yet, her appetite for enjoyment, seemed inexhaustible, so why had these critics not noticed who Valérie was beneath the sobriety of her writing, Mère wondered, and Charles still kept the image of Frédéric before him, Caroline said, and that's why I must not let myself get to that point, and why you need to understand my abstention from food, Harriett, Miss Désirée, who wants to hit rock-bottom, reach the last degree of abandonment, in the pleasure of being held in Cyril's arms, their gaze melting into one, that's the image Charles had of Frédéric in the arms of his black nurse after his fall by the pool, Charles recalled that Pietà, the Black Virgin of pity, leaning over Frédéric's body, he had suddenly lost balance, no freezing rain or surface slippery from pool water, no special reason for a sturdy body to skid like that, it had been melting away for a while now, Charles had always known Frédéric to be hefty and ready for any and all wildness and excess, he didn't realize that his friend was depressed by the onset of old age, the sound of his fall was like something being broken, a machine misfiring, would this difficulty functioning also be mental, even in a man whose genius was well-known, he was the child prodigy, the precocious pianist, the Mendelssohn of the Los Angeles concert-hall dead, there was no way to know, as to the slowly progressing muscular deficiency, this apparition of the Pietà was a recurring one for Charles, the ageing infant Frédéric in the arms of his young Black Virgin who had washed and bathed him, everywhere this image replayed itself for him, the young, voluptuous nurse who arrived at the house on roller-blades and humming a tune, Charles was washing and bathing Frédéric who suddenly said, leave me alone, I just want to sleep, no visitors, I want to sleep for a while, that fall by the pool hurt a bit, and Charles had not thought that love could slip away like that in an image of the Pietà, he needed to go to his ashram to gather himself a bit, perhaps the time for gloomy reflection had come when the soul begs for a resting place, the strengths of the body crying out, no, not yet, it's too soon, and thus arrives an avenging angel that was not expected, exacting all latent, violet-tinged death and decay, the lover who was more than love, the imperishable guardian of declining vitality, Harriett, you think, seeing me struggle no longer, that I'd like to crumble like Frédéric in the arms of a divine nurse, for you do have such patience, I barely let you assuage my thirst with a little black tea, for this body of mine will soon accommodate itself to all its failings without complaint, one must die in harmony, though they want us to think otherwise, the wood is dry and hard, and can't take any more punishment, the bones of the carcass, I dreamed as I was dozing, that I had got dressed up in my black outfit, I don't know why black, because I don't like it, and then you lowered me into a very hot bath, I fought you, for a light snow was falling, oh how I fought you, but you wouldn't listen, why not let me go out in that hospital gown, Adrien and Suzanne will be here after tennis, they'll help me get dressed, but you say they can't get here in this sea-storm, but they'll come, because they know how to get here by boat, get the coffee ready, Harriett, Désirée, quick, get to the kitchen and stop watching me, there's a light snow falling, I recovered quickly, because all of a sudden I was able to run along a snowy road in the night, but still I could hear familiar voices, and at the end of the road was a reunion of friends, the night was not clouded but lit by huge bonfires on the snow, and all of a sudden I saw Jean-Mathieu coming towards me with his red scarf over his shoulders, come, dear friend, all this snow will be shovelled by morning, and we can get out the sleds and horses, come, we never finished our discussion of the painting of the Madonna and Child by an unknown French artist around 1480, she wears a royal crown, sapphires and pearls I think, as you first said, or perhaps rubies, a Madonna both childlike and sovereign, with a mocking smile as she strokes the feet of her child, yet the child seems older than the mother, laid bare, bald head under the halo, appearing to sink into the folds of her ample blue robe, nothing holding him up from the void but the fingers warming his feet, this is how we come into the world, hanging by a caress of the feet, this picture, dear Caroline, was painted in 1480 or 1490, and I'd really like to talk about it with you, come now, and let's get out the sleds and continue our

journey, you and I together at last, Caroline, but why are you
hesitating to give me your hand, think about the painting you
liked, that's how we set ourselves apart from the rest of the
world, like that little bare-headed child, a bit ugly and alone in
the arms of the Madonna holding him only with a subtle
caress of the feet, yes, you were right to say it was painted
in1480 by an unknown French master, I have to tell you now,
you were often right, it was a dream, said Caroline, I'll never
see Jean-Mathieu again, or if I do, when do you think, Harriett,
when will I see him, will it be a cloudy night lit up by huge
bonfires on the snow? In the Vendredi Décadent Bar, Petites
Cendres saw the boy with straight blond hair, he must have
been set free during the night, and he thought, my boy, mine,
he's even charmed the cops, a magician, an enchanter, Petites
Cendres saw him in the street, as he walked with a heavy
heart, not having come up with anything that night, he'd probably have to meet the man from the hotel, the one in whom a
beast lurked, though he was used to this kind of customer, this
one repulsed him, or maybe it was fear of outrage or humiliation, look at that little treasure with his round face like a little
boy, and so well brought up, affable, almost chivalrous toward
a companion who was at least thirty years older, that's what
happens when kids are left alone, they prove attractive to
adults and then inflict redemptive love upon them, if you have
to show up in the New York office wearing a nice suit, then
I'll dress up too, the boy said, anything suits me, if I have to
show up nude, I'll do that too, how do you like that, he
laughed, kids now aren't afraid of anything, I really liked
going out in the boat with you, I didn't even know about
those barges with young prostitutes, isn't it risky, I don't think
I'd go for that, I'd rather be with you, I'm safe with you, in
fact, my parents would be impressed by your taste and culture, that silk shirt really suits you, do you trade in those, I
think it would look good on me too, I like smart things, boy,
we sure have got a tan out here on the bridge, can I have a

taste of your martini, oh you're giving me one, great, I mostly like the olives on ice, thanks, another one would be nice, especially the olives, it's true, I'm going to get a shirt like yours, touch my skin, see how hot it still is from the sun, I feel sorry for those girls lost out on the water, you know, a nut-job, any kind of nut-job might attack them, it's not legal what they're doing, it's better to stay on the right side of the law, I mean you never know, what if someone decide to throw them overboard, what mother would go into town and say, yes, that's my daughter you've killed, who'd dare do that, eh, you think there's any future for them in a profession like that, cruising around out in the open, I feel sorry for them, hey you got tanned too, it suits you, pink cheeks, we have all the time in the world, we could take one cruise after another if you didn't have to be in the office by Thursday, how cool you look, I will too, you've got to do what you want in life, I liked that dangerous swim we took in the shark bay, young people, what do we really worry about except not having money, nope, I really don't like that, I need lots of it every day, I'd really like to have shorts and a camera like you do, is it way too expensive, if you can't, just say so, our skin is glowing, you seem years younger since we've been together, even if it's only been a few hours, most of all, I want you to be satisfied, absolutely, your satisfaction is all that counts, you have to say what you want, said the boy with straight hair, Petites Cendres seeing his round cheeks and the way his hair moved around his face from far off, leaning his elbow on the bar window, he listened sadly to the monologue of dizzying material greed from the boy he called his own, having got a nice smile from him, the kid does alright, Petites Cendres thought, if he was materialist first and foremost, he wouldn't fall victim to his own naïveté, people who plucked his flower knew the price, and it didn't grow everywhere, despite the moment of grace in a smile, Petites Cendres was saddened that this fresh-petalled rose was not for him, poor junkie that he was, who wanted an

undernourished junkie with broken teeth, often broken by
other junkies and nude dancers, often wearing the socks they
tossed to the audience at the end of the show and trod under-
foot on the dancefloor, there was no one quite so hard up as
Petites Cendres, a dope addict inhaling the brown sugar no
one else did anymore for lack of anything better, who'd want
to take that crude brown powder, this generation of nude
dancers stayed clean, didn't fool around injecting poison into
their veins, once in while, not like coke, Petites Cendres
would clumsily line up the spoon and syringe, sick of this
burning furnace of want, nothing, empty pockets, stuck with
the thug that looked like a boxer, such rotten conditions, but
he felt he had no choice but to go to this man and just see
what happened afterwards, brown sugar, smoking heroine
made you want to throw up, while . . . where was Timo anyway, probably somewhere down by the keys, waiting, this
would be when they started dancing and shouting and carrying on, closing time, we're closing in a moment, and in the
wee hours the sun would be burning everywhere, lighting on
faces and faded sheets in the rooms, an indecent sun when
night had honoured, not persecuted, the hungry unfortunates,
so much the better if the kid, my kid, has that self-assurance,
he's tough, and he's only here on the island for a few days,
then he'll follow his companion to New York or somewhere
else, this hell, this furnace of want is mine, I can't leave,
Petites Cendres thought, still everything might still work out
with Timo, I wonder if my boy cries when he's alone with his
multiple-choice video games, a virtual kingdom based on the
real world, with the same corruption, the same serial rapes
and killings, the gamer giving vent to his worst impulses, did
the languid boy cry, stretched out on the sofa with his games,
round cheeks on his hands, saying to himself, I watch because
I'm bored, give me porn or give me crime, manipulate me,
anything so I'm not bored, I quit school too soon, why is that
my fault, I'm just waiting for my lover to get back from the

office, and tonight we're going out, so what did he do all day waiting for his friend, hang out in the streets, work as an escort, already into high-tech, what didn't he have, whereas Petites Cendres was just a poor transvestite junkie with nothing going for him, he thought, with sunrise, life became a handicap, a setback, but at night, everything was the same colour, so did rust-coloured men and lost dogs, jazz sextets improvised in bars on the theme of the soul lamenting its fate with the soft growl of metal, Petites Cendres listened as he thought, spirit, soul, keep going, don't die, all you want is a little more powder, an electric guitar duet, drums, soul, go forward, not back, I'll go see Timo, he must be down on the jetty with a cigarette hanging from his lips, now the percussionists, good group this, I'll be back for a beer, two floors for dancers and one downstairs for skaters, you'd hear the brass at daybreak, forward, soul, onward, Petites Cendres thought, daybreak would mean a handicap, a setback, God who made the world, the earth and the flowers, and me as I am, me, Petites Cendres at the Porte du Baiser Saloon, where's my powder, I sometimes wonder if he cries when he's alone in men's luxurious apartments, that boy of mine, suddenly Petites Cendres felt himself rocking, won over by the music, sliding languidly on the soles of his sandals, he'd go all the way to Atlantic Boulevard, he thought, it was the end of a night like all the others, too bad there was no antidote for the impulse to love or want powder, a night like any other in the furnace of want, except that this boy, his boy, had smiled at him one day, still maybe it was in vain, and I still remember the clouds of flies on the foreheads and eyes of the little kids found by the side of the road, Nora thought, and the lack of running water, even in the hospital, other wings badly needed to be opened, one was donated by an Italian doctor, but charity from benefactors like that was precarious and very rare, a washer and dryer were essential, nothing ever dried by itself in this terrible climate, and because of Cayor worms, everything had to be

ironed, diapers, bed-linen, kids' clothes, what miraculous sunsets and starry nights, yet still the devastating image of children being eaten up by worms was forever present, worms
and bouts of diarrhea on beds and sleeping-mats, the same
distressing spectacle everywhere, sometimes there was a
bright spot in the afternoon when Nora brought milk with
banana-, mango- or papaya-quarters to the bigger ones in
Room 7, some of them suddenly came to life and pushed a
wooden scooter with one wheel missing around in the dirt,
others played with sticks and bits of metal, the little girls
stretching the fabric of their shoes when they had them, Nora
was pained by their weight-loss and thinness when she
checked on them, she remembered the cloudbursts that fell on
the corrugated tin roof over her room at night, the breeze on
her sweaty body through the mosquito-netting, and the death
one morning of a child with severe Vitamin A deficiency,
another suffering from Pott's disease had been saved, or when
she had made funeral clothes in the laundry for the little child
who had died, and what was to be done about those babies
on perfusion who weren't eating or taking in anything anymore, kids infected with AIDS, an entire population was
infected and arriving with all these dying children, wasn't it?
Nora fetched water in buckets along with the mothers of the
children, or those that remained, sick mothers who nevertheless went on working, clouds of flies covered the baby bottles,
this was the despairing picture Nora saw there every day and
never forgot, even back home with her own family, or were
they still her own, my family and friends living out their lives
so far from all this misery, maybe they'd have felt sickened by
these revolting diapers just tossed on the floor before carting
them off to the straw hut near the playground used by the
orphans in Room 9, perhaps they would all have felt some
repugnance for the fact that humanity had sunk so low, with
no hope of progress or resources, for they did not know what
Nora did, they knew nothing of it, despite being told and

shown what she had seen, not the reflection of a nightmare, but inexorable reality, and in the glimmer of dawn on the blinds, the odd, well-shaven young man was there in Mai's room again, from one instant to the next, he'd disappear, he said, because the nanny would waste no time coming in to wake Mai up, since she always slept in too long, listen Mai, the young man said, I've served out my sentence and now here I am, a free man, that's what the court decided, and I can't change that, I'd already done ten years in prison out on the California coast, wasn't that enough, the sentence was twenty, it was my good conduct that influenced the court and the judge, I was once a kid just like you, back in Idaho, always had a dog held close to my chest, small and fluffy he was, and was I a monster, no, my father was a monster to me, and I was just a kid like any other in Idaho, at twelve I was convicted of making obscene phone calls, I learned martial arts, Haïkido and Kendo, so I could get even with a father who beat me up, tied me up with rope, you should have seen me at that age in my white kimono, I remember rope, because I used it later in my rapes and murders, first it was only students, too bad they decided to take the bridges back to campus, bridges and ropes, those were my fascination, when was it my father forgot me all night on a bridge in the cold, when was that, I don't know, but better not stare at my shadow on a bridge when I had on my Hallowe'en mask, the bridges were called Jennifer or Rachel, the names of the ones I strangled, ropes and bridges were all I could think of at home in my bungalow, first the wrists, then the ropes and silence, a real Feast of All Saints, Jennifer Bridge, Rachel Bridge, I had them all, one by one I buried them under the floorboards of my bungalow with a pile of wood I'd cut, sometimes I'd knock on doors and say I was a carpenter looking for things to repair, and then quick, I'd run down to the bathroom and wait and wait, so, if I'm not a monster, what am I, tell me Mai, what's going to happen to me, I'd wait behind the shower curtain, the court decided, and now here I am with you, so close you could hear my breath, want to come to the bridge with me, want to follow me, I've got a Hallowe'en mask in my case, you'll see this scar on my face, when I rape them I get scratched, like in a blackberry bush, their nail-marks, it does me good, if I'm not a monster, who am I, but it isn't me, it's him who never had to face a sentence or a court, who tied me to chairs with ropes, stifled me and my cries with pillows, from then on, ropes were my fixation, you should have seen me at twelve doing martial arts, that was me, the tough guy no one felt sorry for, come with me, I don't want to hurt you, I'm just your brother in his white kimono, I can hear the cocks crowing, soon it will be time for you to wake up, Mai, you've wet your pyjamas again, what will your mother say, I told you not to drink all those glasses of water your nanny gave you yesterday evening, you'll get scolded, they'll call your pediatrician, I got punished too and look what happened to me, Mai, tell me, am I a monster in my white kimono, what will happen to us, you and me Mai, when we're free, and Olivier after hours of writing in his hut, raised his head to the red line over the ocean, how reviving it felt to feel the immensity of water around him, and the silence after all the noise of the party, why hadn't he listened more attentively to Mélanie, especially since she confided so rarely in others, this doltish silence men use to cut themselves off, was that how he'd been with Mélanie in his fear that she would get hurt like other women activists as devoted as herself, even though the house was protected from vandals and thieves, he thought he heard footsteps nearby, there were all kinds of gangs and networks on Bahama and Esmerelda Streets, could they burst in from the park or the street or the suddenly unoccupied space around the pool, were those shots Olivier heard, five maybe, black bandannas over their foreheads, running their knives over him in his sleep, furtive aggressions, drug deals, where were Chuan and Jermaine, although Olivier felt he knew his son, could he have dealings with them anyway, one of them, Carlos, had been accused of homicide, though involuntary, although he had not caused the death of Lazaro, voluntarily or not, he tried to kill me, Lazaro had cried, Chuan welcomed him into her house, and as for Carlos, who, by belonging to a gang had shown his will to kill, even if it was just play, because he thought the gun wasn't loaded when it was, besides, who knows whether Olivier, also a child of the African and Haitian ghettos, might not have been accused of murder himself, voluntary or not, just like poor Carlos, who was now imprisoned by mistake if you thought about it, right, by mistake, the community ought to protest but said nothing, knowing how the town was divided into zones of violence, from the Bad Niggers to the Latino Gang, ten of them with black bandannas around their foreheads, and Lazaro would be one of these, saying, I'm just biding my time, my arsenal's all ready, first Jermaine and his mother, then the man, while he's at his table writing, that black senator no one listens to, just writing out his anger in lacklustre prose, but for us, life is a blood sport, just that, an act of pure violence, Olivier thought he heard footsteps very nearby, although the immensity of water was all-enveloping, and he saw the red line of sun on the horizon from his window, and he heard nothing but birdsong at this hour, he where Chuan and Jermaine were, mother and son had danced the night away, was this the time for frivolity, for laughing and dancing while on the alert, everywhere the tolling of gunshots, alert for the gangs on our doorstep, on Bahama and Esmerelda Streets, Carlos or the others, had anyone really taken into account that they were the sons of slaves, like Bigger Thomas, the hero of novelist Richard Wright, although Olivier wasn't much for reading novels, in fact he was embarrassed that there were so many around him whose books he had not read, he remembered Bigger Thomas, the one they called nigger, and his descent into crime in a white world, for a long time, he thought, wasn't that the only way, that hellish route through betrayal, those with no country, ashamed of petty crime, rape or theft, whether in Chicago, or here in this town, Bigger Thomas or Carlos, all sons of slaves and unable to get over it, although it had been abolished long ago, no, there were still plenty of slavers at work in the world, yesterday Bigger Thomas, trapped and defenceless, today Carlos; whole museums were devoted to the numberless slaves of the past, built along river-banks, reminders that not long ago, along these same rivers, women, men and children had been bought and sold, these structures and buildings recalling the fate of black merchandise, its price often less than that of a chair or a stove, sold in the public square like livestock, what impact would this memory of the shadowy part of themselves have had on Bigger Thomas or Carlos, if not that an entire lifetime was not enough to get away, really free themselves from it, still guilty in the white world that had given them a chance, a historic chance, that they inherited without gratitude, cursing that fortune called racial equality, at long last the triumph of justice, for where was that justice when Emmett Till died at the hands of two white assassins, Emmett Till, another Bigger Thomas from Chicago, but innocent, taken from his bed late at night, beaten, tortured with a Colt .45 in the face, by two men beside themselves with rage who ended up killing him and throwing him into the river, what would Olivier have done if he'd had to identify the disfigured face in his white school shirt and tie, like Emmett's mother, no, he wouldn't have recognized his son Jermaine either, the two men were acquitted by a white court, acquitted and bragging of their victory to their wives, united in this base betrayal of justice, deceitful and victorious, and what would Olivier have done if they brought him Jermaine's body by train, like Emmett's to his mother, upon returning from a family visit to Mississippi and being shown her son's body at the station, who is that, she had asked looking drawn, who is that, what have you done to him, that isn't my son anymore, but this is what she said, you are going to be shamed, because the coffin's going to be open for several days, so nothing can be forgotten, and they said to her, you know, if your son came to this sad end, though he was only fourteen, it is because he whistled at a white woman as she passed by, and that just isn't right, and that's why you've got your son in this awful state, the coffin will be open so the world can see and never forget his dishonour, Emmett's mother said, and pilgrims came by the thousands, joining hands around his martyred body, what would Olivier have done at the open coffin of his son, surely he would have wept every tear in his body like Emmet's mother, but Jermaine was alive, and by noon Olivier would be seeing his son slicing through the waves on his sailboard, fascinating because so different from his father, not an intellectual but a high-liver who rejoiced in physical existence and sought out the joy in life, while his father was more taciturn, his son with wide, slanted eyes under his dark glasses, the living Jerome was the image of his mother, Jermaine, so beloved, Samuel thought a time for life and for love would be time taken away from dance, he wouldn't be just the disciple of Arnie Graal the master, one day he'd be the master and teach choreography himself, wouldn't it have been better for Vincent to dance at day-camp on the mountainside or on a sunny beach than under the close watch of his doctors, he'd have learned to design costumes, he would have been supported by his strengths instead of just being considered too weak, he would have lived in a musical theatre, and Samuel would have helped him learn some basic steps, first tap-dancing, he would have done anything for Vincent to be cured of his cough and bouts of pain, Vincent would have been amazed to hear the metallic clink of tap-shoes, he'd have sung and danced, the forest air would no longer rasp at his lungs, and although Arnie's choreography was admirable, it was exhausting for the dancers as they dropped one by one from high scaffolding into the void, turning over in a gradual but impressive slowness, arms and legs, then head, still more softly, a structural choreography that evoked admiring dread in the way the subject took hold of something in the dancer that became more real than reality when expressed in thunder and blood, Samuel pondered what had been left out, all those high-rise windows suggested by the choreography, glass should have been added to the labyrinths, every window suddenly as mobile as stained glass, with tableaux of characters in the last scene of the sacrificial jump, bustling, alone or in groups toward the jump that ended on cement in the streets, it needed the thousands of faces stuck to the glass and transparent plexiglass forever in an immutable expression of terror so that none could ever forget their imprint, the shroud of their features etched by fire and ash into the melting glass and gradually given a patina by the sun, the rain and the snow, those faces need to be there constantly, between frames of plaster, so the parents, spouses, and children of those caught so unexpectedly under beams and glass liquefied into fiery larvae can make heard to those ears and brows and cheeks in their bloody cut-outs the immense call of their choir, the diffuse lament of their prayers in every voice and language, for what words could say these words, and the wave, the narrative waves of all these faces, for they would have spoken if they could, and one could practically feel the trembling on their lips, the ravaging astonishment on their faces, the pressure from the impacts on their tear-glands, but most of all, they would forever be there in the joints of the glass-work, all those face hoping for deliverance and another life, as if each one were saying, remember, it's me, your neighbour, brother, child, keep the vigil a long time, our faces like those of the saints, don't forget us, but Arnie Graal had been annoyed at Samuel's idea of memory ongoing into the dramatic present, what was one to think of all those who should have been there and all the glassed-in hallways in the buildings, towers and skyscrapers, Arnie Graal's entire people swallowed up into forgetful sleep, though some did not forget and had since rehabilitated by law what had once been a series of massacres against an entire race, so many swollen faces, hundreds of thousands, an incalculable number should have been there, Arnie said to Samuel, including the sacrificed perpetrators of the suicide mission, they too had been duped by their superiors and obsessed by the thought of all those faces, walls of icons, all incinerated, yet still breathing, like images painted onto ivory with eyes that would have cried, all those faces coming toward him while he walked the streets of New York and making his sleep a restless one, Samuel thought that only the art of dance could embody and communicate the amount of lamentation for which he had become the unwilling receiver, he who was born to happiness, this joy of living was part of him along with all those faces, bodies hoisted to windows amid the red-and-white flags or any other funereal drapery, their hands waved from the windows, he would have to live in their place from now on, dance for those who no longer could, and Mère said, as she lay her arm next to Nora's, it's going to be a calm day out on the water, I don't feel the least bit like sleeping now, while you were walking alone lost in thought, I was thinking about my grandson Augustino, you know, he writes, like his father, he writes a lot, oh I really ought to remember more of what he wrote that upset me so much, what was it, I don't remember, it's silly, memory often plays tricks at my age, and what if it isn't just that, she said, relieved that her words were masked by the sound of the waves and Nora didn't seem to have heard her, absorbed in the flight of birds, and Nora said, during my years in boarding-school and those long months away from my parents, I had only one childhood wish that never came true, it's hard to know why such simple wishes can't come true, it was to have a bird sleep in my hand, we had monkeys, lion-cubs and snakes, so why not a little bird to sleep in my hand and go to

around with me all day at school and everywhere, my brother
and I felt so abandoned there, but I couldn't have a little bird,
a small thing to stroke, always gentle and soft and feathery
and good-natured, yet much later on, when my son Hans said,
Mama, I'd like to have a bird, at last my wish came true, and I
bought him a cockatoo, we already had dogs and cats, and
Hans became a Australian-parrot breeder, the house was soon
full of them, is that what happens, after a long wait our wishes
come true exaggeratedly, in an excess of abundance and joy,
yet I still remember how desolate I felt when they refused to
let me have a little bird to sleep in my hand and go to school
with me, the easiest of pets was denied me because I was not
being reasonable, they said, little girls couldn't live in a con-
vent or a boarding-school with birds, otherwise what would
happen to the rules and order of the place? There was a place
for everything, animal, vegetable and mineral, and we humans
over them all, however imperfectly, the nuns asked me why I
had to mix everything together, forgetting I was only five and
my brother four, Mère was listening to her more attentively
than Nora usually did in turn, awkward socially and too read-
ily absorbed in her own thoughts, Nora was thinking she had
brightened up the house with happy moments with the happy
chattering of children and birds all day long, that was not the
truth, she thought, because she had moved with her doll-
house and animals so many times, like a nomad's tent, from
one country to another, depending on her husband's diplo-
matic duties, getting used to new customs again, learning a
new language, as though the childhood exile from Africa were
constantly renewable, though it was also an opportunity for
rebirth whose benefits and diversity she acknowledged, a can-
cerous growth had cast a shadow on her thirty-fifth year, coming through the treatment period, the upheaval in her family
life when all at once the presence of Hans' birds, the ones she
had so longed for, weighed on her, when she had rebelled
and told the doctor, I can't die, my children are young, and

they need me, we've got to stop this cancer from growing, and I'll do it, serenely and hopefully exercizing her rights over her body, she had beaten cancer once, gathering her loved ones around her, children and birds, and ready to leave for Italy, Australia or Africa with Christiansen, saying she'd celebrate her cure with the birth of another child, conceived in Africa, fortified by Christiansen's love, then suddenly Nora said to Mère, I met Christiansen in Europe you know, when we were medical students, though that wasn't what we ended up doing, to Christiansen's despair, he had to spend over a year in hospital after a motorcycle accident, and he had to give up medicine and competitive tennis, though he'd won several trophies at home, and I switched to painting, since medicine had been forced on me by my father, when I met him, I was afraid he was too good-looking for me, what a nasty turn of fate, not to deserve this man in any way, she fell silent, since Mère's expression had suddenly turned irritated and preoccupied, that's bad, very bad, she said, to feel inferior to your husband, my dear Nora, I'm speaking to you as a friend, you are wrong, think of the trials you have gone through with such courage, not only are you a very talented painter, but you speak several languages, a very gifted woman, Mère asserted, like my daughter Mélanie, and Bernard's wife Valérie too, a very free-spirited writer, yet still they're a close couple, just like you and Christiansen, these feelings of inferiority are really not good for a woman, Mère repeated, I don't want you to feel that way anymore, my Nora, because you'll end up believing them, yet still, if Esther was right about this, why was Nora feeling so dissatisfied with her work in Africa since her return, it's because I wasn't able to save anyone there, she said, not the kids with AIDS under perfusion and unable to eat, of course I recognized the bad results of blood-tests, my father had treated, operated on and cured lepers, but where I was, the population had been deliberately infected to wipe them out, a nurse even told me the Ugandan, Rwandan and other militias that occupied and robbed a large part of the country had been systematically made up of AIDS-carriers so the entire population would be infected, when a virus becomes a weapon of war, I guess you can expect a worldwide calamity, so how do we go about centralizing our aid and feeling useful, I wondered, here's a criminally infected population which is helpless, my father never gave up on his patients, he was never put off the way I was, once I was confronted with misery, I never stopped feeling this disgust and nausea, eating the same food as them, cassava and cassava-leaves, I couldn't get it down anymore, I thought about the diapers waiting for me in Room 9, the flies on the baby bottles, honestly, Esther, my father would never have given way to disgust the way I did, where he surpassed me was in never letting himself get discouraged, just being effective and miraculous, but I couldn't get myself to believe in these miracles, when I saw a doctor trying to find a vein to transfuse in a child who would be dead at any moment like a glimmer of light in a wind, all their lives went out like that, I was beyond disgust, I was dispirited, and although I'd once learned to speak Lingala like a native, I suddenly felt myself a complete beginner faced with pain, war is a poisonous energy, evil, hard to combat, and I didn't know how much longer I could hold out with all these dying children around me, there again my father would have been more resolute, I put in twelve-to-thirteen-hour days, my father would never have stopped, he wouldn't have slid under the netting and used perfume to blot out the nauseating odours of the day, he would have been uncompromising, though he still would have been just as furious as me at the priests and the growing number of churches, especially in their pernicious enthusiasm to convert a populace so impoverished and weak, I should have known on this temporary return to Africa I'd never be as strong as he was, when I got a chance to phone Christiansen and the children, which wasn't often, I was in tears and telling them that Amos was gone, he was one I'd

especially watched over, and so was little N'suzi, they were
names and faces in my mind, suddenly no more; mine were
warm and cared for, well-fed, and all they could say over and
over (and how wrong they were) was, we told you so, Mama,
don't go, we knew you'd be unhappy, come back right away,
Mama, I didn't feel any better until I heard the voice of my
dear Christiansen saying, you did the right thing, you had to
follow your heart and go, try and get some rest, you'll feel better tomorrow, you know I'm with you, how did you celebrate
Christmas, and I plucked up courage and said, yes, well, we
gave out presents to the little ones, I was now friends with a
thirteen-year-old boy called Jerome, even though his ex-par-
ents had left him at the orphanage saying he had the evil eye,
I told Christiansen that I still had some belief that I could be
useful here, and I remembered as I spoke to him as though he
were right there with me and so warm, that I remembered
coming home from town the night before and seeing three
funeral processions with drums amid the choking air as I
passed by in the car, why this moment of faith, because after
giving baths to the eight kids in Room 10, I had delayed for a
few hours, or maybe even a few days and even months, who
will ever know, the inevitability of all these deaths, feeding
Joël a little milk or a little camomile through a small syringe
every fifteen minutes, I had also bought some ointment for
chapped skin and some soap at the pharmacy, and ironed the
diapers that hadn't dried because of the rain, I'd also laid in a
supply of cookies, diluted milk and milk-powder, I also had to
listen to the doctor tell me that as soon as the kids were better
fed, they soon felt much better, I'd thought Joël wouldn't
make it through the night, though he wanted to live and went
on to the bottle after the syringe, I didn't tell Christiansen how
afraid I was in the hospital at night when I heard starving wild
dogs roaming around, and nothing about the insects either, I
was all wrapped up in his voice as it said, good night now,
good night, my love, you know we're thinking of you, then

Nora interrupted herself, saying, I know, Esther, I know it's a sign of weakness to always seek approval and love, especially approval, Mère smiled back at her saying nothing, she felt all at once that Nora's spirit had been inoculated with doubt so far back that it couldn't be undone, if only Nora had more contact with women like Mélanie, perhaps solidarity would have stimulated her to suppress this doubt little by little, though her timidity or unsociability and her longing for domesticity when she was home and waiting for Christiansen, perhaps that held her away from others, if Mère had many more years to live, she would have made friends with Nora and advised her, and then who knows, besides, maybe she did have those years in front of her, but why speak of tomorrow when we know we only have today, and suddenly Mère found that today very palpable though frozen, as though she were standing in front of a painting, nothing moving around her, her brain the repository of entire images, an emerald-green sea out at the horizon, and blue-grey closer to the beach where she was standing, Nora's profile set against the rose-pink of the sky, the straight-line legs of the birds, herons and gulls at daybreak, beach chairs piled on one another like pages in a book, and far off the quays, long jetties with the shadows of strolling people not moving, stopped with their bikes when the beauty of dawn stretched out as though there were no more morning or evening, Mère thought, was this the sign that that one's spirit was pausing too, no, not yet, it was surely just an overflowing of delight, a life well-lived, though a life that passed like all others, hers or Nora's, even Marie Curie who had also known doubt, or might it be Valérie getting up at dawn by herself to think about her books, alone with the ocean, the full extent of what she knew belonging to no one but herself for a few moments, not to the husband she admired, nor to her children, Christiansen had told Bernard the night before that women had been taking part in politics in his country for a long time, Valérie's men, Bernard and his friend Christiansen, had spent a long time talking about luxury cars, plush Rolls-Royces, like little boys comparing toys, and avoiding what really played on their minds, knowing that the politics of men was the politics of disaster or at least came very close in its risky tensions, how sweet that lukewarm breeze, was this the hour of the world's beginning, Mère thought, of course, how Christiansen and Bernard, two serious men, bragged about the construction of cars inherited from family members, well, these are the frivolities they chewed over, old-fashioned convertibles, coupés, sedans, bodywork and accessories, this flow of enthusiasm masking what they both felt at the edge of the abyss, what Valérie openly referred to as men's politics of disaster, look at the times we're living in, and they talk about cars, about durability and conserving them, male strength in their voices, making less audible Valérie's voice, or at least what she wanted to say, after they'd gathered around Esther in Chuan's garden during the night, both men knew that dust was their cars' future, though straight out of a rich man's mythology, one of them once so heavily commercialized, but now ageing so badly it had no value anymore, the other, Christiansen's, sold years ago to pay for Hans' studies in botany and zoology, so fascinated was the boy with animals ever since his mother gave him a gold-combed cockatoo, I suppose you'll be a bit like a bird, Christiansen said, when his son finally decided to become a flight attendant, his inner wings always longing for the free flight of birds on high, who knows what dreams our children get from us in our wild imaginings, during the night Mère had thought, so now I'm an octogenarian, and who's going to listen to me now, or will they just think, who is that charming old lady and when's that know-it-all going to shut up, what was a life well-lived, however long it may be, and Caroline said, Miss Désirée, I'm sure it's because I haven't eaten and hardly drunk anything for days, but even during the little sleep I get, I have this nightmare, I am approaching a wooden bridge dangling over a narrow waterway, an obstacle I was afraid of but had to overcome, for I could hear my own heartbeat, even though I'm locked up here, then I see, or rather hear, a woman coming towards me, limping on the wooden floor of the bridge, thump-thump, towards me, hard sounds, it's her, an invalid, coming slowly towards me, I knew that even if I yelled, you wouldn't hear me asleep in your armchair after reading your psalms, can't you hear her yourself, the sound of her leg as it drags along the boards of the bridge, can you hear her calling me, Miss Désirée, Harriett, can't you hear me, Miss Désirée, Harriet, no, how could you, when there's a sign between us, like in the old days, that says, only Whites allowed here, though my family rebelled against that vicious law, and my mother said to me, we're against racial segregation, I hold out my arms to you on the other side of the gate, how dare you separate a child from her black nurse, how dare you, shouted my mother, I'm here with you, said Harriett, you must sleep, say with me, the Lord is my shepherd, and I shall fear no evil, repeat it with me, Harriett said, I can't hear you Caroline, you and those prayers of yours, you wrote on the walls, where will you spend eternity, when the Whites used to laugh in the streets and on the sidewalks, only Whites allowed here, they've separated the two of us, yelled insults, is the hour that Whites call eternity, and the gazelles return as quickly as they left, the antelopes my husband and I shot in the desert, then cut off their arched horns and opened their snow-white bellies, who, who is it, the falconers have trained their birds of prey against me, but I don't know where to run, Harriett, Miss Désirée, will they feast on me, and I remember that bullfight I filmed in Lima, are there three horses I harness and ten men waiting for me with the clean-up crew to remove my beaten body from the arena like a bull turned over on its side while the crowd exults, they snatched the box, the case with the ashes from my hands, and Adrien still whispers in my ear, we know how much you loved him, come on, the boat will take you into port, come now, and on board the boat I saw the young man I had photographed in the night before his suicide, he was standing, and he too said, with graceful, welcoming gestures, you know they talk a lot about it, but there's almost nothing to it, here, do you recognize that music the Academy of Music played in the ruins, *Così Fan Tutte, Così Fan Tutte*, the dark mourning over all Europe, *Così Fan Tutte*, but dear, why are you wearing black, you hate black, Jean-Mathieu tells me, I do hear him though I can't see him, come dear friend, he says, we have so much to tell one another, why such silence between us, is it Charly, violent and jealous, is it her drugging you by degrees, a little more each day and each night, is she the cause of so much unhappiness, Charly, I told you to beware of whatever seemed new or fresh, didn't I, Caroline my dear, for when the falconers send their birds of prey after us, what can we do, what? Oh really now, what's all this fuss about, said Miss Désirée, Harriett, I'm here, how can I make you feel better, not by taking me in your arms like Frédéric with his Black Madonna after his fall by the pool, said Caroline, oh no, Harriett, do you hear the bell, should I change for dinner, Adrien, Suzanne, Bernard, Valérie and the others must be here already, how thoughtless, Harriett, what a mess the house is in, Charly's been out all night, you see, do you think you could wash my dress and my hair, what an untidy mess when Charly's out all night with that uncouth bunch of boys and girls, she's so young I can't forbid everything, has she fed the cat and the dog, that's a bad habit she has going out at night, but I can't stop her, and Chuan went into the cabin her husband was writing in, too bad he'd missed so much of the party, she thought it was a great success and was smiling with joy in the red dress, which was by now a bit wrinkled from going to-and-fro the kitchen and dancing with her friends and towards the end, with Jermaine, whose love she shared of music that was not passive, jarring and unnerving maybe, that was his way of expressing himself, she looped a strand of very short, dark hair behind her ear, was this a little bold and intrusive to surprise him like this, or just affectionate, if she didn't, he'd get into one of his dark moods, write all day and be rude to his guests, except for Mélanie, who had he talked to, really, it would be impolite not to say goodbye to them all, at least to shake a few hands, her feet were cramped in these patent-leather shoes, perhaps they were too tight and low-heeled, and she was going to say to her husband, as she placed her diminutive hands on his thoughtful head, come on, we have to get out of here, have you forgotten that this morning's the flotilla, there will be yachts, schooners, all kinds of sailboats from far off, more than a thousand, she'd say to him, your friends are on the beach already, and you're shut up here in your office, Esther told me how delighted she was, the party was a great success, what more could anyone want, except maybe for these shoes slung too low, by noon Jermaine would be on his surfboard, his vacation from university would soon be over, then how long would it be before she saw him again, would they always be close, not like Christainsen and Nora's son, always in flight, she'd have been very apprehensive to see Jerome go off like that, does our child need to love books the way his father does, is it even that important, her husband even declined to read his friends' novels, she'd have to point out to him it seemed rude, honestly, you've got to read the novels your friends write, the poets too, we've got quite few among our friends, what are you going to talk about when you meet them and haven't read their work, he'd scowl back, only history interests me, what we've been and what we are, that's concrete and irrefutable, the very life we're made of, this whiff of lemon under the trees, a splendid party, Esther had said, modestly adding, I really don't think I deserve all this when you consider the world as it is, my dear Chuan, oh why think about it all the time, came the answer as Chuan cast a limpid eye on Mère, as long as you're alive, it's only today that matters, these night even, as far as I'm concerned, Esther, there is you, that's all, you and the friends I want to see around you, and if I thought any differently, I suppose I'd already be with the things that are laid waste, and that's not what I want, no, absolutely not, come dance with me, do you think I'm not too stiff for that, Mère asked, I won't let you have time to hesitate, Chuan said, see, here we go you and I, and Mère had danced with Chuan's son holding her by the shoulders, so they all laughed, Chuan, Esther and Jermaine, all three dancing together, definitely a wonderful party, Esther said, and Chuan, despite being tired but also a little tipsy, smiled with joy, perhaps it was the smell of the acacias, the African lilies, the lemon-trees, and all that wonderful champagne they had drunk, though she'd forgotten to eat some of the wonderful things at the banquet, so busy she'd been with her guests that night that she hadn't noticed the time go by, and she'd danced so much, shaking, eyes closed when she danced alone, closed to fleeting electrical sensations, though she enjoyed their density, as though dancing had inflamed every one of her senses, leaving no room for stiffness or for rest, Chuan simply had too much to do for that, a demanding husband, a bit tyrannical and demanding, she thought, her career as a designer, of course, he wouldn't mind her visiting him in the cabin, well perhaps just a little, he'd be morose at first, but almost tender afterwards, she'd place her hands on his head, and he'd say, you know, Jermaine has larger, stronger hands than mine, but you've got hands like a little girl, where does he get them from, that smell of acacias was what made Chuan feel so good, just a little tipsy perhaps, very little, but as Mère had said, the party was a huge success, a triumph, they did say that Chuan could pull anything off, Mai felt she'd wet her pyjamas again, not having woken up at cock-crow as she often did, in daylight everything shows, her nanny would say as she took her to the bathroom to strip, in daylight everything shows, Marie-Sylvie de la Toussaint would say, where's Mama, thought Mai, of course it's always me that has to clean up and fix things, Marie-Sylvie would say as she pushed Mai toward the bathtub, this can't go on, no, it can't, are you still a baby, Mai, the boy with the hat came into my room and I got afraid, Mai would say, what boy with a hat, oh no, this is not going to go on, I'll have to tell your mother, this time I will, it's got to stop, I'm going to have to wash your behind and your back, you ought to be ashamed, Marie-Sylvie would say, what would happen if I weren't there, and Mai whimpered with sadness and shame, the boy with the hat came into my bed, she'd say, the soap and the blue foam mixing with her tears in the bathtub under Marie-Sylvie's rough hand, clean but dressed in shame, Mai would say through her tears, he got into my bed and wanted to sit on me as he always does, but because he was heavy . . . stop lying, Marie-Sylvie would cut her off, you have to look good for your parents, this time I won't tell them, don't you ever do it again, I told you, when you hear the cock crowing, you need to get up right away, Mama, where is she, when all at once Marie Sylvie asked, it isn't true is it, this story about a boy with a hat, it's just one of your fantasies, isn't it, she couldn't dismiss the fear that her crazed brother had come back again, He-who-never-sleeps and his Mexican sombrero, tell the truth, you're making it up, aren't you, she would say, shaking Mai hard with her bony hands, but get no answer, nothing from Mai, too bad she wasn't a boy like Augustino, she'd have beaten adults, especially this nanny Marie-Sylvie who didn't even like her, thrown her out, put her back in her boat out onto the ocean, right to the bottom, for Mai recalled what her father had said, you must share, share Marie-Sylvie with Vincent, but I don't want to, I don't want anything chopped up, I want it all, she'd sighed, not to share my fruit ice-cream with Emilio, though he was so brown and so cute when they played on the beach together, that was a few years ago when they were both only three, the Cuban Emilio and his father, athletic and brown himself, with a sudden white flash of teeth, like Emilio himself and like a mystery solved on both their faces, Emilio, pensive and looking for seashells while his father played volleyball, the most agile of the six players reaching for the ball over the net, Emilio's father and Emilio, Mai said, he's the one, he's my father, will you play with me, the best volleyball player in Cuba, and your father plays volleyball too, right, no, I don't want to play with you, Mai had answered Emilio, ashamed all at once of her father as the man on the restaurant terrace in white shorts, looking distinguished and writing outside in a notebook or on a sheet of paper, everywhere, as though seeing him write all day around the house were not enough, or going off on some solitary retreat in Europe, saying, I'm off to write, as though it were not already unbearable for Mai to be forbidden to touch his papers or his computer, even when he took Mai to the seaside, he skipped away to do some writing, forever writing, then suddenly her father's voice would ring out, come on over here, I've got ice cream, both of you come on, and Mai had thought, why not two ice creams, because there's Emilio and me, two ice creams, but Papa had said just one, and when it was time to have some fruit-flavoured ice cream, Papa had said, here are two spoons, but there's only one ice cream, Mai had complained, two spoons and one ice cream, I want mine all to myself, Papa, and he had said, that's so you share, that's why there's only one, understand, Mai, you have to share, that's the very first lesson in life, by which time Emilio had swallowed the whole thing himself so fast it hurt him and he made a face, I said share, her father had said again, I hate that word, she said, look Papa, Emilio's eaten it all, and Emilio, recovering his breath, said, I can eat it all by myself because my father's the best volleyball player in Cuba, I don't like that word share, Mai told her father, although she had long ago pardoned Emilio when she saw him on the beach with his father, he's the one she'd have liked to lick all over like an ice cream, him and his salt-water-and-sand smell,

his 'brown torso, almost naked, while Mai had to put on a
dress for dinner, she'd have liked to be encrusted under the
salt on his skin, winnow through the envelope of his muscles
in the sunlight, hold between her fingers the shells he took
home in the evening when the sun sank on the sea, or was it
home, when night fell on the net and on the players, and the
swings stopped in the children's park on the other side of the
street where the cars still went by in a cloud of sand, or was it
home, sharing Emilio, dividing him up, no he was hers, all
hers alone, she told her father, my Emilio, just mine, well, he
won't be if you don't stop biting his ears, her father told her,
be kind to him, you have to share him with others, what
others, Mai asked, Emilio's all for me, that word, share, when
she thought about it, was really awful, Papa said it often, in
fact that's all he seemed to say, maybe, though, Marie-Sylvie
would be easier-going and say to Mai playfully the way she
talked to Vincent, don't worry about it, these things happen,
don't think about it anymore, it was going to be a fine day,
and Mai could go to the beach and play with Emilio, both of
them wearing trunks so the sun would burn her chest, and the
pyjama would end up in the laundry, and Marie-Sylvie would
talk to her the way she would to Vincent, don't think about it
anymore, I won't tell your mother, go play now, your father's
waiting in the car to take you to the ocean and see Emilio, no,
Chuan thought she wouldn't want her son always up there in
those planes like Nora's son, nor have him learn to fly like
those young people flying a light plane with only a few seats
along the Connecticut coastline in the thickening fog, then
suddenly losing control and crashing into the sea, the precious
human cargo scattered over the water, whether princes or children adulated in glory, each one suddenly the poorest of all,
drowned and without fortune or baggage, whose fresh flesh
was suddenly corruptible and reduced to tatters by sharks,
good thing Jermaine was the practical type, feet on the ground,
Chuan thought, when you realize how quickly disaster can

strike in our lives, whatever it might be, no telling, before Chuan had been born, how many mothers, parents, lovers like her and Olivier, had waited for their daughters and sons to come home from school in Hiroshima, wondering, will he come back alive in this August heat like an oven, when a black fog rose to the heavens with bodies awash, will Jermaine come back alive, but imagining those horrors from before Chuan was born was to slip over to the side of desolation, never to know calm again, never be peaceful or pacified, Chuan claimed for herself and for all victims of that August day in what was once her country, Japan, peace, pacification for herself or for Olivier, no, she thought, it was for Jermaine, anything for the present in this life, Jermaine, the only line of pacification amid the extent of desolation, if one dared to look, but Chuan did not dare anymore, simply rejoicing in the success of that night's celebration, Chuan in her red dress was smiling in satisfaction and joy, now all that remained was to hope Olivier was in a pleasant mood, not uneasy or anxious, that arrangement of green apples in a crystal vase would certainly please him, she'd also decorate his office with orchids, when she told him, Olivier, maybe it would be a good idea to join our friends on the beach, it will soon be time for the flotilla to sail past, yes, it would be spectacular, haven't you worked too much all night as it is, you know it was a big success, this party for Esther's eightieth birthday, really, and he would grumble in a neutral voice, being elsewhere, oh yes, it was fine, just fine, and Chuan would be a bit disappointed but say nothing, putting everything into the pretty arrangement of green apples and orchids she would use to brighten up her husband's office, and on the quay, the silhouettes of people out strolling and cyclists barely seemed to move when seen from afar, from where Mère and Nora walked side-by-side on the beach, these silhouettes in the distilled light of dawn on the water seemed almost motionless, I'm not the man you want, Timo was saying to Petites Cendres, I use, but mostly to

make the customers feel good, rich folks are into that, you'd
be better off going to Bogotà, you're not going to survive
Bahama Street, besides you're so badly got-up with that corset
over your jeans, it's really ugly, I told you before, Ashley,
appearance is everything for customers, it's my top, Petites
Cendres said, you know I can never quit Bahama Street, no
choice, Petites Cendres thought, in an hour I've got a date
with the old sadist, and he'll say, be a dog, lie down in front of
me, and I'll hit you a few times, I love seeing your stinking
kind suffer, you'll do anything for a little stuff, won't you, a
brutal, low-down kind of guy he is, and Timo was smoking
with the cigarette dangling between his lips, you look like a
banker, Petites Cendres said sadly, I'm just the way the Lord
made me, even if the street-girls laugh at me at night, high-
heel divas, he said, I know you don't hang out with them,
especially for the flotilla, they're going to get themselves up as
pink flamingos and swans, Timo said with a note of disdain,
my going with men too is just coincidental, and I don't choose
just anyone, right, Petites Cendres said, I saw Reverend
Ézéchielle in her church, and she said, pray little man and
you'll be saved, I heard her singing voice say, I bear you in my
heart's faith, if you are downtrodden and nobody's son, think
of Ézéchielle, the pastor of your church who bears the unfor-
tunate that you are in her heart's faith, take the hands of the
people to the right and the left of you, for in my church, all
are equal, and we sang hymns, Ézéchielle said, blessed be
you, can you not hear the sound of trumpets in the sky or the
voice of angels, for I've come to this church to tell you about
the land of blessings from which all suffering is banished, and
she held me to her huge bosom, Petites Cendres said, and she
exclaimed, blessed are those like you, Petites Cendres, the forgotten of the world, for you will see God before I do, for I,
Reverend Ézéchielle may have the sin of pride in me as I go
everywhere preaching, and your heart may be humbler than
mine, for every day you are in the mire, and I am honoured as

the pastor of the church you come to, whoever you may be, blessed be you, Petites Cendres, you, rejected of men, how can you believe that crap, said Timo, condescending, religion's a fraud, that's what I've always thought, every Sunday I go to the temple at the Cité du Corail, and I pray, and dance with the Reverend Ézéchielle, that's how they put the miserable people to sleep, Timo said, you'd better go meet your client at the hotel, I am expecting someone, another pusher, no one shoud see us together, better get going Petites Cendres, Timo said with his cigarette between his lips, I don't want to play doggy for that filthy creature, thought Petites Cendres, I don't want him to order me, let me mount you like a horse, nigger, I picked you up in that hotel once, and you were going around the hallways with a trolley of soiled sheets, I said come in here to my room for a minute, take those sheets off my bed, and I practically grabbed you by the throat to kiss you, pathetic, they only let you do the lowest jobs in that hotel, hierarchically inferior, as they say, you and the other negroes, I told you, give up on dignity, and I'll give you all the money you want, you obeyed, because you knew I was stronger, then said that thing that earned you a slap, I think all the men who put up flaming crosses in front of black houses and the huts they live in the South, where I come from, haven't been put in jail, like you, the Ku Klux Klansmen are still out there free, yeah, you're still free with your torches and your guns, I give up, I'm through, but one day you'll get your punishment, you had the nerve to talk to me that way, Ashley, Petites Cendres, and I told you you'll regret it, I can make you spit blood if I want, you despise me, well watch out, I could make a sacrifice out of you and leave you in a garbage bag, your life means nothing to me, I can fix you good, so you'd better give up, I don't want to see this guy who humiliates me, Petites Cendres thought, it'll be pathetic, I know, and suddenly Petites Cendres felt better thinking of the round-cheeked boy, a vision of paradise, he held onto his dignity, even between two policemen, yellow cap on his head, upright, hiding the handcuffs under his cotton shirt, proud and dignified, and he'd been freed so quickly he was already in the arms of another lover, leaving for New York, or about to this morning, he was the immersion of love and had smiled at Petites Cendres as if to say, patience my friend, I'll be back, patience, I'm thinking of you, a vision of paradise in this pale light of day on the ocean, thinking about him, Petites Cendres marvelled, Timo said, I told you, leave me alone, that's how it was, Timo slapped him on the back, there was nothing left but for Petites Cendres to go back to the hotel and the man who was waiting for him, dragging his sandalled feet to the moorish-styled hotel amid coconut-trees and palms, he knew all about the basements under that imposing façade, for a long time his shadow had inhabited those subterranean places among the sheets and bed linens, transporting them from one floor to another in heavy, grey canvas bags on trolleys, that's how he had met the perverted stranger, he thought, and started losing his soul, because that's what happened when you were a slave to a master and his perversions, still sometimes he had no choice, he thought, he'd probably die without his powder in the morning, and I also had this dream, said Caroline, standing on a rock out in the ocean, I saw Charly set fire with her cigarillo to the letter I had given her for Jean-Mathieu before he left for Italy, though it was a dream, it was very detailed and fantastic, so exact I'd have thought it was true, I could smell the smoke from the cigarillo as it burned the paper and those words where I told Jean-Mathieu, I beg you, my friend, come back and see me, I admitted my feelings for him, it was all there, stopped by flames, and I even felt myself burning, I too was damaged and altered by fire, it was torture, is it possible this crime really was committed against Jean-Mathieu and me, that Charly was actually insane enough to burn that letter I gave her for him, in my dream, I asked her, and she answered insolently, I had no choice, it was Jean-Mathieu or me, what's done is done, and then yesterday in the mail you placed on my table, there was a letter from Cyril, saying, if Charles has decided to go back to Frédéric, it's because of you, your friends and you are the cause of our break-up, you think you had a right to interfere and split us apart, what can you know of our relationship in your little circle of snobs looking down their noses at what isn't theirs, what Charles was escaping from with me, Charles, whose extreme sensitivity you know well, would have loved to have your approval, but we didn't get that, did we, because to you I was unworthy of him and his genius and his aristocratic air, I was nothing but an actor, maybe even a mediocre one, because you never saw me act in the theatre, did you, as I read this letter, I felt flung to earth, the earth of conflicts in words where no one is ever right or wrong, Cyril, the young man in anger, was confusing me with one of my friends, maybe Adrien, who had hurt him with some ill-advised remark, for Adrien had said to Charles, you'll stop writing with this boy around, do you even know who he is, do be careful my dear Charles, but I did know who Cyril was and had actually seen him act in a theatre where he was both actor and director, but it's as though for a long time I hesitated to see him as vulnerable as myself since he'd fallen in love with Charles, I blamed myself for having let Charly make me vulnerable too, it was time, old age that played against me unfairly, I told myself, how could this ardent young man, arrogant and awkward, have felt his dignity hurt? Nevertheless it was true, he was persecuted within that famous circle of friends who subtly, almost imperceptibly, held him at arm's length, but Cyril quickly felt brushed aside, maybe I was the only one to invite both Charles and Cyril to my villa, a new couple, misunderstood and about to feel personally devastated like me, no one tried the way I did to love them, but I couldn't figure out how, everything I did seemed awkward because I was thinking about Frédéric at the same time, and I had to be loyal to him, so Cyril and I got into the muck of word-conflict, odd places, often on comfortless theatre sets, he'd produced *Phaedra*, a street version done as a musical with the songs played and sung by marginal people like bikers emerging from dark alleys and subway stations, that was how the handsome and rustic Cyril saw it, as if to say, that leather-clad Hyppolitus is me, this is what I am, none of this vulgarity works for me, Adrien announced, and other critics joined in, no doubt crushing the young man and putting him into such anger that Charles could do nothing to reason with him, what Cyril accused me of was really the fact that Adrien was my friend, a false friend of Charles, so none of us in our brilliant bourgeois circle had understood a thing about their fiery union, Cyril wrote me, we were self-involved narcissists: Adrien and Suzanne, basking in outdated glory, Jean-Mathieu and me, just as complacent and stuck in the past, I cried when I read Cyril's letter in words that this leather-armoured Hyppolitus used without nuance to slice me up, country boy, no, alright, he was not a country boy nor crude the way the others saw him, he was like me, vulnerable and torn, when Charles left him it was in pieces, he was life's fresh beginning, so he got carried away with telling us who were at our end, of course, that was it, the end, and as Charles would say, he alone was right, being young, that's what we all refused to admit in our jealous fears. You touch on taboo subjects, Adrien said to Daniel as they walked along the beach, Suzanne strolling along behind them and humming to herself as though remote from the weightiness of their intellectual debates, oh how this splendid dawn air gives me a lust for life, she seemed to murmur as she hummed and freed her hair from its turban, I mean the will to live a long life, very long, don't pay any attention to my wife, Adrien said at once, she denies the existence of death, these subjects are what are sometimes so unpleasant in your book *Strange Years*, he went on imperturbably, you know what I mean, when you write at length about what you call scatalogical art, or what nowadays you might better call scatophilia, but that's what it is, said Daniel, sensing the breath and embarrassment in Adrien's voice so close to him, it's a form of commercial art, I talk only about what I see, Adrien went on, I confess it disturbs me, these words and images you come up with, wishing Daniel would walk a little faster and keep up, is it really necessary to write down absolutely everything you see and feel, like for example, the story of that young English artist you met in the Spanish monastery and who does performance art with his stomach rumblings, a whole show made up of sounds from the gasses in his digestive tube, is it really appropriate for this artist, if he deserves to be called that, to make a living from the exploits of stomach and intestines, to be invited to play in different countries, do you really feel the need to write down every manifestation of what you call scatalogical art, you say yourself it is everywhere, but what I don't understand is that you don't condemn these aberrations, instead you describe these manifestations in minute detail, but they're constantly there in our faces, Daniel said, thinking of the lofty verse written by the older man, indeed what a contrast it was, the English student's stomach noises, all the gurgling in his guts, of course it was normal for Adrien to be disturbed, even shocked, Daniel thought, but still more scatalogical was the page in a circular that defined the couple, man and woman, by their proximity in the bathroom: he, not visible, to the left, but represented by the raised toilet seat against a backdrop of clean tiles, some big, brown, unlaced boots beneath the bowl; she represented by a bowl with the toilet seat down, prettied up with a crushed and faded bouquet of roses, and open wardrobes with an array of shoes and accessories, and thus lived man and woman side by side, with their intimacy exposed for all to see, well, I don't want to know anything about all that, Adrien said, I'd rather hear about Rembrandt and his water colours, you do that too in your books, and let man and woman be as they are, Adrien suddenly felt himself getting tangled up in words, no longer knowing just how to explain what he felt so vividly, not bathroom creatures and primary objects, that's not what men and women are, but something sacred and indestructible, there you have it, he went on, the man-woman couple cannot be compared to any other thing, but just then, Suzanne caught up and started smiling, what are you going on to Daniel about, my dear, she asked, what do you want to educate him about this time, the truth of course, said Adrien, just the truth, here in this town we have all kinds of multi-formed couples and marriages, you know how tolerant I am about that, even our friends and loved ones, but the solemn couple made up of a man and a woman, the celebration of their union in marriage, surely that's the strongest relationship, the most unshakeable, the most naturally convincing union, he said, but Suzanne could not help laughing provocatively at her husband's emphatic speech, at that instant it seemed unforgivable that they had so rarely seen or invited Charles and Cyril to their house, such an exceptional couple they seemed, despite the fact that Charles was still unalterably attached to Frédéric, just as she had been for years to Adrien, she was thinking she'd have liked to have a lover like Cyril, still with Adrien there, perhaps she was just tired of Adrien's moralizing about love, twenty years earlier, before they were married, he'd said the contrary, hadn't he, he'd proclaimed the freedom of their living together, allying himself with all those marginalized couples, maybe, she thought, love was as sudden in its inspiration as poetry, a state of heightened consciousness one should not fight against, besides, how could Charles have refused the combined inspiration and fecundity that was Cyril, that of the poet and his friends reviving inextinguishable flames, the same way that thirst is inextinguishable, living on infertile soil was the anomaly, not thirsting after an intelligent and gifted creature like Cyril who fixed you with his azure gaze, still an anarchist and an incendiary thing, Adrien added, look at the ravaged life of poor Frédéric, and look at what Cyril does on the stage, having Phaedra played with insidious ambiguity by a man, a Phaedra dressed as a soldier is who we see, man or woman, well, there's no doubt about it, I translated Euripides myself, and Phaedra is the daughter of Minos and wife to Theseus, it bothers me a lot to see an actor just fool around with it out of pure vanity, wanting nothing so much as to draw attention to himself by provoking people, Suzanne thought it was abominable not to give in to the thirst to hug Cyril and travel by his side, so much more so because he could recite bits of Charles' work from memory, to refuse his presence, indeed, why was it they had never invited Charles and Cyril to their home, what sign of mistrust was it on Adrien's part, Suzanne herself had often invited Cyril to breakfast with her on her terrace by the sea, but remembered now that he had politely declined, surely because of Adrien and his review in a town newspaper, it really is inadmissible, she suddenly said to Adrien, that we've never invited Cyril and Charles here this summer, but, my dear, he said, we hardly get to see them, they're always on the go, I worry about Charles' health with all those trips, he's not a young man like Cyril anymore, it was as though Charles had forgotten all about how delicate his health was when he and Cyril had left for India, Suzanne said again, it was a mistake, an irreparable one not to have them here, who knows what will happen next, or when we'll see them, oh come on, Adrien said, nothing's that irreparable, they'll be back soon, and Charles will be just as head-over-heels about that boy he hardly knows, unlike us, whom he's known since his youth, but Adrien's mind had already moved on from Charles and the couple he formed with Cyril that had so haunted him, and was observing Daniel and wondering why the writer let himself look so rundown, still polite, Daniel had rolled up his jeans and the sleeves of his shirt open to a vigorous torso, Adrien saw his coal-black eyes shining beneath the blue-grey glasses reflecting the colour of the sea, neither a smug nor a pretentious

writer, he was just disarmingly natural, but managed to irritate
or annoy Adrien without knowing why, surely it wasn't Daniel
himself that got to him, serenely striding along the shoreline,
but his book *Strange Years* that rubbed against Adrien's self-
esteem, I feel somehow annoyed when I read you, Adrien
said, pulling his hat down to his nose to block out the sun,
although there wasn't much this early at daybreak, one gets
lost in your maze like the twists and turns of medieval
churches, there seems to be no way out, you skip from one
subject to another till we don't know where we are, in these
meandering constructs and interwoven paths it is all there, but
we don't know why, music by the Viennese Alban Berg, paintings by the Frenchman Georges Seurat, and the anxiety of
time arrested and slowly dissolving into a reddish mist in *Un
dimanche à la Grande Jatte*, that same dissolution of time we
are sensing this morning, all of us soon to be together here by
the sea, dawn or morning, time already seems to be ahead of
us, we appear and disappear like oil stains on a canvas, that's
what you write, isn't this the inspiration of Charles and that
corrosive salt of his, the salt of dissolution and disappearance,
or of that thinking I detect behind Seurat's painting, quite
ironic, as though a walk on the beach or a picnic were a pre-
lude to a one-way trip to eternity, and all of a sudden you
inundate us with your legal and political ideas, as if we hadn't
thought about all that already, Kandinsky's painting, you talk
about that too, first you confess to your fears that there are
dictators who are barely getting started, just gearing up before
making torture constitutional, an allowable necessity, and in
the end there is nothing you don't get us to believe, of course,
sometimes you're right, unfortunately it's certainly true that for
more than four thousand years men have been executed in
Iran because of their sexual orientation, people are killed
every day for the misdemeanour of being different, what sort
of world are we living in, he sighed finally, but don't go writing that all this might happen here, in our society, Daniel's

musical ringtone went off, and Adrien turned to Suzanne, as though she had saved him from the meanders and mazes in Daniel's book, and feeling tender that she was still close and listening to him, he took her hand, and mopped the sweat beading on his brow with his handkerchief, how hot it is, dear, he said, and Daniel heard Vincent's thin voice saying, Papa, come and get me, when am I going to see you, Papa, remember that Sunday on the sailboat when the sky turned black and I had this violent, hacking cough, you saved me just in time, Papa, you carried me to the hospital in your arms, you're a hero for saving your son just in time, one second more, and it took so long to tie up the boat, and you kept saying, breathe, son, don't stop, we'll soon be at the hospital, one second more, and in that second I knew you were the hero to save me, it was a very long second, because tying up the boat in the rolling waves wasn't easy, you said, above all Vincent, don't stop breathing, you must know, Daniel said, what saved you son was the oxygen tank the doctor handed me, not me myself, it was life he had in his hands, Daniel was unhappy that his son's voice was practically a whimper, Papa, where are you, where are Mama and Marie-Sylvie, when am I going to see them and Samuel's boat *Southern Light*, Will in the wheelchair is happy because we got a visit from some actors, there's even a kid on a gurney because he had a bad attack during the night, really bad, like me on the boat, when you saved me, Papa, they say it's an independent theatre company with actors from all over who've come to entertain the kids who are sick, but I'm feeling better, Papa, I don't want to stay here anymore, it's fun when we play-act, or sing and dance, and I was OK enough to dance with a black musician wearing necklaces of all sorts of colours that tinkled in my ears, I felt for sure I was cured, Papa, will you come all the way to the mountains in Vermont to get me, Papa, with this homesick refrain, his voice went out like a little silver bell to his father and Marie-Sylvie, Papa, *Southern Light*, had the phone actually rung, had Daniel really heard the voice of his son, were the waves already drowning out Vincent's hesitant voice, his contained tears and his cough, it must be unthinkably hard to hear that your twenty-year-old daughter or son or both at once had been killed in the front of their armoured Hummer, a sheet over their remains, to hear it from a suspicious voice no parent wants to hear, in a murderous month with treacherous combat, to hear from this suspicious voice that you will never see them again, son or daughter, they had enrolled, and you couldn't stop them, in other times they had done it to pay for university, they'd fight forest fires, then suddenly safe, or so they thought, in their armoured Hummer, enrolled to fall in combat, killed in an ambush, what would Daniel have done if this shadowy voice had said, we regret to inform you that Vincent, the weaker one, and Samuel, we regret to inform you that your children, peacekeepers in the front of their armoured Hummer, have succumbed to their injuries, they left their unified families, Daniel thought, a world of model students, of playing in the schoolyard with their blonde Labrador, hoping one day to go to university, often poor or sons of workers, just kids, they left for the horror, stiff in the uniforms they would be buried in tomorrow, experienced in their warlike tasks, serving without knowing who, and dying without knowing why, just sensing in their fragile limbs, at the back of the neck, in the front of their armoured Hummer, that they were falling under enemy fire with no crowd to attend to them, a mother and father in a stupor, maybe a twin sister to survive them, suddenly deprived of identity with the other, as though having lost the use of an arm or leg, they would say she was the hundredth or two-hundredth to die, never this many girls since World War Two, never, fifteen-year-olds, sixteen-year-olds, twins, still close, flirting and wild, then suddenly the laughs shared with the brother or sister were gone, so was the flirting, so was the drinking, one wrote to her father, Dad, it'll soon be nightfall on the Tigris, forget about the fun and games when I was fifteen and wanted to go out with a different boy every night, I'm afraid, dear Dad, but I have an ideal, and it tells me there are things worth dying for, if I were to have an accident on patrol, remember these words I'm e-mailing you, I'll write tomorrow, now I can hear the crackle of firearms nearby, you have to expect, Dad, that all convoys will be attacked, though not every night or day, don't forget I'm going to register at university, that too is my ideal, more than any other, and as you often say, a family with lots of kids has no other choice, I'm not a soldier, I'm a peacekeeper, tell my twin sis I miss her a lot, I've never lived without her, even if we are always fighting, I miss sleeping in the same room with her at night, I want us both to register at the University of Madison, Julie wrote that she wanted to come out here with me, that we'd be safe together behind the lines, tell Julie, my dear twin sis, please, don't come out here, it's no place for you, there's too much burning near this post right now, too many suicide-bombs, I'm sending you a picture, Julie, the person you saw on TV targeted and shot on duty wasn't me, more gunfire, I've got to go now, dear family, till I see you on Easter furlough, what could a mother or father think re-reading these words, knowing now that the Easter visit had never happened, that they would never see their kids again, did it all have to replay over and over like the shootings of the cousins in Poland in 1942, when Great-uncle Samuel, for whom Samuel was named, died in the village of Lukow, Lublin, did it have to replay like that with a girl falling far from her sister in her armoured Hummer under enemy fire, and why was there always to be fire and enemies, with the young guard, her unwilling surrender and death, the rabbis prostrated themselves over and over, and near them, Great-uncle Samuel with bullets in him, if death gave way to life, why continue firing ceaselessly until the very seed is gone, thought Daniel, the root that still held firmly to the earth when tenacious life could not be put an end to, Suzanne thought she'd write to her daughters tonight, and she'd do it

behind the Chinese screen so Adrien would not see her from
his workroom and ask her, as he often did, for advice on one
of his translations, dear girls, she'd write, your parents are in
top health, and my hip fracture's no longer causing me problems, so we go to the tennis court every day, but I often think
of Jean-Mathieu and Caroline, I love life and your father too
much to . . . no, she'd write this instead, do you remember
that letter I wrote you to tell you about my decision, or was it
our decision, I don't remember, because I never really got to
discuss it clearly with your father, well, anyway, today I'll tell
you my decision, do you recall that the freely chosen end of a
beautiful and enlightened life is not suicide? *Daleth*, a door
open onto a shining sea in Hebrew, is a word that opens up to
light, even if it sounds sombre and final, it isn't, believe me,
and the drawing of a white lotus on this letter represents
Chinese Buddhism, still Suzanne had only just said to Adrien
and Daniel in a radiant burst of sincerity a few moments ago,
what a splendid dawning this was, how it gives you a taste for
life, long, very long life, and her friends had rejoiced in her
good humour, which seemed stable and constant in her, well,
not quite yet, one of her daughters was in England, the other
in Germany, and the son, still a bit lost and dreamy, with no
profession — and this caused his father to despair — no,
Suzanne just could not inflict this solution on them all, even
though she'd planned on it, this was not the time to write to
them when they were scattered far and wide, and her journalist daughters were doing so well, no, this isn't the day or time
she would choose, because, because, ah the birds were
singing, and her husband was looking at her tenderly, yes, I
must say again, what a dawn, what a splendid day, but we
ought to get a nap before going out for tennis, Adrien, seeming to note the unusual intonation in her voice, repeated it
too, yes splendid, and another among many, that's what's
amazing, he exclaimed, suddenly relaxed by the sea air, all of
a sudden, when you think about it, isn't every instant miracu-

lous, though he did regret not being at his worktable and leaning over his dictionaries the past few hours, each of these children, Nora told Mère, for however brief an appearance they made in my life, was like a little sun, perhaps no ray or light from within their heads, sometimes no real brain function, like Thérèse, age four, who couldn't walk or talk for several months, making us think she was autistic, but she wasn't, she started to sing when you rocked her a little, one night we were sitting together, the nurses and I, with babies on our laps near the door to catch some badly needed air, when we heard her sing, there were lots of patients everywhere, on straw mats, on the floor, we had so little space, but we all heard her singing like a stream in the night, at that instant, as she sang, it's strange that I did not have more faith in myself, in that minimal effort that was not futile in the face of the desperate fate of what once was my country, I knew that I should have devoted my entire life to them all, yet still Greta begged me to return before her baby was born, I knew I'd never have time, Thérèse needed rocking day and night, needed to be held up a few seconds every morning so her little legs didn't buckle, needed to get her over the scoliosis, needed to have an operation, but already she was happier to be alive, our little sunshine, I'd have so little time, one evening I suddenly got a forty-degree fever, the start of malaria, I was in the laundry, thinking we needed more than a hundred diapers a day, I was criticized for wasting them, but these sick kids were constantly having diarrhea, and they needed them, whenever anyone made the slightest reproach I just fell apart, I'd even bought diapers in town on my own, then suddenly as I was ironing in the laundry room, the fever hit, I also felt there was very little cooperation or organization, in the kitchen, for example, the two hotplates for the baby bottles were out of order, the pots and pans were worn out, and the bottles or the semolina would burn, so I bought a saucepan in town, and I got blamed for that too, and I told myself maybe I was the biggest defect, I talked about buying a pot in town in a country where a father earned sixty-five dollars and had to feed a family of six, still, I suppose because I was a mother, the most afflicted children around me felt something like a will to live, some even held on a long time, I was just there for lack of strength in lives prematurely eclipsed, the courageous efforts that would eventually prove vain, but, said Mère, you were there that's all that matters, Nora said, it might have been only thirty-seven at first, but I had a bad cough, and I thought, it's nothing, the kids have passed their colds on to me, I'll feel better tomorrow, I had such little patience, when the Italian priest called for me to get some water to baptize one of my dying kids, I told him, maybe you should treat them instead of inflicting this idiocy on them, a baptism for a two-year-old, he will go to heaven, said the priest stunned by my fury, no, it wasn't patience I lacked, it was pity, I should have felt sorry for this priest so tormented by the misfortune he saw all around him, he said, you've been working since dawn, go and get some rest, he had God, I had nothing, not even feelings of pity, I had witnessed, helpless, the child's baptism, the water running over his wounds, he would die in my arms that afternoon, you can't imagine how long it seems when a child dies in your arms, baptismal water or witches' relief, it just prolonged the agony, then next day, there was another little sun to help me forget, Jerome, I sometimes gave him a can of sardines in secret, or a piece of bread, hoping to improve his diet, telling him all the while how he warmed my heart, I felt bereft of everything, the voices of my own children, of music, of beauty, of culture, isn't it scandalous to feel that, like Ibsen's Nora, far from her loved ones, imprisoned with nauseating smells, even a fan wouldn't have helped reduce the odour of curdled milk and dirty diapers, and above all, my fever kept up, and I was so dizzy I couldn't stand up, I didn't dare tell anyone, in a kind of fog I asked the priest, I'm so thirsty, has the tanker-truck come yet, go and rest, he told me kindly, we'll have water tomorrow, the truck couldn't get down the road, the driver's on holiday till tomorrow, so go get some rest, then you won't have to worry about the children's baths, see, no water, that is hell, I told the priest, just one chamber-pot full of water for nine babies, no, there is worse, he said, having to cut sixty Cayor worms out of the feet of little Daniel the way I did yesterday, or watch strips of skin fall off some of them like scales off a fish, but that's not hell, malnutrition that can be treated, he said, and skin treated with tetracycline can be brought back, and of course mosquito-netting to keep the flies out, I listened feverishly, feeling myself curl up inside, how had I come to this, I said to myself, so useless in every part of my body when I was needed, how, why, I needed to speak to Christiansen, explain it all to him, I knew the almost maternal understanding he could express, something my friends benefitted from as well, I remember once Valérie went to see him in his New York office and consulted him as a friend whose past experience would have been soothing sup-port, I wasn't born yet when you were a child resistance-fighter in Norway, Valérie said to Christiansen, but what disturbs me is that time of false peace, our country house with little sisters and their father bombarded, I was still going to have a com-fortable life alone with my mother, Mother said, you've got a future ahead of you, no point looking back to the past, you'll only find pain there, get hold of yourself, but I rebelled and said, those before me are responsible for the state of the world they've left behind, nothing but destruction, what a sinister inheritance, and if nothing changes in human politics, it will be just as bad for my children, we do each inherit that notch in the flesh that is our responsibility, don't we, Valérie asked Christiansen, if it really were a time of peace, things wouldn't be falling apart all around me, life gets cut down, a crime, isn't it, what would my father and sisters have become if the knot of their lives hadn't been slit, the dishes and crystal glasses were still on the dinner table, one wall was cracked and burnt

where they all sat, my mother was in Paris, and that wall had
to become a crater, this link between you and me,
Christiansen, has been buried for years while you were a little
boy fighting, buried under the same ruins that cover my family, yesterday and today, Bernard, who knew nothing of all
this, and our children are the result of the uncertain, threatening peacetime, a very happy family nevertheless, but what if
there were an opening for those who still don't admit their
guilt to come back through, wouldn't we be wiped out like
my family, orphaned, my mother and I, Christiansen listened
to Valérie, his experience of the past never without its uses
and sometimes helpful if possible, could only tell her, Valérie,
we live in the present, that is where you are a writer, but you
are right, when some inherit a world of blue skies, while others nearby have foundered, there is very little peace with this
pain and mystery from the past, but these are your tools for
casting light, thus I knew I could explain to Christiansen as
Valérie had done, my feelings of defeat and my desire for tran-
quillity and a world of blue skies, a place to heal myself, now
was the time to settle this, Christiansen simply said, come
home dear, but Greta and the others got worked up and said,
we told you it would be too much for you, Mama, you always
act as though you're twenty, Christiansen was coming to meet
me in Europe where I'd go into hospital, God what a mess, I
thought, I was leaving my second family, second set of true
children, Garcia, Jerome, all the others, living or dead, I was
infected with malaria and who knows what else, I suddenly
seemed like one of my father's lepers, I'd stay away from too
many tearful farewells, where is Africa now, will I be going
back, though I felt so incompetent, I forgot to tell you, Esther,
I'm now the grandmother of a little boy, Greta had no great
difficulty with the pregnancy, my universe was well-ordered
and intact, then at once Mère said to Nora, could we stop and
look at the sky, it's all so beautiful and peaceful when people
are asleep in town, but Mère felt she should put her trembling

hand on Nora's shoulder, Nora didn't notice a thing, a thin shoulder it was under the lace dress that seemed to float around her body, a body that, as Christiansen said, had changed a lot, and Nora herself was no longer the same, she wanted to console her and say, Nora my dear, believe me, I have intuition, and you will go back to Africa where you believe the work is not done, Nora was so delighted to hear this that she embraced Mère, wondering why Esther seemed to tremble a bit, perhaps it was all the excitement of the party, perhaps she'd caught cold in this heat, or was it Nora's fever returning to her temples, would she come out of this fog feeling as alive as she did before, running here and there with inexhaustible energy, Mélanie heard Marie-Sylvie's voice from the tiny, phosphorescent green phone, Mai wasn't in bed or even in her room, Mai, where was she, Marie-Sylvie asked, Mélanie was going to catch up to the group on the beach, but Daniel, Adrien, Suzanne, Chuan and Olivier were already so far ahead, their shadows melting in the first misty rays of sun, so far along the shore she'd do better to head back to the house quickly, if it was true this time that Mai had really disappeared, not just hid in the shadows of the black almond-trees with her cats or up a tree eating fruit, Marie-Sylvie had said, I don't see her anywhere in the house, the backyard by the pool, or the garden, but she was right there when she woke up, I had to change her pyjamas because . . . Marie-Sylvie wouldn't say what Mai had done, I haven't seen her since then, she said, Mélanie went quickly to start the jeep and hit the accelerator, faster, faster, traffic was smooth at this hour, not many cars and pedestrians, that's how it happens, they're up in the morning and then disappear God-knows-how, you see them playing on a carousel at kindergarten or at nursery-school, then suddenly nothing, too bad there were no passers-by, Mélanie would have asked every single one, have you seen her, she's my daughter, perhaps she's just run off again, maybe she's gone to the stadium again, you can meet the wrong people there, it's happened before, yes, no, I forbade it so strongly, Mélanie thought, so where is she, that's how it happens, there's no one around, then someone shows up in a car and opens the door, the worst thing would be some secret meeting at that enormous stadium, so long that Mai could easily get lost in it, like that day on The-Island-Nobody-Owns, she'd fallen asleep under the Australian pines, but in the hour before her father found her, what had happened, no one knew, and even with the help of a psychologist and a pediatrician, they still knew nothing from her about that day, mustn't alert Daniel or Mère yet, above all, it might just be another one of her games, there was that brother of Marie-Sylvie's who'd been spotted hanging around the gate wearing a Mexican sombrero, although Mélanie wasn't worried about He-who never-sleeps, they would still search everywhere under the trees with Augustino, who was rubbing his eyes, because he hadn't slept either, and with the dogs, OK, probably none of it was true, and Mai was probably close by, and her mother would smother her with kisses and say, my angel, I'm sure this has been a long night for you, but it was such a happy one, especially for your grandmother, you're convinced she'll be there for you and Vincent and Augustino tomorrow and always, but it just isn't so, why weren't you sleeping, Mai, I put you to bed and read you a story myself, maybe it was nothing, Mélanie thought, maybe just a moment of fright that we sometimes get thinking of our children, a sense of imminent danger, Mai, where was Mai? Mama, I've done everything I could, Vénus wrote to her mother, I defended my brother like you told me to, the minute I saw his hairy head in the mangroves, the minute I saw my brother, I said, God have pity on you, Carlos, even if you hide on the Captain's boat, I'm afraid for your life, because there's a traitor here, an informant, and it's Richard — Rick, Mama, you don't know this awful guy, but he was the manager of the estate for my devoted husband William before he died at sea, he turned Carlos in, Perdue

Baltimore, who works at the Department of Corrections and Probation, and I will do all we can for my brother, Mama, right now at the Juvenile Detention Centre, he's beaten and mistreated, Perdue Baltimore says we have to do everything we can to make sure he isn't transferred to adult prison in Louisiana when he turns twenty-one, because that will be the end of him, he won't just be a delinquent accused of manslaughter, locked up with other convicts often younger than he is, some of them twelve or thirteen, but an inmate in an adult prison he can never get away from, you remember Perdue Baltimore, Mama, born in Barbados to George and Rita, university graduate, she says she can put a word in for Carlos at the Department of Corrections and Probation, she's already done a lot to reduce the mistreatment he's getting from the prison staff, once an officer tried to choke him for refusing to obey, but you can't tame Carlos with violence, you know that, Mama, even the Correction Centre, though it's a prison for young people to be held until they're twenty-one, it's still a hellhole, airless cells made of concrete, dark, stinking corridors, the sound of water dripping from the showers day and night, the endless shouts of the guards and of prisoners fighting, they use sticks too, Carlos along with them, he had to be in solitary confinement for twenty-four hours to calm down, do you know, Mama, how many fights there were between guards and boys last year, nearly four hundred, Mama, no, it's inhuman, sure Carlos shouldn't attack the guards the way he's done to get even with them, they call the twenty-four-hour cell the Hole in the Rock, Perdue Baltimore says there's no way Carlos can be rehabilitated if the guards are so violent with him, Carlos is so young that violence will just breed fear, and there's no future for him, and when he's twenty-one, he absolutely must not be transferred to adult prison in Louisiana, because it'll be hopeless, I've done everything I can, Mama, remember a long time ago, I held a charity bazaar, and now the kids on Bahama Street have been inoculated for

smallpox and meningitis when they reach school-age, I sold
my house for Carlos, the home of my husband, Captain
Williams, I sold his boat too, but still I'm in debt, even if Perdu
has helped me with credit, I don't know what will happen to
my brother without her, because there was no one to help us,
they all said he was a criminal who deserved to be in jail,
never mind that he was innocent, he thought the gun that
Cuban cook gave him wasn't loaded, but no one believes me,
especially because of all the trouble he's been in with the law
before this and his involvement with gangs on Bahama and
Esmerelda Streets, when he was a messenger and drug-runner,
remember, Mama, how it kept you up at nights and how you
said that Pastor Jérémy and you were pious parents always
ready to serve the Lord, how could this happen to our family,
it's not like we were in Chicago where so many black kids are
lost in riots, and the judges are indifferent to what happens
when they're thrown into prisons and correctional centres,
Perdue Baltimore says there is so much criminal activity on
those streets, it's hard to know everything that goes on, there
are a few good sheriffs who do their job well and try to keep
teenagers out of jail, but there are also a lot of unemployed
fathers on Bahama and Esmerelda who don't set a good example, you said, this isn't Los Angeles, where you can get killed
by some street thug while decorating your Christmas tree, but
when they caught Carlos, they laid him flat on the grass in
front of the house and handcuffed him behind his back, it was
a shame, Mama, and while my brother, your son, was still
down, a police officer put his knee on him while he raised his
head to me and said, help me, Vénus, his mouth half open, he
was so afraid, I remember the tattoo on one arm, it was Polly
the dog, and on the other it was arrows and knives, I've done
everything I can to help my brother as you asked, I have no
house, and I now know my husband William died defending
my honour when they laughed at him out on the sea for
marrying a black, fifteen-year-old escort, Rick says it was

about drugs and a settling of accounts between enemy captains, I know we loved each other, and he was a brave husband and captain, Perdue Baltimore says I've got to study the way she did, work days and study nights at Collège de la Trinité, my dachshund and iguana and I can live on a houseboat together, I've sold all the captain's paintings except for one, he's got quite a reputation as a painter on the Island, but a lot of our nicest household things have been stolen, and I know Rick is the one, he's a low-life, I can't tell you all the things he's done to me, he was always harassing me, and I had nowhere to go except off in a boat on the canal, you have no idea, Mama, Papa forbade me to cross the threshold of your house because he was so put out about our wedding and my life as an escort, when I sang with Uncle Cornélius at the Club Mix, but what else could I do, I'd so love it if Papa would let me sing again in the temple where he preaches on Sundays at Cité du Corail, everyone says it's Pastor Jérémy who brings the lost sheep back into the fold, to me it's like Papa, Carlos' father, who is in prison and has only us, his family, to stand by him, why have you abandoned him, you asked me to help Carlos my brother, and I have, justice is expensive, I have no house, nothing anymore, if only I could sing at the synagogue or the Baptist church or the temple at the Cité du Corail, our father's church, I haven't seen anyone in the family for such a long time, not even the Toqué, Deandra or Tiffany, the twins must be big by now, and I may only be a sinner, as my father would say, but I'm your daughter, you're living all cramped together, and I told you to come and live on my husband's estate by the canal with the vines and water-snakes, while I still had it, when Captain Williams was still alive, and we fed the hummingbirds and passeriformes out of our hands each morning, it was a paradise here, real paradise till my husband got killed out at sea and his boat came back flying a black flag, and that crooked manager he put his trust in, Richard, Rick, turned the place into a serpents' nest, day and night he harassed me, even though I had a gun under my pillow at night the way the captain told me to, I didn't want to use it, I often thought I could get Rick out of the house, but I never did, then Mama had written to Vénus that it was true, that Pastor Jérémy judged his daughter as a sinner, he'd forgotten she was an escort at the Club Mix and didn't really know what that word escort meant anyway, just as long as his daughter was decent, no, it was when she married Captain Williams and became an accomplice in his illegal cocaine and crack trade, surely she knew that, and besides the captain was an old man for such a young girl, and it made no sense, the sin was in the marriage Vénus should never have agreed to, the pastor acknowledged his sorrow at Carlos' imprisonment, but his family had not abandoned him, they'd all go to see him soon at the Detention Centre, Toqué was making progress at school, despite a congenitally infirm leg, and the twins Deandra and Tiffany, all would soon go and take packages of clothes and cigarettes for Carlos, he'd have liked to see Polly, but they couldn't take her, nor Oreilles Coupées, the latest dog that Deandra had rescued from the Island animal-killer, but they would go and see him, it was awful for Pastor Jérémy to see what was written on his worn blue shirt, No. 340, Block 3, and to see his son behind bars, every Sunday he prayed for him in the temple, and weekdays too, and although the pastor was disappointed in his sinner-daughter, she was once again welcomed into the house, she could come back and see her family if she wanted to, she could sing on Sunday at the temple in Cité du Corail, for our children are indeed also the children of God, said Pastor Jérémy, of course she could sing in church, but Jérémy recommended she dress more modestly and less transparently than before, for all was vanity, and Vénus must be decent to sing the psalms, Carlos was a thorn in his father's heart and an affliction to his mother's spirit, those syringes and drugs, that was evil, said Pastor Jérémy, but saddest of all was that he had nearly killed Lazaro that day at noon, so what if it was a game of vengeance between boys from rival gangs, Carlos was paying for his foolishness now, a thorn in his father's heart and an affliction to his mother's spirit, unless Perdue Baltimore could pull off a miracle, he'd be sent to an adult penitentiary next year, they had to write to the governor and the Department of Corrections and Probation, to think that Carlos and Lazaro had been great friends before these gang fights, gone boxing together on Saturdays, Pastor Jérémy would pray in the temple for the governor to show clemency to his son and give him a chance at rehabilitation, Lazaro's mother too was heart-struck about her son's refusal to forgive Carlos and his dedication to revenge, what's going to happen to our kids on Bahama and Esmerelda Streets, still Perdue Baltimore could accomplish a miracle, Venus thought, and she's going to intervene with the Department on Carlos' behalf, begging the judges for clemency, Carlos must not go to the Louisana prison with murderers, Vénus remembered selling all her husband's paintings but one, and that she'd take her dachshund and iguana, for in a few hours she'd be leaving, saying goodbye to the estate by the canal, nothing left or very little, but that picture would go everywhere with her, her sensual husband had painted for her with so much love that the passion appeared proudly on the canvas, it was the one he'd painted on their wedding day, it showed them in an embrace, and Williams had lent his own sea-sunned pink tint to the body of Vénus and taken on her black skin colour for himself, to show her how inextricably linked they were, that picture was the sign of their permanence as a couple, each was the other and away with prejudices, yes, I've done all I can, and I'll still do more, Vénus had written to Mama, and Pastor Jérémy had said to his wife, if I ask the governor to pardon my son's offense, I must do so myself, let Vénus come back here to be with her brothers and sisters, and Vénus thought how, after all these years, she'd see the house low under the palm trees which had never been trimmed, the freezer that still hadn't been moved away, although it was supposed to long ago, and the yellowing Christmas trees, well, they would still be there nearly fried by the sun, and the parasol over the games table, the dice polished by storms, under it the hens and chicks pecking away, for Pastor Jérémy had preached to all in his sermon that it was time for the lost sheep to return to the fold, even if it might pierce his heart like a thorn to think of Carlos and afflict Mama to her very soul, what future do Bahama and Esmerelda hold for our children, would there one day be an end to these gangs on the streets, and the millionaire captains who had invaded the town for the flotilla, Lazaro thought as he rowed his boat after shutting off the motor, the sea appeared smooth, hardly a ripple, and the movement of his oars and a soft rocking was all, in a few days he'd be with the men and their swearing and their nets on the shrimp boat, but it would only be for a while, he wasn't going to spend his life here on this island with his mother Caridad that he no longer wanted to see nor hear her complaining, his mother, a convert to freedom and the moral deviance of the other women, imitating them when she should cover her head and face, saying like the others that women's rights had been trampled on so often in Muslim countries, she took part in their conferences, listened to them and said, the time of the Inquisition is over, she was loathsome to listen to now, and as for Carlos, well, who knows when he'd get out of jail, but Lazaro would be back for revenge, he'd love to get into his cell and kill him by surprise, yes, but he'd wait, the time would come, and that's what upset his mother still more, for, she said he was just like his father Mohammed, unable to forgive, irreconcilable, brutal like his father in Egypt, these millionaire captains from Europe and Scandinavia with their regattas, now they owned the Island like some country getaway, it was disgusting, Lazaro thought, I'd rather see nuclear submarines than these boats, these vacation ports for a few days, and these sailors drunk on beer every night, gorging themselves with women and rum, they'd all set sail and make ready on the horizon, boats like *Anchor, Conqueror, Sea Pioneer*, with their Pathfinders, Pelicans, Hydras and Yamaha models, speed and engines, it was outrageous to have them in town, this was the world of upstarts his mother was drawn to, rich and materialistic, forever complaining about archeological museums, treasures and statues being destroyed over there in the country that once was ours, she would say, they're going to destroy all the treasures of antiquity, and that's how it was at Sarajevo, antique works killed the way they kill horses, nothing, not a thing would remain, and how was humanity going to remember, no memory of vases and statuettes, nothing, no libraries, no monuments, tomorrow there would be no memory of Mesopotamia, nothing, what I worry most about, she said, are the vandals, but Lazaro thought this was a memory of humanity that should be lost or burnt, he too loved birds and only birds, pelicans and seagulls flying over the fishing boats, but this Western society his mother had chosen was not for him, it was disgusting that his mother Caridad didn't realize that the laws of his father Mohammed were the only just ones, she wouldn't wear a scarf, she dressed like all the other women in *flagrante delecti*, she never would be purified, and the fact she defended all the laws promulgated for the freedom of perverts was a crime, this woman was no longer his mother, nor the wife of his father Mohammed, in our society, my father's and my cousins', these evil elements are eradicated, it was just law, Lazaro would be a fighter for all laws designed to purge all that was harmful or degenerate in this world that his mother had chosen, renouncing her own in the process, on the beach appeared groups of people strolling nonchalantly, no doubt people who'd been partying all night, thought Lazaro, filled from their banquets at all the tables he had to wait on disdainfully in his white apron, saying to the masters of the house, I'll just get the seafood you ordered, when he'd rather throw it at their feet, and their son looking down at him with false candour, underhanded no doubt under those slant eyes, what did this over-praised son know about child graves in neighbourhoods near the front lines, kids armed in towns under siege, nothing, not a thing, it was far away in some vague and dirty place abandoned to packs of dogs so hungry they would, they did, devour spent projectiles, no windows left in the houses, except maybe metal shutters and bars through which you could see still more packs . . . of kids wielding weapons, playing with them the way others might a guitar, lining them up along their bodies, what did he know about any of that, this papa's boy and his friends laughing by the pool or on their surfboards in the afternoon, while Lazaro was out on the shrimp boat with coarse men, no truce in the captured towns, the strident noise of loudspeakers in the night, to no longer belong to this race, to flee from them and nonchalance on the beaches, on the water's edge, look at them forming into groups to watch the boats sail past, elsewhere groups were forming for guerrilla tactics, in mountains or near the frontlines, and pretty soon they'd hear yells of attack right by their houses, let's go, strike now, for there is joy in blood, but in their pools, out on the sea, in their gardens and at their well-laden tables, they wouldn't hear any of the shouts, and here they were, huddling together for protection, forging shelter down there, the mountain camps were waiting to welcome Lazaro at the Irano-Turkish border, the march would be long and hard through fog and snow, some find their joy in blood, Lazaro thought in his boat, the sound of the water keeping time with the movement of his oars, it's everyone's tribal need for vengeance come true, they feel glorious humiliating prisoners taken in combat, dragging them by the feet along a muddy road, you poisoned wells with dead goats, you're nothing but a Taliban, they don't see the face turned upward and begging to live, blinded by the joy of blood, they force the man to take off his pants, then assassinate him over and over again, bloody legs inert on that muddy road, the prisoner's chest filled with multiple holes, it's a land of unjust suffering, it's my land, desperate combatants with the same colour eyes as me, the same colour skin, Lazaro's brown hands kept a calm rhythm as they rowed, fixing the shore with his gaze, eyes closed off and fleeing the shadows there, the people waiting on the wharf, like those prostitutes on the quays since early nightfall, soon to flaunt their disgrace in broad daylight, not one of them, he thought, really deserved to live, and Chuan, who had convinced her husband to come down to the beach with her, said, let's go find our friends, knowing full well that Olivier was still thinking about his article on the fifties and the long fight for racial equality, what was it they said back then, separate but equal, that was before school integration in Boston, so Olivier could never be torn away from the seriousness of his thoughts, even on a day of celebration, he was one of those who can never forget, but Chuan thought forgetfulness a nobler faculty from which a compassion could emerge, perhaps even a form of generosity and magnanimity, she'd taken him by the hand, you know what I'd still like to have in the garden, she told him, knowing he wasn't listening, but always enthusiastic when she talked about her floral arrangements, compositions she pictured in full detail, a cascade of images she rejoiced in, it would be a harmonious cascade of daisies called white swans and cinquefoil — that supposedly look like lambs' ears or lobes — over by the fountain, wouldn't that be charming, we'd also have tulips, and at nightime, those white flowers would all shine like the moon and perfume the air, we'd have borders of amaryllis, and Olivier thought that for him, angels were black angels, victims of arson in the night of October 16 in their house in Baltimore, but where would he be without Chuan's floral pieces, her patience, her gentleness, what would he have done, a man forever living in the furor of the past or his ability to keep that lifelong fury going, without Chuan and Jermaine, all he possessed after what Chuan called the existence of things destroyed, yes, of course, he said, all those flowers would shine and smell sweet in the night, you're right Chuan, and we could have a rosebush near the patio table, next to where the yellow frangipani flowers would bloom, there's where we could have cocktails, and you could have your awful after-dinner cigars with Bernard and Christiansen when our friends come in the autumn, and winter would still be luminous, this is our future Olivier thought as he listened to his wife, there is always a future as long as we live, too bad we have so little faith, yes, you're absolutely right about those white flowers, Chuan, he said again, breathing in the sea air, and you know, I think this night has come off beautifully, a fine party that our friend Esther will never forget, Olivier was feeling a sort of contentment with life, yes, that's what it was, not simple forgetfulness or erasing of memory, Chuan's richness and generosity were enlivening, he thought, and after saying he'd see the doctor, just a brief visit to get his eyes checked, Samuel's teacher said he'd be back for the evening rehearsal, Samuel didn't know where Arnie Graal was now, not in the set-storage warehouse, nor below stage, where Samuel was used to seeing him, nowhere, the sudden absence, a separation, was announced today on a colour tele-phone screen, thought Samuel, a fun menu over an integrated digital camera, a message list, this colour-burst of technology suddenly blended into black when Arnie wrote to Samuel his student, don't try to find me but don't cancel my production of *A Survivor's Morning* in Berlin this fall, for you are my succes-sor now, I told you one day I would lance the abscess, well it's done, I'm going blind and won't be able to dance any-more, I also told you my *A Survivor's Morning* was conceived for those leaving us, but I do not want to leave like those I accompanied with my twenty dancers, my choir of women and children, I don't want that because my whole life has been like a song, even when I worked in the hospital laundry at night, a song, because I danced all day from Amsterdam to

San Francisco, as you will do later on, be bold and never stop dancing, Petite Graine, you said when you lost Tanjou, a family friend, as I lost my dancers in my last choreography when the walls and windows in my towers blotted out their shadows one by one, leaving us only with cut-out shadows, you prefer not to love anymore, not Veronica, nor any other woman, always afraid that a beloved face will be swallowed up tomorrow or some time afterward, like these walls of icons, you said, all burnt up with Tanjou, you're wrong, Petite Graine, you still have a lot of growing up to do, for in life, persecutions live among us, and you yourself don't know if you're on the side of persecuters or among those who could be persecuted for crimes committed by other generations, as you (286) told me too, your parents brought you into the world for happiness, so never stop loving or dancing, Petite Graine, don't try and find me, I don't want to fall like those I accompanied in *A Survivor's Morning* with the choir of women and children, I want to be left alone and listen to some major works I've worked on: Stravinsky and Prokofiev, you can add some weightlessness to the Berlin performance of *A Survivor's Morning*, so there's no groping about, be brave then, Petite Graine, little seed of a man, go, persist, be tenacious, could it be true, thought Samuel, he'd never see the student Tanjou again, nor the itinerant Lady of the Bags, perhaps not his black dancer-friend Arni Graal either, Arnie had always said he didn't like being alone, an eye check-up with his doctor, they said, and Samuel would never again see the flamboyant artist in the theatre, nor in the set warehouse where Arnie hung out alone, nor in the murky depths below stage where he designed and conceived his shows, never hear his baritone voice, was it that of a preacher whose auguries were too direct and disturbing, with his bone amulet shining beneath his black shirt, but where would he go with everyone expecting him each night, how could you go on and love when the breath that has given you love and dance has left you, how

could Samuel transpose an art that was not his own but
Arnie's, Arnie who had taught him everything, the dizzying
heights of his dance steps, the long fall past the walls where
the faces and bodies reappeared, Arnie's blind fall to the concrete streets, to whom would Samuel explain that tied and
bound bodies with covered faces slept with him at night,
and that they were all living, their hands had been tied, and
Samuel could hear them breathing beneath the rough fabric
over their faces, they slept and breathed, Samuel thought, a
convulsive sleep, were they awaiting interrogation, having
nowhere to live, or were they ghosts held in chambers waiting
to be whipped and tortured when they awoke, even they did
not know why they were there, but wordlessly they begged
Samuel to lend them blankets and the glass of water by his
bedside, for they were thirsty but could not drink, they were
hungry but could not eat breakfast with him, how can you go
on like this, Samuel thought, when you think you're fast
asleep in your sheets, you dream you're walking on water,
weightless or almost, water finding its way, unwavering,
beneath your feet, and suddenly heads fall from the wall onto
your sheets, bodies wander some way off, tied and bound or
sometimes seated with their feet out in front of them, closely
watched by dark shadows, that must be how they've been
photographed or filmed, if the eyes in these heads went out
and the mouths cried out, I don't want to, no, I don't want to,
call someone, I don't want to, call my mother, my son, isn't
anyone in charge here, how can you go on with the rolling
and rubbing of those heads in your sheets, and even when
Samuel left his apartment and ran down the stairs into the
street, they were still there, all those naked bodies seemingly
nailed to the front doors, as though the city were a prison
colony, it rained and snowed on these soaking bodies,
whether single or stickily clumped together in obscene positions they didn't want to take, a shiver of fear ran through
them all, up against door- and window-frames, pitifully tied to

one another with electrical wire, and when Samuel awoke
they had all disappeared, he searched through the sheets to
see if there might be a head still unstuck from its body, the
eyes begging him to let them live, but when he opened the
blinds onto the street, he saw it was a beautiful summer morning, Veronica had written to him saying, come back, and his
mother urged him to come home for a few days and see
Vincent, who would soon be coming home, almost cured too,
his mother wrote, Samuel, better to count the days when
Vincent feels well than the others, then he can react since he's
been in the mountains, he coughs a bit less, and he swims
now too like all boys his age, I still won't let him go out to sea
with Marie-Sylvie, though, I'm sure it's too soon, his last attack
really scared all of us on Papa's boat, then walking in town, if
Samuel were never again to see Tanjou or perhaps even Our
Lady of the Bags, who'd been replaced by someone else, a girl
without sweetness who had brushed him aside with some
choice words on his way out of a store on some avenue
where opulence reigned supreme, as she said, but it was true,
so why blame her for saying what she thought, she who slept
in cardboard boxes and dirty alleys, Samuel stopped by to say
hello every day to her who'd been buried under the rubble
with Tanjou, Our Lady of the Bags, and suddenly with the
blossoming of the lilacs, tulips and roses in the parks, who
could tell if what was tomb-scaffolding yesterday, or now had
the appearance of smoking ruins with so many dead, might
not be a fortress or fortification where, instead of a glass
citadel provoking more attacks, trees and gardens and the
perpetual flowering of lilacs and tulips and roses might rise
skyward, so nothing would be bastioned and devastated anymore, this smiling geometry would take over the city, lush
green in the sun, thought Samuel, and Petites Cendres turned
back, all dishevelled and sad and still without his powder until
Decadent Friday, he thought, when the bar was deserted,
though you could still hear music in the street, a few notes

from a piano and a man singing in a smoky tavern with nobody in it, just a sweeper picking out a few notes, haven't you got anything for me, Petites Cendres called out to him, no, nothing, he said, hey listen to this song, son, *Unchain My Heart*, oh let my heart not be in chains anymore, son, and yours neither, hey, where you going, it'll soon be time for the churches and temples to open, better go pray, son, I ain't touched coke since I got old, not like in the old days when I played in Cornelius' band at the Club Mix, look at the scarecrow I turned into with that powder, don't do like me, Petites Cendres, everywhere they threw me out, even the Club Mix, now all I do is sweep up other people's garbage, don't let your heart be chained, son, that powder's the devil, I'll score some before 11:00 this morning, Petites Cendres said, I've got a customer waiting at the hotel, huge guy, monster belongs to an S-and-M crowd and masturbates alone with his porno films while he's waiting for me, he'll be ready when I get there, what gets him off is us Blacks, insulting us and messing with our heads with a lot of sharp demands, that's what he wants, the sweeper repeated again, don't let your heart be chained, I wanted to be Ray Charles, and look what powder's made me, skin and bones, it swallowed everything I had, son, don't you do like me, I'm lucky I can barely play a few notes, listen, *Unchain My Heart*, it'll be carnage with that guy, you'll come out of there all bloody, God help you, son, just go your own way, I got to sweep now, then as he got close to the imposing pink façade of the hotel, Petites Cendres felt tears on his cheeks, why am I playing doggie for this bastard again, he thought, why am I going to let him spit on me again, where was that vision of paradise, the round-cheeked kid who'd smiled at him, he'd have given anything to see him again, he had nothing to give, even that selfish Timo hadn't given him a cigarette, yeah, but wasn't today the day the cruiseship came into port with fifteen hundred sailors, deckhands and crew, red and yellow balloons going up, a regular deluge of visitors in town from Germany, Scandinavia, the world, under their collars handsome, muscular and bare-chested, and at the temple, Reverend Ézéchielle had said to Ashley, Petites Cendres, halleluliah, eternity is for the poor, the beaten down and the oppressed like you, Ashley, next to God, you'll never be alone, and in that eternity there will always be powder, Petites Cendres thought to himself, and I'll have my boy, he won't be going off to see his silk merchant in New York, it'll soon be time for the temples and churches to open their doors, the tears trailed down his cheeks as he dragged his sandalled feet toward the hotel with its imposing pink façade, do come down, Mère had written to Renata, we'd so love to see you, and it was aboard a flight like this one, Renata reflected, that ill-fated Flight 491 after it stopped over in New York, that all those kids in the French class had died so pitilessly on the Honduran mountain, who could tell why little girls in taffeta dresses, whose parents were waiting for them at the airport, had to disappear in the thick fog over the treetops that day, when Renata, getting off in New York for an international conference on the death penalty, would be spared their cruel fate, not thrown from a plane and robbed of her life, a life that already seemed long to her, while these little girls were not yet ten, of course nothing was fair in life, she thought, those who were spared were often incredulous that the life taken from the young and fresh could be turned over to themselves for a longer time still, is this really how it was, or was there some other tragedy still to come, Esther, who claimed to be a distant cousin of Renata's, nor Mélanie her daughter, nor the grown children, and the youngest, Mai, whom Renata still didn't know, none of them knew Renata would soon be coming to see them and telling Esther she wanted to surprise her for her eightieth birthday, the family was so small, the pretext would be a holiday by the sea with her husband, or maybe no pretext at all, just the wish to see them all again very briefly, not making a grand entrance like before in a satin vest revealing

her tanned and naked skin, just to be that distant relation dis-
creetly reaching out her hand before embracing each one,
almost melting into Esther's timid silhouette among the pink
laurels around the entrance, saying, here I am, Esther, I know
you weren't expecting me, but I wanted to see you because it
allows me to rekindle respect for the past, I remember our
Polish cousins, Daniel's father Joseph, it's time to commemo-
rate every one of you, your blood is mine, even if I don't feel
that I actually belong to anyone in particular, I know you see
me as a little haughty and perhaps brusque, I know, I know,
you're not pleased that your daughter Mélanie is so close to
me, but we have so much in common, or perhaps Renata
would simply say nothing, they would all notice she'd started
smoking again, though very little, they'd be aware of her old
gesture when she fished out her gold cigarette case, though
less ostentatiously than in the past, yet still the same defiant
look, they'd be indignant, Esther especially had little tolerance,
I'm not in convalescence anymore, Renata would say, I'm
entitled to life's pleasures now, and I do control how often I
do it, she most of all wanted to speak with Mélanie and relieve
herself of some of the weight of her judicial responsibilities,
Mélanie was an influential female leader also working with
justice, especially with regard to women and children, but
there were others like Nathanaël, narrowly spared a life sentence after being convicted at fifteen of the murder of a small
boy when he was eleven, the clemency of a governor, whose
own delinquent son avoided prison, had saved Nathanaël
from too harsh a sentence and allowed him to be supervised
in a juvenile detention centre, but what was going to happen
to Nathanaël in future, and what about all the other accused
minors, considered incorrigible by the judges who oversaw
the support to their upbringing, applied the law, and incrimi-
nated them like adults for the damnable things they had done,
and they were evil acts, Renata thought, but the perpetrators
were children whose minds were not yet formed, how

Nathanaël had wept when the judge said his actions were not just childish mistakes that got out of hand playing with a younger, more fragile child, a little girl defenceless against the strength of a teenager, no, they were acts of indescribable cynicism and brutality, when Nathanaël had acted without really knowing what he was doing, and with the multiplied strength of a boy his size, Nathanaël and his parents had cried, knowing he had killed by accident with sudden and exaggerated out-of-control force, what would happen in future to Nathanaël with no governor to take pity on him, and to his brothers facing down the judges in court, Mélanie, a delicate soul, would understand that Renata was one of the harassed and scrupulous judges, and was relying on her to help put things in perspective, what would she do as a woman and a mother, how would she judge Nathanaël and the kids from underprivileged backgrounds, born to the oppression and misery of the ghettos, later, at the open window of her room looking out at the Caribbean Sea, Renata was to recall the execution of a black by lethal injection in a Texas prison, it was so long ago, but she'd always been convinced of his innocence, since proved by DNA, so she'd not been wrong, and thousands of innocent people had mistakenly been executed by lethal injection or the electric chair, she'd realized that day that no court could ever come to grips with these crimes of negligence, crimes of a justice system designed not to see, what tears were in store for Nathanaël's parents, Renata thought, how many poor people who had committed no crimes would be subjected to the death penalty, what tears, Renata thought, and Caroline asked again for her chair to be brought closer to the window so she could see the sunrise over the water, no, it won't be night, and I won't wear that black outfit you ironed for me this morning, you know, Harriet, Jean-Mathieu and I will be replaced by others, that's the way it is, the friends I use to have over, Bernard, Valérie, Chistiansen and his charming wife Nora . . . Christiansen, a Nordic god, it was so good to have them around, all of them, writers and humanists, Valérie in particular, the philosopher-novelist who knows all about the drama of living; Nora's a mysterious, secretive painter; Bernard and Christiansen are so full of learning and humanism, and the friendship that unites them all, life and the friendship that enlightens their painstaking work, yes, they will supplant us, Jean-Mathieu and I, and it's good that it should be so, if I'm stepping out onto the bridge now, standing upright before the crossing, yes, if I have to . . . leave, then I'd like them all to come and live here in my villa, write and eat at my table, and you must always be ready to welcome them, Harriet, and where will Frédéric, Charles and I go, what will happen to Charles now that he's let Cyril go, tell me, where are we all going to go now we're being replaced, but you have to believe it's for the best, and it is for the best, but tell me the truth just this once, Charly's in the house, isn't she, you just didn't let her get near me, did you, but she is here, isn't she, just behind the door, be truthful with me, I heard her footsteps and her voice saying, Caroline, now we're even, out of each other's debt, let me back in to take care of you, lay my head in your lap like when I pretended to serve you, though I lied to you and didn't really, Caroline, it's true I burned your letter to Jean-Mathieu like in your dream, please let me back in, Caroline, I heard her, she was there, Caroline said, and you told her, shut up liar, get out, we don't want you here, where are my hat and gloves, I've got to go out, they're all expecting me, Adrien, Suzanne, Frédéric, and as for dear Charles, why take Cyril away from him, his life, there he is alone at dawn to write, he describes it as he lives it, dawn and his fountains to quench all thirsts, beyond the Gates of Hell that Botticelli painted as if he were right here with us, the living through an immense fall, tumbling one on top of another from the walls that were supposed to shelter us, to a death they know nothing about, and Charles will write and write, heart-struck with these spiritual torments that Botticelli and Dante in his violent poetry shared, he will write, and why take Cyril away from him, the dawn and the rivers to slake all thirsts, and I even know how Charly was dressed, Caroline said, even if you won't tell me, Harriett, she was like those characters of Newton's, impenetrable and sophisticated in their indolence, did she show up in her black evening jacket with purple nails, the way she did when she went out dancing with her friends night after night till she dropped, tell me now, is that how she looked when you saw her, and Harriett — Miss Harriett — answered with cautious slowness, yes, she was wearing her black evening jacket, she came, but I didn't let her in, I couldn't, she would have hurt you, in fact, I escorted her back out into the street, and do you know what I saw, a beautiful new car and a frail elderly man waiting for her, she's a chauffeur again, that girl is evil through-and-through, said Miss Désirée, she's going to abuse that old man the same as you, Caroline, you were so good to her, oh no, I wasn't, Caroline said, I wasn't all that good to her, but perhaps I could be if she agreed to see me again, I'd be another woman, but I've got to get my best things on, someone's waiting for me on the bridge, who knows, maybe it's her, not that sordid, lame old woman who's waving to me, how dare she call me, they'll all come and live in my house, and you'll make them welcome, won't you, choose the best wines for Bernard and Valérie, for every thirst must be satisfied, and that will be your role, Harriett, when I'm no longer there, I'm sure it's time to go toward the bridge while the sun is still out to find my way, then, when night falls, remember, the birds of prey will return, is it already the hour of the predators, Harriett, Miss Désirée, when no one, not even you, my faithful nurse, can watch over this child of yours, is it already the pale hour when I must go to the bridge? Even you, most faithful Harriett, Miss Désirée, cannot follow me, Adrien, burning hot under his hat and annoyed by all the sand in his shoes, was saying to Daniel, you really do walk fast, I know you're used to running several hours each day, I used to do it once too, isn't this the wharf where your wife is supposed to meet us, oh yes, about your book *Strange Years*, I still wanted to say this, believe me, I'm speaking in all honesty as a friend, in all this illuminated foraging there is very little echo of hope, you call Andy Warhol one of the most amazing portraitists of our time in his obsessive multiplicity of portraits and self-portraits, but why, what is the point of soup cans and his self-portrayal as a bourgeois woman, I have to admit he has a fine hand for plasticity, but as a pop artist he might have more of the attitude and aptitude on the counter-cultural scene he's so good on than actual talent, and do we really need to know that Stalin had a weakness for gangster and cowboy movies, perhaps out of prudery, to get away from anything sexual, or that he talked about literature during decadent banquets with his friends the torturers, all of them monsters as sentimental as himself, you remember what Dostoyevsky wrote about this sentimentality of the worst members of our species, I mean, what are you getting at, that even those who gave rise to the Great Terrors in this world can fall victim to this revolting sentimentality that moves them to tears in a gangster movie, while they can kill ten million Ukrainians with famine and not shed a single tear, well, yes, that's partly it, said Daniel, suddenly seeming impersonal beneath glasses reflecting the sea, for he'd not been listening to Adrien for the past few moments, where is Mélanie, he asked with concern, weren't we supposed to meet here by the wharf, over there, I can see her, said Suzanne, it's going to be a magnificent day, and look at the boats all lined up on the horizon, oh it's too bad Caroline can't get out to join us, I still think of Jean-Mathieu each morning when I re-read his books, the most important thing is that we think about one another, that's eternity, isn't it, Daniel dear, it's the only way not to die, I've always said to Adrien, I'm a believer in death, Daleth, a door opening out onto the bay, and the light like this morning, and Mère said to Nora, I remember now what it was Augustino wrote at the very beginning of his book, or at least he said it would be a book, he often writes all through the night, which drives his parents crazy, not me, though, I'm not bothered by it, he wrote, we might get up some morning and recognize nothing around us, wonder if this country is our country, and even if it is still there, we might get up some morning and think, where is the familiar terrain, where is Cleveland or Cincinnati, where are our cities by the Pacific Ocean or the Gulf of Mexico, where would we go if we had no cities or houses or fire or bread, where would we go, and who would open the door to us, one morning as we get up, we could discover that we had nothing, and say to people around us, will you open your doors to us, and if nobody does, because they're afraid we'll steal the little that remains of their cities and houses and bread and fire, then what will happen to us, and Mère fell silent, for the sky was hot and shining, it seemed so sweet to be alive that she forgot the increased trembling in her right hand, Nora was kneeling by the water, it was a sublime summer day, and she said, I'm going back to Africa soon, touching the green water with her hand and refreshing her eyelids and her brow, an accomplished life would surely be one like Nora's or Marie Curie's, Mère thought, an unknown adventure ahead of one, or would it be existence in the face of uncertainty and hope for happiness, or all of this together, it would soon be time to go back up to the house and see Marie-Sylvie, Augustino and Mai, it would soon be time, thought Mère, and Mélanie was starting up the jeep, pressing the accelerator, Mai, where was Mai, but why was she so nervous, Marie-Sylvie had asked, she's on the swing in the garden with her cats, I scolded her a little bit, look, there she is, not even washed or combed, and she's ignoring me, and Mélanie hugged Mai, saying, why do you always have to scare me, you didn't go back to the stadium, did you, you know Papa and I told you not to, I don't want him to come back, Mai said definitely, though her face looked pathetic and frowning, I don't

want Vincent to came back, no one talks about anyone but
him, I'm the baby, not Vincent, and Marie-Sylvie's just going to
spoil him again, but Papa and I love you every bit as much as
Vincent, said Mélanie, thrown into confusion by Mai's words,
it isn't true, Mai replied with the same assurance that so dis-
armed her mother, it isn't true, you're all lying, except
Augustino, he doesn't, but he says I'm too young to be his
friend, he's afraid I might wreck his books, Mélanie took her
daughter in her arms, now, now, she said, caressing her hair,
why don't you go play on the beach with Emilio and forget
about all this, it's a little early, but do you want me to take you
over to his house, now Mélanie and her daughter were
headed for the beach in the jeep, and the radio was playing
Britten's *War Requiem*, Mélanie said it was their friend Franz
who was conducting, did Mai remember him, listen to those
choirs and soloists, she told her daughter, who seemed to be
asleep on the seat and didn't answer, it's so moving, Franz is a
musician who has gone through so many states of being to
give us this music, and you know, they say that in the most
beautiful music like this there is often a note left out, but I
don't think there's one, some great musicians live such crazy
lives that they end up getting killed, or they die in extreme
poverty, the missing note, because they've given over their
lives to music, Mai woke up in a leap of joy and opened the
door, shouting, Mama, that's him, Emilio, over by the volleyball net, and when she caught up with him, all at once laughing
and gay, Mélanie felt relieved, now she really knew where Mai
was, in a circle of sand she was making around Emilio, his skin
brown from the sun and his teeth sparkling more than ever in
his delicate face, see how cute he is, Mama, and in this circle
he's all mine, Mai exclaimed to her mother, at last Mélanie
stopped being afraid that her daughter was not really there,
not at the stadium nor walking the streets telling passers-by
that she had no mother or father, Mélanie was thinking about
seeing Renata that evening, unbelievable, wasn't it, that they

wére executing kids of sixteen, kids with parents like Mélanie and Daniel, who didn't know when they would see their children again, if ever, or perhaps see them die stoically in the glassed-in execution chamber with flames shooting through their sons' electrocuted bodies, maybe sometime soon even their daughters', look Mama, it's the flotilla, Mai cried, look, and Mélanie tilted her head to the sun, thinking about a life of struggle that was just beginning, how sweet it was still to be young, willing, determined in such a virulent world, and Ari told Lou, who was sitting on his lap, isn't it great to be on your own boat with Papa, it is our boat, you know, and I'm going to show you how to sail it, *Lou's Slipper*, listen to the waves, hear that, Lou had on the same outfit she wore when Ari took her to the gym each morning, where's Mama, I want Mama, she said, you'll see her on Thursday, Ari said, you see her every day from Thursday to Sunday, but today and tomorrow you're here with your papa, Mama, I want Mama, Lou sniffled reaching her arms out toward the marina where she had seen her mother head for the car, I want Mama, those were big birds on the wharves, she thought, and kittens she'd run around with, slapping her feet on the planks of the wharf, the marina, Mama's car, Mama's reddish hair, the litter of kittens, the landscape was receding, while Ari's boat — soon to be hers — moved seaward, the ocean that felt like nowhere, the huge place she didn't want to go, even on her father's lap, then she stopped crying, maybe he was right, she would be with her mother and her brother Jules on Thursday, her father kept saying, look how beautiful it all is, so beautiful, and in front of Pastor Jérémy's low, flat house amid the yellow grass, there were cocks and hens and chicks pecking away, Deandra and Tiffany were taking pictures for Carlos of Polly and Oreilles Coupées the dogs, if only they would stop wagging their tails, Polly should remember, they'd see Carlos and give him the picture on Sunday.

ACKNOWLEDGEMENTS

My thanks to Francine Dumouchel and to Marie Couillard for their constant and solid support, and to Claude for his enormous confidence.

ABOUT THE AUTHOR

Marie-Claire Blais is the internationally renowned author of more than twenty-five books. She is a three-time winner of the Governor General's Literary Award for Fiction and has also been awarded the Athanase-David Prize, the Medicis Prize, the Molson Prize, the Writers' Trust Matt Cohen Prize, and Guggenheim Fellowships. She lives in Quebec and Florida.